Rorey's Secret

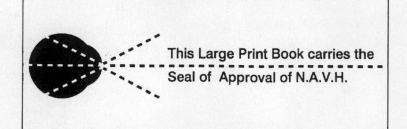

This Large Print Book carries the
Seal of Approval of N.A.V.H.

Rorey's Secret

Leisha Kelly

Thorndike Press • Waterville, Maine

Published in 2006 by arrangement with Baker Book House.

Thorndike Press® Large Print Christian Historical Fiction.

The tree indicium is a trademark of Thorndike Press.

The text of this Large Print edition is unabridged. Other aspects of the book may vary from the original edition.

Set in 16 pt. Plantin by Elena Picard.

Printed in the United States on permanent paper.

Library of Congress Cataloging-in-Publication Data

Kelly, Leisha.
    Rorey's secret / by Leisha Kelly.
      p. cm.
    ISBN 0-7862-8619-9 (lg. print : hc : alk. paper)
    1. Depressions — Fiction. 2. Neighborhood — Fiction.
    3. Large type books. I. Title.
PS3611.E45R67 2006
  813'.6 — dc22   2006005614

With much love to my brothers and sisters:

Curtis Scheuermann
Sue Minton
Carla Steinbeck
Grant Scheuermann
Eric Scheuermann
Sean Scheuermann

And their families.
God bless you all.

As the Founder/CEO of NAVH, the only national health agency solely devoted to those who, although not totally blind, have an eye disease which could lead to serious visual impairment, I am pleased to recognize Thorndike Press★ as one of the leading publishers in the large print field.

Founded in 1954 in San Francisco to prepare large print textbooks for partially seeing children, NAVH became the pioneer and standard setting agency in the preparation of large type.

Today, those publishers who meet our standards carry the prestigious "Seal of Approval" indicating high quality large print. We are delighted that Thorndike Press is one of the publishers whose titles meet these standards. We are also pleased to recognize the significant contribution Thorndike Press is making in this important and growing field.

Lorraine H. Marchi, L.H.D.
Founder/CEO
NAVH

★ Thorndike Press encompasses the following imprints: Thorndike, Wheeler, Walker and Large Print Press.

1

Julia

October 15, 1938

I had chicken to fry, lots of chicken, because it was Willy Hammond's birthday and all the Hammonds would be over for supper.

Lard was sputtering in the skillet, and I was flouring the chicken pieces when I heard the crash behind me.

"Oh! Mama, I'm sorry!" little Emma Grace wailed.

She was the youngest Hammond, too young to remember her own mama, and she'd been calling me that ever since she could talk. Now she was looking at me with her big brown eyes all teary. All I could do was sigh as broken glass and globs of home-cooked applesauce spread in a lumpy puddle across the floor.

"Oh, Emmie."

"I didn't means to, Mama. I'll clean it up." She jumped down from the chair, not quite missing the mess. She was always willing to help. And she was seven and a half already, though she still seemed far younger.

"You'd better let me get it, honey. The broken glass could cut your fingers." I handed her a dish towel. "Step back, okay? And wipe your shoe."

She smeared the applesauce around on her toe a bit and watched me scoop most of the mess into the dustpan. "We got more applesauce?"

"Yes, we've got more," I assured her. But we didn't have another bowl like that pretty one. It was simple enough, nothing that would have cost much, but it had been Emma Graham's, little Emmie's namesake. Everything that was Emma Graham's was precious to me, and it hurt just a little every time another piece of her was lost. But the broken bowl had been an accident, and I wasn't about to say anything more.

"Can I frost the cake?" she asked me, grabbing another bowl off the counter without waiting for my response.

"You can help with that in a little while," I said quickly and set the butter frosting back on the counter carefully. Then I noticed that the tears in her eyes hadn't faded away.

"Am I a dummy?" she asked, her little lip quivering into a pout.

"Oh, Emmie, no. You're not a dummy. Accidents can happen to anyone. It's all right."

"But Teddy Willis says I'm a dummy. Like Franky."

Teddy Willis was only six and a little big for his britches, but this news bothered me just the same. I already knew how much teasing Emmie's brother Franky endured. At fifteen, he still could hardly read, but he kept on trying valiantly. He was tough skinned enough to endure even the taunts of younger children. But Emmie was a tiny thing, and far from tough. Elvira Post, her teacher, had already told us that she wasn't catching on to much of anything. I hated to think of little Teddy, or any others, picking at her over something she couldn't help. It didn't roll off her the way it did Franky.

"Emmie, you know Franky's no dummy. He made that chair you were just standing on and quite a few other things around here, he and Samuel. He's already working, and working harder than some grown men. He's good at a very lot of things, and so are you. You don't have to worry about what anybody says."

"But I can't read, and Teddy can! He read three whole sentences today, an' Mrs. Post said he was comin' along swell! She don't never say that 'bout me." She looked down at her shoes. "She said I might be like Franky."

"Well. Both of you are kindhearted and helpful. You're alike in that, which is more important than a lot of things I could name. Would you mind counting out the silverware for me?"

She scrunched up her face. "How many?"

"All of you are coming for supper, except Joe, of course. Even Lizbeth and Ben will be here, and Sam and Thelma and little Georgie. You lay out enough for everybody and tell me how many." I knew she could do it. Because just like with Franky, for Emmie, numbers weren't a problem. Unless they were written down. Both Franky and Emmie could cipher in their heads and remember what someone had read to them. But Mrs. Post had long ago despaired of Franky ever reading a line on his own and had asked us to school him at home so she could concentrate on the other pupils in her one-room school. And now she was wondering about Emmie too.

I could hear the thundering footsteps of one of the boys running across the porch. Ten-year-old Bert came bursting in the back door with two tiny kittens in the crook of his arm. "Look, Mom!"

Bert was second youngest and the only other Hammond child who didn't call me Mrs. Wortham most of the time.

"Cute," I told him. "But where's their mother? She won't be too pleased with them disappearing, now will she?"

He didn't pay the slightest attention to my question. "Why wasn't they born in the spring, huh? Like calves an' pigs? How come cats'll have kits any old time? Seems foolish, them birthin' 'em whenever they do, even when it's gonna get cold! At least these'll have a month or two 'fore the snow comes."

"God will take care of the kittens, Berty. They always seem to manage just fine. Take them outside, please, so I can finish dinner."

"Harry's started the milkin'," he told me, still standing there petting those teeny kittens.

"Well, good. That much less for Mr. Wortham to do when he gets home."

Behind Bert, Sarah came in the back

11

door, carrying a basket of freshly dried clothes. She eyed Emma and the dustpan still in my hand and the chicken needing attention on the stove. She smiled. "Need some help, Mom?"

"Please. Or Lizbeth'll come breezing in here thinking we've had our feet up all day."

Emmie laughed. "Why would we put our feet up?"

Sarah put the clothes down by the sitting room doorway and turned her attention to the chicken. She looked so tall for thirteen. Taller than me already, but I thought maybe she'd stop growing like I did at her age. She had my straight brown hair, and people in town said she looked like me. But Sarah was going to be more of a beauty, I could tell. She was turning heads already, which was enough to make my Samuel nervous.

I was just about to dump the mess from my dustpan when a car horn made me jump. Who in the world would come honking? Sarah and I both craned our necks, looking out the window to see who was pulling in.

"Sam!" Berty yelled.

Indeed, the oldest Hammond brother and his family were coming up the drive in their rattletrap Model A. But something wasn't right. Sam wasn't one for any sort of noise that would call attention to himself. And that made me a little squeamish inside, thinking about his wife and the baby to come. I dried my hands and hurried outside.

Berty and Emma Grace had run out of the house before me. Katie looked up from where she'd been pulling turnips in the garden and started walking our way. Harry came rushing out of the barn with the milk pail swinging. Almost I said something to him about being more careful, but I didn't. Hammond children helped with the chores when they came over, same as we were always helping at their house. Like we were all one. No sense doing any criticizing.

When Sam Hammond stopped in the drive I knew before he got out that all was not well. Two-year-old Georgie was bouncing up and down on his seat as usual. But Thelma, his mother, was not looking so good. I wished they'd gone honking into Belle Rive for the doctor instead of to my house.

"Good evening, Mrs. Wortham," Sam called. "Thelma's not been feeling the best. Sorry to trouble you with the horn, but I sure appreciate you coming out."

Thelma shoved the car door open before Sam got around to her side. She was heavy with child, and even sitting forward took some obvious effort.

"Stay there a minute, Thelma," I told her. "I'll come to you."

"Oh, Mrs. Wortham, I just want to come in and put my feet up. I'll be all right."

"Are you feeling any pains?" I questioned, needing to know but hating to ask in front of the younger children.

"Not so much. I been nauseous more than anything."

"And weak," Sam added. "She's been weak."

I wondered again if I might persuade them to visit the doctor in town or even go into the hospital at Mcleansboro, but we'd been over all that before. Young Sam wasn't as bad as his father when it came to doctors. But he and Thelma had already told me that a pregnancy wasn't the same as some disease. They didn't really want a doctor, and especially not a hospital stay. Sam and Thelma wanted me and Thelma's mother, Delores Pratt, to be the ones delivering their children.

I'd missed out on the first one, having the influenza at the time, and Delores had managed just fine with the help of a neighbor. But here they were now, making me pretty nervous. They were confident in me, because I'd helped dear old Emma bring little Emmie Grace into this world. But that had been necessity and my only experience. I'd never meant it to be the start of any midwifery of my own.

Standing beside the car, I could see Thelma's bulging abdomen churn and wiggle in front of me.

"Oh my," she said.

"Baby kicking?"

"Seems like she's ready to come clear out the side," she said with a laugh. "But I believe I'm feeling some better."

Sam wasn't so sure, and neither was I. Thelma was perspiring heavily, though it was becoming noticeably cooler with the clouds moving in. Georgie climbed up on his mother before anybody could tell him otherwise, and she winced.

"Are you still feeling faint?" Sam asked her. "Mrs. Wortham, she was feelin' faint. Is that a normal thing? She don't rest enough, that's what it is. She can't rest when I'm off to work, with Georgie runnin' around. I come home, and she looked like a shallow breeze could just knock her plumb over. I carried her to the car, and we come right over. Can we get her inside?"

"No, no," I wanted to say. But I knew there wasn't much sense in sending her out on those bumpy roads again. If she wasn't in labor now, that would surely bring it on. Straight to bed for a while; maybe that would help. And if the labor started, I'd chase Sam Hammond out the door in a hurry to fetch me the doctor, like it or not.

Thelma wanted to walk in, but Sam picked up his once-dainty bride and carried her, which I heartily approved of. She was supposed to have a couple more weeks to go, at least we thought. No sense in too much activity hurrying things.

"Me! Me!" Georgie yelled. "Carry me!"

His father didn't seem to hear him, so I swooped up the little tike and started for the house.

"I wa' appasauce!" he told me, and I remembered the mess I'd not quite finished cleaning up. Maybe Sarah had gotten it. She'd stayed inside, and she was always extra good help. Which made me think of Rorey. The oldest Hammond girl still at home, she was supposed to be around here somewhere, but lately she was doing just as little as she could.

As if reading my mind, Harry yelled, "Hey, Rorey!"

I looked but couldn't see her anywhere.

16

"Whatcha doin' up a tree?" Harry laughed and then bounded on into the house with the milk pail, not too full, obviously, or it would be spilling all the way. Twelve years old and he still could hardly walk for running everywhere he went. He'd been a pill when he was younger, that was for sure.

"Looky! Looky!" Georgie screamed in my ear. Thanks to his pointing, I finally saw Rorey sitting two stories up in our sweet gum tree, a book across her lap. Her diary, almost surely. And she was writing in it, scarcely looking our way for all that was going on.

"Supper before long, Lord willing!" I called to her.

"Oh," she said, barely loud enough for me to hear. "I'll be down pretty soon."

"I hope so." I shook my head. A thirteen-year-old up a tree and paying the rest of us no mind. She'd better get down before her father arrived or she'd catch the dickens from him. But I didn't feel like warning her.

Thelma was doing some moaning when I entered the house. More of the baby kicking, I hoped. Sam had moved pretty quick and gotten her clear into the sitting room, out of sight. Hurrying to catch up, I completely forgot about the floor. I got as far as the table with Georgie wiggling in my arms, but before I knew what was happening, my feet flew out from under me, and I landed hard on fresh-mopped floor. I was stunned speechless for a moment, wondering if falling with a toddler in my arms might have hurt the poor child. Sarah ran over to my side.

"Oh! Oh, Mom! I didn't know it'd be so slick!"

She tried to take Georgie from me, but he would have none of that. At first he looked as stunned as I was. Then he burst out laughing.

"Do again! Do again!"

I'd have laughed with him if it hadn't hurt so bad. Thank God, though, that it wasn't Sam and Thelma falling down in a heap.

"Are you all right, Mom?"

"Oh yes," I assured my daughter, and Harry, who by now was staring at us from across the room. "I'm fine."

"Do again!" Georgie squealed some more. "Fun! Fun!"

"No," I told him simply. "Not fun for me. Harry, come and take Georgie so I can get up."

I felt a little stiff. I could imagine what a

sight I was, going in to see to Thelma after drying the floor with my backside. But I went anyway, feeling a little better as I walked. And I made Sam get Thelma to my bed instead of the rocking chair where she'd wanted to be.

"Really, Mrs. Wortham," she tried to tell me. "I'll be just fine. I just need to sit a spell."

"That's wonderful. And I'm not disagreeing with you. I just don't want to be taking any chances. Sam's probably right. You need to get off your feet more. Might be a good idea to ask Dr. Howell —"

"Mama's comin' out next week," she assured me. "I'll be just fine till then."

"Well enough," I agreed. "But while you're here, you stay in bed, just to be sure. We'll take care of Georgie for you."

"Thank you, Mrs. Wortham." She smiled and mopped at her brow. "Goodness. Still pretty warm, isn't it? And already October."

I didn't bother telling her that I'd been feeling autumn's chill in the air for days now. Not strange at all for her to be warm. I'd been warmer when I was with child too. Back when I was carrying Robert, I'd nearly frozen Samuel by kicking covers off the bed all that winter.

Thelma plopped her shoes at the foot of the bed and said she didn't want anything but a little sheet tucked in over her. "I oughta be up helpin' you cook supper," she told me. "And here we come bringin' nothin' at all but more for you to do."

Before I could answer we heard the awfullest clatter from the kitchen. Sam just turned his head, but Thelma knew her little boy pretty well, and she clucked her tongue. "Georgie, I'd just about wager. So sorry, Mrs. Wortham, for whatever he's done."

His little child voice was laughing plain enough for us all to hear. "Boomie! Boomie!"

I left Sam reaching for Thelma's hand and ran to see what Georgie had gotten into this time. I should've known. A whole stack of baking pans lay littered across the floor, and Georgie was plopped down in the middle of them looking delighted with himself. I should've tied that cupboard shut when I knew he was coming. He'd done the very same thing the last time he was here.

Harry was just standing there helpless. "He didn't want to be held," he explained. "I didn't think it'd hurt to let him walk around a little."

"It's all right. Just better to take him in the sitting room so he doesn't get too close to anything hot, all right?" I did my best shoving all the pans back into the cupboard with little Georgie standing at my side, merrily enjoying all the noise I was making at it.

"Boomie!" he chuckled again. "Boomie!"

Sarah was pulling the hot rolls out of the oven to put on the warming shelf, and Harry didn't move an inch toward taking Georgie into the next room.

Emma Grace strolled back inside, and I was glad to see her. She was always obliging. "Emmie, please help Harry entertain little Georgie a while. Can you find that rag ball we made?"

Having a job to do made Emmie smile, but Harry immediately protested.

"Ah, if Emmie's gonna play with him, why do I have to?"

"Just keep an eye on them for me," I insisted. "Till we have supper ready."

Harry rolled his eyes. "Why me?"

"Because Sam is with Thelma, Berty's outside, Katie's in the garden, and Samuel and your father and the other boys aren't in from the field yet. But they'll be here any minute, and it'd do well for you to be found at something helpful."

"Oh, all right," he said. "Oughta be Rorey doin' it, though."

I couldn't argue there. She was the one who owed us a bit of helpfulness, to be certain. But she was off in her own world again. If I hadn't needed Sarah's help so much right then, I might've sent her out to see about Rorey. Maybe then they would've gotten to giggling and talking the way they'd been doing since they were six, and come in together ready to set their hands to business.

With Georgie occupied and Thelma resting, I turned my attention back to the chicken, hoping I could get the meal further along before everybody else showed up ravenously hungry. Kate came in with fresh-washed turnips and started peeling them for me. Lizbeth should be here any minute. She'd be bringing food and her helpful hands, and I was looking forward to her visit.

Georgie squealed from the next room, and I ignored his cries to make sure all the chicken was frying. But then Thelma gave a holler, and I couldn't ignore that.

"I'll watch the chicken, Mom," Sarah said, looking a little white.

I ran to the bedroom to see what in the world was wrong. "Baby kicking again?" I asked hopefully.

"No," Thelma said weakly. "I — I don't think so, Mrs. Wortham."

"It's the pains started, then?" I was feeling a little weak myself.

"I don't know!" Thelma cried. "It weren't the same kind of feeling I had before."

She tried to get up, though I don't know why. She was straining, pulling herself toward the edge of the bed, when her water broke. She looked up at me with fear plain in her face.

"Lay back down," I told her. "And don't you worry about the mess. I'll get everything cleaned up right around you." I turned my eyes to young Sam. He was looking pretty scared himself. "I wish I could say for you to take her to the hospital," I started to say. "But —"

"No, Mrs. Wortham," he interrupted me. "We can't pay a hospital. Besides, Thelma don't want that."

"We might not ought to move her now, anyway. But I think you should go and find Dr. Howell —"

"No!" Thelma protested. "Don't send Sammy. Please! I want him here with me."

She grasped at her husband's hand like it was some kind of life rope. I thought she was probably right, that he ought to stay.

At least she was having no complaint about me wanting the doctor brought in.

"George and Samuel will be back any minute," I told them, trying to sound calm. "Lizbeth and Ben will be here before long too. I'll send whoever gets here first. And I expect they'd better stop and see about picking up your mother too?"

Thelma nodded, reaching her free hand for the quilt I'd scrunched up out of her way. "So cold in here all of a sudden," she said. "How'd that happen?"

"Oh, honey, you're wet, that's what it is." I yelled into the next room. "Sarah! Will you bring me some towels?"

I had no easy time of it, stripping the bedsheets with Thelma still on them, but I didn't want her getting up. Sam helped her off with her wet clothes, and I got her one of Samuel's nightshirts, knowing anything of mine would be too small. I made up the bed again with two sturdy old tablecloths underneath the bottom sheet. Sarah briefly stood in the doorway to hand over an armload of towels, but she didn't linger long enough to ask a single question.

"You tell me," I said as she was leaving, "just as soon as your father gets here."

Tucking the quilt around Thelma, I thought, *Why in the world couldn't Samuel just have stayed home working in the woodshop today?* I knew he and Franky had a few orders to fill. Sure, there was harvesting to be done, poor as the crop would be after all the dry weather, but I would have far preferred him to be here. As it was, there was nobody but Sam and me who could drive, and we were both pretty obligated to stay.

Where were Lizbeth and her husband, Ben Porter? They were never very late getting anywhere. If they were here, I could send Ben right back to town and have Lizbeth help me till the doctor came.

Lord, help us! How hard it'd been for Lizbeth watching her siblings being born, especially Emmie Grace. Wilametta Hammond had felt something "different" at that birth, and I felt almost faint thinking about it. The baby had been breech. Emma Graham had been there to do the midwifing, and she had her trouble bringing them through, but she did it with more strength than I could muster. How I wished I had dear old Emma with me now.

"I'm awful trouble to you, ain't I?" Thelma asked.

"No." I sniffed. "I was just wishing I had Emma here, that's all."

"Right here in her old room." Thelma

25

nodded. "I never did figure I'd have me a baby right here in my old Sunday school teacher's room. I wish she was here too." She scrunched up her face and tried hard not to holler, but I knew pretty plainly what she was feeling. Sam did too.

"Maybe I oughta check the field and send Pa or Kirk on into town for your mother," he suggested. "Wouldn't take me long. I'd be right back."

God must've favored keeping Thelma's husband at her side, because she didn't even have time to protest the idea.

"Mom!" Sarah called from the kitchen. "I can see them coming!"

I didn't know for sure who she meant, but I didn't wait a minute wondering. I ran straight on out, clear out the back door. And I could see Samuel coming across the field with four more, all of them looking like men. I knew which one was our Robert, and I could tell George Hammond by his hat. The other two, William and Kirk, were so easily the tallest. I didn't take the time to consider where Franky could be. I just went running out to meet them with my apron flapping in the breeze.

"Juli, honey, what's the matter?" Samuel called as soon as we were close enough. It wasn't every day I came out of the house

26

running, that was for sure.

"I need you to hurry to town," I told him between puffs of breath. "Thelma's water broke. She's about to have that baby, and I don't want to be without some help. She wants her mother, but I think we need Dr. Howell too." I stopped and took a deep breath. "I'm sorry I don't have the supper ready yet."

Samuel smiled. "I couldn't expect you to be cooking. I'll go. Now try and relax."

As I hurried back toward the house I could see Rorey scurrying down out of that tree. George hadn't seen her. I knew he hadn't. But I didn't say anything about it.

Berty came running out of the barn with the old gray mother cat in his arms. "Mom! Mom! Looks like she's been in a fight or somethin'!"

"Tarnation, boy!" George exclaimed at his son. "Let the cat take care of herself. You's about to be an uncle again."

Bert set Ladycat in the dust and stared at us. "Really? Already?"

"Lizbeth's comin'," Kirk told us quickly, and I turned my head to see their little car coming down the road.

"Thank the Lord," I whispered.

"Send Ben," George suggested. "Be good for him to get hisself involved."

It was a departure for George to be so obliging about calling for a doctor, I knew. But George had changed some since his wife died.

Lizbeth was clearly surprised to see so many of us outside. She grew a little pale when I told her what was going on. "You go with Mr. Wortham, will you please?" she asked her husband. He answered with a nod.

Robert and I helped Lizbeth carry their covered dishes. Unlike Thelma and Sam, they had the time and energy, and the means, to share their cooking. And no little ones running around yet.

"Go ahead and take our car," Lizbeth ordered. Ben stayed in the driver's seat, and Samuel leaned and kissed me before piling in.

But Lizbeth didn't say another word to Ben, and he backed out the drive in silence. They'd been so close in their two years of marriage that even at a moment like this I noticed the quiet between them as something strange. But I couldn't say anything.

"Might rain tonight," Berty told us. "Look at them clouds. It ain't rained in a long time."

Lizbeth glanced his way. "I hope it does.

But with a baby comin', it's not somethin' I'll be dwellin' on."

When she walked in the kitchen, she took a quick look around. Sarah was at the stove, Katie was still cutting turnips, and Rorey had come in and started setting plates on the table.

"Oh, Mrs. Wortham," Lizbeth said with a sigh. "Here you are again, right in the middle of helpin' us out."

"I was just thinking how glad I am that you're here to help me."

She went with me straight in to see Thelma and gave her older brother a hug before sitting on the edge of the bed.

"Lizbeth," Thelma said, trying to sound casual. "How's the teaching comin'?"

"No complaints." Lizbeth smiled. "But I hear you're fixin' to make Pa a granddaddy again, and on Willy's birthday too."

"Yeah. Somebody should tell him I'm sorry for spoilin' the party."

"Won't bother him any. He'd rather be fishin', anyway."

Thelma laughed. "He oughta take Georgie and all the boys."

"You feelin' all right?"

Thelma didn't respond to that. "Where's Ben?"

"Gone with Mr. Wortham to fetch your

mother and the doctor."

I couldn't quite discern the look in Thelma's eyes, but she forced a smile. "I'm glad you sent 'em 'fore they could come in an' see me in this nightshirt. You keep all them boys outta here, will you?"

She was trying to make light of everything, but just as she finished talking, she squeezed at the quilt with one hand and at Sam's hand with the other.

"Pretty good already, huh?" Lizbeth asked. "How far apart?"

"We don't know," Sam told her.

"Haven't timed them," I admitted, wondering where my head had been. But maybe it didn't matter if we knew that or not.

Georgie came bursting in the room with Emmie Grace right behind him. "Auntie Lizbef!" he called. "Auntie Lizbef!"

Lizbeth scooped up the little boy and planted a kiss on his forehead.

"Look at you," Thelma told her after a big breath. "You oughta be a mama. Been thinkin' 'long those lines?"

"No." Lizbeth shook her head emphatically. "I'll leave you the pleasure."

"Auntie Lizbef p'ay wif me?" Georgie was asking.

"In a little while, sugar," she told him. "I

want to sit with your mama a minute first."

"Is Thelma sick?" little Emmie whispered to me, understandably surprised that Thelma had come over and gone straight to bed.

"No, honey. She just needs to rest because the baby's due."

"Oh." Emmie looked at us with a very serious expression. "Does that mean it's time to get borned?"

"Yes," I told her. "But not quite yet. Not for a few hours, so far as we expect."

"Oh. That's a while." She turned on her heels and ran for the kitchen. "I want to frost the cake!"

I could hear George Hammond and the big boys coming into the kitchen, and they were surely hungry. "I'd better feed this crew," I told Lizbeth. "Wish I'd had the food done in time to send something along with Samuel and Ben."

"Oh, don't worry about it. We'll save them somethin' hot. You need anythin', Thelma? Cup a' tea or anythin'?"

"No. Nothin', please. Sammy, you go ahead though, if you want."

"I'll take a plate when the time comes," he said. "Everybody else here?"

Of course he knew their brother Joe was away with the army at Fort Campbell in

Kentucky. It was a bit of a worry to all of us, but just a part of life, seeing boys become men.

"I haven't seen Franky yet," I told him. "Maybe he stopped at your father's place to finish up some chores." I wondered on that a little. Franky had been working field with the rest, and I would've thought they'd manage chores at the other farm together before any of them came back here. But maybe Franky had offered to finish up so the others could come on.

George stepped in the doorway with a smile for his eldest son. "What you s'pose you got there?" he asked with a chuckle. "Twins?"

"Lordy, I hope not!" Thelma exclaimed. "One's enough work."

Young Sam disagreed. "Mama used to say that if one takes up all your time, then ten can't be any harder."

Thelma squeezed Sam's hand again as another pain swept over her. But it would surely be a while yet, and Lizbeth was with her, so I started for the kitchen. George followed me, looking a little anxious. "These times," he said, "they never was easy. Don't you think Sam oughta step outta there? It's gonna be a womanly situation, 'fore long."

Most people felt that way, I knew. But I figured it ought to be up to the mother. "He can stay just as long as Thelma wants him to stay."

"Ain't it bad luck?"

"Why would it be? God made him the head of his house. I see no reason he shouldn't be watching over them."

"I always used to be pacin' around outside. Even the ones that was born in the winter. Wilametta shooed me out. Blamed me for ever' one a' them babies."

I had nothing to say to that. I didn't remember him arriving at all until after Emma Grace was already born, but there was no telling about the other nine.

Sarah was mashing the potatoes, and Rorey was standing right next to her, stirring Lizbeth's pot of green beans. Funny how she could make herself look like she'd been working all along. Emma Grace stood on a chair, anxiously holding the frosting bowl.

"Just a minute, Emmie," Sarah was telling her. "I've got my hands full."

Indeed she did, making gravy, tending the chicken, and mashing those potatoes, practically at the same time. Bless her.

"You want me to help with the cake?" Katie asked, setting two kinds of pickles and a jar of rhubarb jam from the pantry next to her generous dish of raw turnip slices in the middle of the table. Bless her too.

"I want to frost it! Please!" Emmie begged.

"You're gonna need a hand," Katie told her. "That's a big job."

Emmie nodded her agreement, and I waved them on. Sometimes I didn't know what I'd do without Sarah and Kate. They were my best helpers. Katie was not yet thirteen, a relative we'd taken in about six years ago, and she seemed to make our family complete.

I moved to the stove, offering to take over with the chicken.

"Are you sure?" Sarah asked me. "Doesn't Thelma need you?"

"She will. In a little while. I think I can feed the rest of you first."

I'd husked a pot of sweet corn earlier, and the girls had moved it to the back burner to get some heat. Wouldn't need much. Most of the kids would eat corn on the cob raw, they loved it so well. I lifted the lid, just to see if the water was bubbling.

"Reckon Franky'll be here in time for dessert?" It was Robert asking from the doorway.

"We can very well wait for him, Robert John, as you ought to know. Is he doing the milking at home?"

"We did the milking over there, Mom. He went to find Mrs. Post. Said he was going to get another book from her."

I nodded. Just yesterday, I'd finished reading a Dickens novel to him. He'd be anxious to have something new in the house, even if he couldn't read it for himself. And besides, it was Friday. He always went to see the schoolteacher on Fridays, begging a book or a map or something for me to go over with him at home. I should have remembered that. Franky was always hungry for something more.

William sneered. "Why's he bother?"

Willy had always hated school and didn't go anymore unless his father made him, which was far too seldom. Today none of the older boys had gone. Like most of the teenagers in the district, they were helping with harvest.

"Franky likes books," I told them. "You boys should read, or at least listen, more often."

Robert and William both frowned. Somehow they'd gotten the notion that it was babyish to be read to and sissy to be caught with a book on your own. From

Willy, such an attitude wasn't any real surprise. But my own son? He'd always been such a good student.

Rorey sided with them. "I don't know how Franky can stand that stuff you read to him. It's dead dull, if you ask me."

"And stupid," Willy added. "Franky just don't want to admit he's stupid."

Even from the corner of my eye I could see little Emmie Grace turning her face toward me. Her father, Franky's father, had come in and was standing right beside me, taking a whiff of that chicken, and he didn't say anything. But I couldn't let it go.

"I don't want to hear another such word in my house," I told them. "There's not one of you stupid nor even close to it, and I don't want to hear of it again! You know Franky. You know he's got a special talent, and he's sharp as a tack —"

"I sure have appreciated you and Samuel feelin' that way," George finally decided to break in. "Don't know what Franky'd ever a' had otherwise, if you know what I mean."

I was suddenly so mad I could have hit him with the pot holder I had in my hand. How could he be so blind? Instead of standing up for his precious son and rebuking William's cruelty, he was practically endorsing the unkind words! Didn't know what Franky would've had? Indeed! I happened to know that George didn't read any better than his son, though he claimed it was because he'd never been to school.

"Way I see it, your Samuel give Franky a future," George continued. "Folks is startin' to know his work now."

"The whole business was Franky's idea," I reminded him. "WH Hardwoods might never have happened —"

"Do you want walnuts sprinkled on the cake?" Katie suddenly asked.

"Sure," William told her. "Do what you want."

I looked at both of them and back over at George and decided to let it drop about Franky for now. There were other things to think about, and it wasn't helping anyone to have me arguing with George Hammond.

I started wondering just exactly how long ago Ben and Samuel had left and when they could possibly be getting back. They had about ten miles to the doctor, and maybe a stop for Mrs. Pratt. It'd be a while, unfortunately.

We set out all the food buffet style, since there wasn't room for everyone at the table. Folks could sit wherever they wanted to. Kirk and William were itching to get started and pretty upset at Franky for the delay. He should've been here long ago, they thought, since he'd left to find the schoolteacher way before they started for home.

Oh, well, I thought. *He's surely on the way.* Their house wasn't very far. And Elvira Post wouldn't keep him long, with her ailing husband wanting supper. She seemed uncomfortable around Franky most of the time anyway, though she freely supplied him with books. He couldn't be much longer.

I went in to check on Thelma while we waited. She was sweating again, but the labor pains seemed no worse. William and Robert impatiently started a game of checkers. Rorey traipsed around the kitchen a few times, trying to look useful, and then went out and sat on the back porch. Finally, after quite a while, she hollered, "He's here!"

She must have meant Franky, of course, but she didn't say so. I glanced out the window and was immediately glad I did. Franky's limp looked far worse than usual. He was hurt, I could tell.

I rushed out the door, thinking that surely George was right behind me. But when I got to Franky, it was Kirk speaking

38

up at my side, and I saw that George hadn't even come outside.

"Fight! You was in a fight!"

Franky didn't say anything in reply to his brother, didn't even look his way. Instead, I saw his gaze resting on Rorey, who hadn't moved from the back porch step.

He was banged up a little, with one eye going purplish and a cut on his lip.

"What happened, Frank?" I asked him. "Goodness, are you all right?"

"I'm all right."

Kirk smiled hugely. "Fought back this time, didn't you, Franky? Finally had enough?"

I knew how some of the other boys in the area treated Franky, teasing him mercilessly when they got the chance. But how had he encountered anyone today? School was let out already, and I wouldn't have expected anyone to be between here and the Posts' farm. Neither Elvira's husband nor her brother-in-law would have let such a thing go on anyway, if they'd seen it.

"Who was it?" Kirk persisted. "Bobby Mueller? Or the Everly twins? I heard they was doin' some work on Mueller's farrowing house."

"Be quiet, Kirk," I commanded. "Franky, can we help you to the house?"

"I don't need help. Better wash up, though, 'fore Pa sees me."

"Ah, he won't mind much," said Harry, who'd suddenly come up alongside us. "If somebody fights at you, you got a right to fight back. He knows that. Looks like you got whupped, though, Franky. Did you get whupped?"

Franky looked from one brother to the other but didn't say a word, and I didn't feel like pressing him for any explanations. Maybe I could talk to him about it later. Maybe. When no one else was around to be enjoying the story.

Franky handed me the book in his hand. "Sorry if it got mussed. I might have to make it up to Mrs. Post. She didn't really want me to take it, anyway. Didn't think I'd understand it."

I looked down at the volume and smiled. *Silas Marner* by George Eliot. Why was it so hard for others to see the searching mind that made Franky want to reach out for books like this? I knew he'd sit just as long as I'd let him, soaking up every word the way he'd done with all the other books I'd read.

"Ugh!" Kirk said quickly. "What do you want with that book, Franky? No wonder people tease you. You're just plain odd."

That didn't deserve a reply, and Franky knew it. I tried to take his arm, but he wouldn't let me. He limped the rest of the way to the house all on his own, pulled off his shirt on the porch, and washed up best he could. I tried to help, but he'd barely let me touch him. He looked in Rorey's direction just once more, and she went back inside without saying anything. I wondered what was going on between them.

Franky wasn't hurt badly, but his eye was getting blacker, and the cut lip made him look pretty awful. The knuckles on one hand were banged up too, leading me to think that maybe Kirk had been right about him fighting back, as out of character as that seemed. I wasn't sure why his limp was worse, but somebody had lit into him pretty frightfully, and I really would have liked an explanation.

"Kirk," I commanded, "get me some warm water from the kettle on the stove. And Harry, run and get one of Robert's shirts for me, will you?"

When they were both gone, I tried to dab at Franky's eye. "Will you tell me who did this?"

He smiled just a little. "You're a real good mom, Mrs. Wortham. But don't fuss on me, okay?"

41

George stepped out the back door, and I hoped he'd be gracious. Seven years had gone by since his wife had died, and he'd relied on Samuel and me for so much. Most of the time, he'd tried to do his best for his children. Surely he could find a way for Franky now.

"What's this you've got yourself into?" he started immediately, much to my dismay. "Here we are, all waitin' while you go galavantin' after some book, and then fightin' on top a' that! It's your brother's birthday. I shoulda knowed to refuse lettin' you go over there. What's the use you gettin' books anyhow, Franky?"

I opened my mouth to say something, but George didn't give me a chance.

"And now you're tyin' up Mrs. Wortham out here when she needs to be in there with Thelma. They's havin' that baby, maybe tonight, and you ain't been no help at all!"

"Will you go gather up the kids," I told George, trying to be calm. "Say a prayer and start them eating. I'll be in in a minute."

George didn't budge. "I'll see to my son, if you please, Mrs. Wortham. You go on in and be with Thelma, 'fore she gets to frettin' 'bout you not bein' there for her."

I hated to go, I truly did. But as if on cue, Thelma gave another yell, and I scarcely had a choice. Franky was tough, after all. And he'd told me he was all right.

Jesus, help us, I prayed on the way to the bedroom. *What's happening today? Thelma's baby to deal with. Franky in a fight. Lizbeth and Ben and Rorey and little Emmie Grace. And even Robert. Seeming not so happy, nor so wise, as I thought we all were.*

Thelma was sitting up when I got there, looking pretty worn.

When she scrunched up her face again, Sam about jumped out of his skin. "Ain't there somethin' we can do 'bout the pain?"

"The doctor might know something," I told him. "But there's not much I can do right now but wait it out, the same as you. And pray. I can do that."

He nodded, but as soon as I was done with a prayer, he stood up and started pacing. I wondered if he might not be more comfortable outside like his father had said. But I didn't say so. It wasn't my place or George's to decide something like that.

"You need you a baby too," Thelma told Lizbeth between puffs of breath, but Lizbeth just shook her head.

43

In a little while, I was aware of the big boys eating in the next room, little Georgie fussing for his mother, and Sarah gradually settling him down. Thelma tried to drink a little tea but couldn't manage much. She tossed about on the bed, trying to find a comfortable position. Then, strangely enough, the pains seemed to just stop. When we were expecting another contraction, it didn't come.

"I better rest while I can," she said.

She curled up with her head on the pillow, and within a few minutes she was asleep.

"Is that normal, Mrs. Wortham?" Lizbeth asked me.

"I don't know," I had to say. "I hope so. We did pray for her to have less pain."

Sam got himself a plate but scarcely ate a bite. I couldn't eat either and kept watching out the windows, thinking that Samuel and Ben ought to be coming before long. Surely they'd had plenty of time to get to Belle Rive and back.

I started pacing worse than Sam and George put together. There wasn't much talking going on in the house. Not even between Rorey and Sarah, who were sitting together but silent. George cut the birthday cake, and most of it disappeared without any comment. Hammonds were never ones to give birthday presents, but when I offered to start reading Franky's book, George said it was Willy's right to decide what he wanted to do. Willy chose a radio show, which pleased almost everybody. But Franky went and sat outside.

"We'll jus' stay till Samuel gets back," George assured me. "Be bad luck all a' us in your hair any longer than that."

For a long time it had seemed the most natural thing in the world to have Hammonds in my living room and Hammonds such a big part of my life. But that night it suddenly felt strange again, like the first time, and I hardly knew what to do.

2

Sarah

Mom had her hands full. And it worried me a little seeing her anxious, so I did what I could to keep Georgie quiet and Emma Grace occupied. I ended up on the floor with them, playing dolly in the corner while the radio show was going on. Rorey followed me over and sat down too, but she just pushed the dolly away when Georgie tried to hand it to her.

"Franky's such a sourpuss," she whispered so quiet that not even Emma Grace heard, and she was on the other side of me.

"He's not so bad," I defended. "Just a little different, that's all."

"You just don't know." She scrunched up her face. "He's not *your* brother."

"Same as. He's over here all the time. Between school and work —"

"School's worth nothin' with him, and you know it."

I was used to her saying whatever she felt, but I could easily take offense to that. It was *my* mother trying to teach him, after all. "He doesn't see it as nothing. Mom says he tries real hard. And he's sharp too, on most subjects."

"Yeah," she scoffed. "Long as he doesn't have to read it for himself."

"I don't see why it matters to you."

"That part don't. An' he does make some nice wood things once in a while."

"So how does that make him a sour-puss?"

Emma Grace looked at me. She was hearing us now.

"Oh, Sarah." Rorey rolled her eyes. "You're so simple sometimes. It's not his school or work. He's just such a puritan! He got all riled up just 'cause me and Lester Turrey were talkin' the other night."

I had to hear more, but I knew Emma Grace shouldn't. "Emmie, run and get the dolly's blanket, would you?" I said quickly. She looked at me funny, but she got up and obeyed.

"When?" I prompted Rorey. "When were you talking to Lester Turrey?"

Lester was an older boy. Almost eighteen. He'd quit school last year just when Mrs. Post was about to kick him out. He was an awful lot of trouble.

Rorey leaned toward me and whispered even more quietly. "Last Saturday night. I snuck out to the bridge and met him. Didn't know Franky'd see me and take it in his head to follow."

"Does your pa know?"

"No. An' I made Franky promise not to say nothin'. Lester's my boyfriend. I'm meeting him tonight too. Don't you tell."

For a minute my head felt like it was swimming. For the life of me I couldn't see what Rorey would want with a big lug like Lester.

"Promise me, Sarah," she pushed. "You're my best friend in the whole world."

"Where are you meeting him?"

"In the barn. At midnight. Promise you won't tell. You'd get me in an awful mess of trouble. I think it might've been Lester who busted up Franky today. He said he might, just to make sure he wouldn't wanna follow me no more. Franky don't know, though, that we're meetin' again."

I was suddenly uncomfortable. No wonder she didn't want me to tell. We weren't old enough for boyfriends yet. She wasn't even fourteen till December, two whole months away. My mom and dad would be just as upset as her pa. "Rorey, are you sure about this? We're not old enough to be seein' boys."

Georgie was pulling on my sleeve, and Emma was on her way back to us. Katie was coming our way too, from across the room. "Mama was thirteen when she started seein' Pa," Rorey informed me importantly. "So it's not so strange. Promise me you won't tell, Sarah. Promise me. Hurry up."

I felt sort of squeamish inside, like my innards were arguing over having to hold this kind of information. But Rorey was Rorey. My friend even before first grade. She wouldn't do anything too stupid, surely. "I won't tell," I whispered just as Katie and Emmie were sitting down.

"Tell what?" Katie asked us.

Rorey shook her head. "Nothing." She'd no sooner tell Katie any secrets than she would one of the grown-ups. She'd never liked Katie as much as she liked me.

Emmie spread the blanket out and tried to get Georgie to play along like we were all at a picnic. Rorey's pa and all the bigger boys were so caught up in their radio show that they might not have even noticed if we'd been talking about Lester full out loud. Only Franky was outside someplace.

And I felt bad about that. I felt bad that probably he'd followed Rorey innocent, just wondering what she was up to, like a brother would. And then to get beat up for it, if it truly was Lester who had done it. But whether he had or not, I didn't like Lester, no matter what Rorey thought. He'd been a bully at school. He was still a bully. And I didn't want anything to do with him.

I wished Rorey hadn't told me. I wished she wasn't foolish enough to be sweet on somebody like Lester, who was four years older than her. Franky might be in for a lot of trouble if he was trying to protect his sister.

I swallowed kind of hard, thinking about that. I kind of wished he'd tell. But I knew he wouldn't, not if he'd promised. Not any more than I would. But there ought to be some way to let Rorey's pa know. Or the rest of her brothers.

"You be the mama, Sarah," Emmie was telling me, putting baby Bessie into my hands. I looked down at the doll I used to drag around with me every place, and for the first time I wished I was Emmie's age again. Being thirteen was getting kind of complicated.

3

Julia

Thelma stirred before long, and the pains were back, but I was confident we had some time before the baby came. The big girls were playing dolls with Emmie and Georgie, and Lizbeth and Sam stayed with Thelma. So with everybody else sitting and listening to "Spiral Hayes and the Dew Drop Gang," I stepped outside to check on Franky.

At first I didn't see him in the dark. He was clear over by the apple tree, sitting silent with his back to the house. He liked to be alone often enough, but this night I worried about him.

"Franky? Are you feeling all right?"

He turned his head just a little. "Yes, ma'am."

He didn't volunteer another word. I stepped closer. "Do you want to talk about what happened?"

"No."

"I'm sorry you're not getting much sympathy from your family."

"It's not a night for that."

I had to marvel at him. No hard feelings toward them. He just accepted it all as a matter of course. Picked on, beat up, and ignored. All in a day's work.

"Franky, I could heat you some water if you want to soak. A chamomile bath would help the soreness —"

He shook his head. "You have enough to do. I'm all right."

"Are you just going to let somebody hurt you and not say anything at all? And let them get by with it?"

Finally he faced me. "I guess you don't understand. The way I see it, talkin' about it wouldn't do no good."

I was absolutely incensed. "But you're no dummy, Franky! No matter what they say! You're —"

"It wasn't about that."

His words stopped me cold. What else could it be? Mild-mannered Franky, always minding his own affairs. "Tell me, Franky. Please."

"I can't. I swore I wouldn't."

"Swore? To who? Franky, what's going on?"

"I wish you'd quit your worrying. It's not no big deal."

"You came limping in all bruised up, and you tell me it's no big deal? Why, Franky? Tell me —"

Lizbeth opened the back door and hollered for me. My stomach squeezed tight as a knot.

"You better hurry back in," Franky said quietly.

And I turned and left him, suddenly very angry at his father and his brothers. All of them, for just leaving Franky out here alone.

The radio show was just ending and George was standing up as I came in. "Gettin' later," he said. "I know I tol' you we'd wait till Samuel got back. But he'll be along any minute, and it's high time we got ourselves outta here."

I could hear Lizbeth back in the bedroom, urging Thelma to take a breath.

"I wanna stay!" Emmie protested.

"Ain't no use none of us stayin'," George maintained. "We been here too long a'ready. It's jus' with no radio over to home, it give William a little treat. But Lizbeth's here, and they're gonna have more help'n that 'fore long. We'd be complicatin' things to linger. Time to be gettin' out."

I went into the bedroom, glad they were

going. I didn't want all the kids hearing any more. Things were getting harder for Thelma, and we had a ways to go. "Take what's left of the cake with you," I called out to them.

"Oh! Mrs. Wortham!" Thelma exclaimed as soon as she saw me. "I'm ready for this baby to be here."

"I know you are, honey."

"Can't I stay?" Emmie's voice was persisting out in the sitting room. "I wanna see the baby!"

"We can see it in the mornin'. That's good enough," George was telling her. "Hey, Sam!"

Sam had been petting at Thelma's hair and jumped at his father's call. "What, Pa?"

George didn't stick his head in this time, just called loud enough for Sam to hear. "You're welcome to come along and rest over t' home with us if you want. You hadn't oughta be in the middle a' things anyhow! Samuel'd be glad to bring us the news later. Or they can send Robert."

Sam Hammond looked genuinely insulted at his father's suggestion, and I was glad about it for Thelma's sake. "No, Pa. I ain't about to go nowhere."

"Suit yourself. Bad luck, if you ask me."

I shook my head, and Thelma was shaking hers too. "Don't listen to him," she whispered. "You was there for Georgie, and he's strong as a bull elephant."

"I know." Sam sighed. "I know. It's just Pa says it ain't what's done, me stickin' around you so close. He gets testy at times like this."

I was feeling a little testy myself. Worrying. Over the baby, of course. A little over Franky. And now I was really wondering what could be keeping Samuel and Ben. It was almost 8:00, and they'd been gone more than two hours. A blessing that Thelma wasn't further along by now.

"Ah —" she started to cry out but then just clenched her teeth together.

"Are you pushing? Thelma, are you pushing?" I could feel my heart thumping through my chest. Maybe I'd just *thought* we had time.

"No. I don't think so," she told me when she could breathe. "Oh!"

There it was again! *Lord, have mercy! These pains are close now. Samuel, Ben, Dr. Howell! Where are you?*

"I wish I was pushin'!" she groaned. "I wish it was done!" She grabbed for Sam, missed his hand, and got hold of his shirt.

"Why didn't I think about this part?" she

55

lamented. "A wonder any woman ever has more'n one!"

"They make up for themselves," I reminded her. "Don't they, now?"

I could hear George ushering all his clan out the door. Little Georgie started crying, and I heard Sarah taking him upstairs.

Robert poked his head in. "It's been awfully long, Mom. Dad wouldn't stop for nothing else. You think I should go after them in the truck?"

Ordinarily I would have said no, but this night was different, and I knew he was right. I'd tried to talk myself out of worrying over it, but I knew they'd been too long. And now I wondered if maybe they were lying smashed up along the road someplace. Maybe Ben had been hurrying too fast.

I couldn't voice such a thing, though. "You'll probably just find them coming up the road," I told him as calmly as I could. "But go ahead and go. It won't hurt anything. Drive carefully."

If George Hammond had waited two minutes, I might have sent one of his boys with Robert. But it was surprising, really, that George had stayed as long as he did.

Robert seemed glad to have something constructive to do. He was out the door in seconds, and I prayed I'd told him right.

"What are you hopin' for?" Thelma suddenly asked her husband. "Another boy?"

"I don't much care," Sam said quietly. "So long as you're both strong as Georgie."

She wiped at her face with a hanky Lizbeth must have given her. "Did I sleep long?" she asked me.

"A while. I was pretty surprised you could sleep at all."

"Gettin' my strength up. Gonna need it." She grunted as a pain swept over her again. But then it was finished, and she tried to smile. "We oughta call this one Sam, honey. Just to confuse everybody. What would Mr. Wortham think? Or maybe George again, wouldn't that be somethin'? I could call one name an' turn three heads."

"You're gettin' goofy again," Sam told her. "Jus' like last time."

Lizbeth went to the kitchen. It sounded like Katie was doing the dishes, and I knew that whatever else Lizbeth was doing, she'd be making sure we had plenty more warm water. I could hear Sarah singing upstairs now too. She'd have Georgie asleep pretty soon. Probably on her own bed. I looked out the window, hoping to see the headlights of Ben's car. Robert was already gone, and there wasn't a sign of anyone on the road.

Thelma was panting and sweating, and I felt like time was standing still and we'd be going on forever in her painful cycle, one wave followed by another and another. Eventually she gave up trying to smile or talk in the moments of calm in between. She was getting weaker, the pains were getting stronger, and I was getting really worried. I kept hoping to find the baby's crown of hair, to get this over with before the doctor got here, but I found nothing when I checked. I took to bathing Thelma's forehead with some cool water until Lizbeth came and relieved me at it.

I noticed for the first time that I was sweating as much as Thelma. My heart was thumping like galloping horse hooves as I went walking around the kitchen, trying to figure whether we had everything we might need. Clean scissors held in the lamp flame to cut the cord. Bias tape to tie it off, just like Emma had used. Towels and clean sheets and water and . . .

Suddenly a noise outside. Our old dog, Whiskers, came running up from the barn and gave just one gentle bark, the way he always did when greeting a car coming up the drive. I ran to the window, just about falling over myself hoping. And when I saw two sets of headlights coming up the lane, I almost shouted. *Praise the Lord! Finally our help!*

I ran out the back door, not waiting for them to get inside. I figured the doctor should know just exactly what had happened so far. I could tell him everything we had ready, how Thelma'd been doing. I ran to the car, almost tripping over iris stubble in the side yard on my way. Samuel jumped out from the passenger side and caught me in his arms, starting to talk at the same time I was noticing that there was no doctor with them. Nobody at all.

"Juli. Juli, honey, I'm sorry," he said quickly. "The doctor wasn't at home, and we couldn't find him. The neighbors weren't sure where he'd gone, but they said they'd send him our way when they saw him come in."

I was shaking in his arms. Dr. Howell was a busy man, despite his advanced age. He might've been called anywhere. What would we do without him?

Ben stepped out of the car and solemnly went for the house.

"W-what about Delores?" I asked.

"We tried to find her too," Samuel told me. "We went clear over to her son's place.

He said she might've gone to Frankfurt, calling on Lora Bloom again. He's going after her. They'll get her here as soon as they can. We went after Dr. Hall in Mcleansboro, but he couldn't leave the hospital tonight with a woman there birthing twins and a man from the town that'd just come in sick with his heart. Dr. Hall said we could bring Thelma in if she can be moved. Do you think we ought to try?"

"She doesn't want to be moved, Samuel. And tell you the truth, I don't know how she'd stand it over these roads. She seems so weak. I'd be afraid the baby would come halfway there."

I took a deep breath, thinking that now was the time to be extra strong. But I ended up bursting into tears, and he had to help me inside.

"It'll be all right, Juli," he said. "We can do this."

"I can't. I don't even want to."

It was silly for me to argue. Of course Samuel knew that. But he was patient and reassuring anyhow. "Relax. We'll be praying. Thelma's healthy. They'll be all right."

Dear Samuel. Wise and unruffled. At least he was here with me. At least I had that much.

★ ★ ★

If Thelma even noticed that the doctor wasn't there, she didn't let on about it. She was bearing down and pushing when I got back in the room. Breathing in hard little gasps, she looked me straight in the eye. "This . . . baby . . . she's . . . she's . . . comin' . . . right . . . now!"

She screamed and pushed, and Lizbeth tried holding her hand the way she'd done with her mother, but Thelma pushed her away. "Sammy!"

Sam Hammond leaned close, looking afraid to say or do much of anything. "Yes, honey?"

"Are you glad? Are you glad?"

"About the baby? Yes, I'm glad."

"Me . . . too . . ."

She yelled again, and I felt like I was going to pass out. But Thelma kept pushing, and I stayed with her for what seemed like hours but was surely shorter. And that baby came right on, headfirst like it was supposed to, screaming and squalling like it should. I was so relieved I could barely see straight. A girl. A teeny thing. Didn't take Sam and Thelma two minutes to name her Rosemary and start kissing each other. And all I wanted to do was kiss Samuel and cry because it was over.

Ben and Lizbeth decided to go on home once we had everything cleaned up and mother and baby were finally sleeping. I hugged Lizbeth, so very glad she'd been there, but she shook her head.

"I did nothing at all, Mrs. Wortham. You know that."

Ben was looking at her just a little uncertain, but he reached and patted her hand kind of quick, and she gave just a hint of a smile. I wasn't sure what their problem had been earlier, but hopefully it was fixed now.

I was standing at the back door watching them go when Samuel came up and closed his arms around me. "You did well, Juli Wortham. You make me proud."

"Oh, shush! I was fit to be tied, and you know it."

"I know I love you."

That easily, I melted completely. He was hugging me close, kissing my neck, sending little shivers of delight all the way to my toes. Wonderful. I hugged him back, loving every minute of it. We kissed full and warm until I saw Robert come in the kitchen behind us.

Our near-grown son looked awfully embarrassed to see his parents carrying on so. He ducked his head and was about to turn away. But I stopped him.

"You need us for something, Robby?"

"Um . . . no. I was just wondering if you might want my room tonight, and I'll sleep on the floor in the sitting room. Thought it might be easier that way."

"Thank you, Robert," Samuel told him, not letting go of me. "That's very generous of you."

Robert gave his father an indefinable sort of look and left us alone, shaking his head.

I could hear the baby stirring again, and I went to check on her, hoping she'd be anxious to suck. Emma Graham had told me there were two things you've got to know for sure: if a baby can suck and if the mother's strong enough to let it. They tried. It was a start. And I ended up rocking the baby a while as the father sat holding Thelma's head and talking too low for me to hear.

It was sometime around midnight when I left them all in our room. Robert had stretched his covers out on the sitting room floor. Sarah and Katie had gone to their room and were surely asleep with Georgie, the house was so quiet. Samuel and I tiptoed upstairs.

Most days we were so tired when we

went to bed that we couldn't do anything but hit the pillows and go to sleep. But that night was different, and neither of us had a thought of sleeping.

"Maybe I should've stayed down there," I whispered to Samuel. "In case the baby —"

"Shhh. Sam's there. If they need anything, we'll hear them." He pulled me gently across his chest and petted my hair with his callused hand.

"I thank God for you," he whispered.

"Oh, Sammy. I thank God for you."

I lay against his shoulder a while, and we were both quiet. *This is the way things should be,* I thought. *No matter how much of the day crowds over your mind, there should be times just like this to wipe away the load.*

I would've been sleeping soon. I would've just floated away into dreams of bliss. But Samuel suddenly stiffened beside me. He lifted his head, looking toward the window.

"What is it?"

"I don't know." He sat up, still looking out the window. And I could see an eerie glow in the sky out across the timber.

"Fire," Samuel said, springing up and grabbing his shirt. "That's at Hammonds'."

He was dressed before I could even

64

think. I jumped up and dressed too, but he told me I had to stay here, that I had a newborn in the house, and Thelma, and they might need me.

"Robert John!" he yelled. "Sam! There's a fire!"

He ran down the stairs two at a time, and I could hear Sam Hammond and Robert stirring down below. Sarah stepped out of her room, looking bleary eyed, and asked me what was wrong.

"A fire at Hammonds'. I just hope it's the barn or one of the outbuildings and not the house."

Katie came up behind Sarah, looking so sleepy I wasn't sure she heard. But Sarah stared at me, looking scared. "I can help. Mom, I can go help."

"I'm not sure your father —"

"I can sit with Emmie Grace! None of them will have time for her if they're fighting a fire! She'll be so scared —"

"All right," I told her. "All right, go. Hurry. Your father won't be waiting on anything."

"What about me?" Katie asked. "You want me to go too?"

"You oughta stay," Sarah told her before I could answer. "In case Georgie wakes up and Mom's busy with Thelma or the baby."

Katie nodded. I nodded. And quick as anything, Robert and Sarah and Sam Hammond piled in the back of our truck, and Samuel wheeled it around and went racing down the lane. I'd never seen any of them move so fast.

I wished I could have gone with them. I suddenly was afraid not to be there too. But I knew that Samuel was surely right. It was too soon. Too soon to leave Thelma and little Rosemary. They seemed weak, both of them. Not bad. But enough that it wouldn't do, me leaving them.

I stood in the kitchen and cried, wishing I had Samuel with me still to hold. What would this mean? Losing a barn, maybe, or worse yet, their house. I prayed that all those Hammonds were awake and out and that we didn't lose not one of them.

I could hear sobbing somewhere else in the house. Thelma. The poor dear. I ran to her and found her crying on the bed. "Thelma, honey, are you all right?"

"I'm scared!" she cried. "What if it's the house — oh, Mrs. Wortham, what if they're all inside?"

"They're not. You just calm down. They're not. That's all there is to it. You hear me?"

She was shaking, and I tried to calm her,

but I was probably shaking a little too, at least on the inside. I started praying out loud, and she got calmer and calmer. Pretty soon Katie came downstairs with Georgie awake in her arms. I thought surely they'd all go back to sleep, but they didn't. They just sat. We all just sat, until the baby woke up and there was something I could put my hands to.

4

Sarah

The barn was burning. I should've been relieved it was the barn. But all I could think
about was Rorey.

"In the barn at midnight," she'd said.
"He's my boyfriend."

Oh, God, I should have told.

Sam Hammond and Robert jumped out
of the truck before Dad even stopped it.
Fiery little embers were all over the sky like
fireflies, and the Hammonds had already
started dousing the porch roof, trying to
save the house. Emmie was standing by the
well hugging at her doll while Harry kept
pumping water into one thing after another.
Dad yelled for me to take Emmie clear to
the pumpkin patch and stay with her. He
was counting heads. Pulling our buckets
out of the truck, he kept checking. Harry's
there. Frank's over there. Mr. Hammond
and Kirk and Willy and . . .

I kept looking for Rorey, feeling tighter and tighter inside. Finally when I was just about to bust, I saw her standing in the barnyard, just staring into the flames. She wasn't doing a thing. Maybe she couldn't. She was just standing there, looking. I didn't see Lester Turrey anywhere, and I was too scared to ask if he'd been there.

"Where's Bert?" Dad was calling toward Mr. Hammond, and I looked up. I grabbed hold of Emmie's hand so I wouldn't lose her and pulled her toward the pumpkin patch, looking every which way, hoping I'd catch sight of Berty safe and sound. Some of the goats and a pig were just running around loose, but everybody was turning their attention to the house.

The barn had gotten too much ahead of us already. With no more folks and no more water than we had, there wasn't a hope for it. But all those frightful embers were flying over and landing on Hammonds' new porch. It would take some doing to keep the house from burning to the ground.

Emmie was tugging at my shirt. "The cows get out?" she asked me tearfully.

"I don't know," I told her. "I sure hope so."

Berty bumped into me suddenly. I

hadn't even seen him coming.

"Hold on," I told him. "Where you going?"

"I found Bess," he said, sounding funny in his voice. "I gotta go back for Imey."

Bess and Imey were calves. Berty loved his calves. He was running toward the barn, to the north section, where the flames weren't touching yet. I tried to grab him, but he got away too quickly. And I thought sure nobody else had seen him.

"Dad!"

My dad turned his head. I pointed to the barn. "Bert's going after his calf, back into the barn! He —"

I was going to say he looked okay. I thought maybe he'd be okay. That part of the barn didn't look touched by the fire at all yet.

But Dad turned on his heels and ran. Right in there after him, and then I was scared. Berty ran in after a calf, and Dad ran in after Berty, and Mr. Hammond and Robert and all the rest were so busy saving the house that they didn't even know. I squeezed Emmie's hand till she hollered and pulled, so I had to ease up and just stand there watching. I knew how it was supposed to end up. Berty would come out, pulling his calf. And Dad right with him, giving him an earful for risking himself over some dumb animal.

I waited. I waited. And then I heard the most awfullest crack, and I couldn't stand it anymore. I started screaming and screaming. The others turned to look, but they didn't know what they should be looking for. Something gave way in the top of the barn in the south section, where the flame was the worst. Something gave way, and it leaned and crashed in on itself, a whole chunk of the barn falling down in a heap of smoke.

I was screaming and Emmie was screaming, and suddenly Robert was grabbing me.

"What's wrong?"

"Dad! Dad! He went in there!"

I let go of Emmie's hand and tried to get past Robert. I was going to go straight in. I was going to go find Dad, but Robert grabbed me.

"He went in!" I screamed again. "He went in after Bert! He's in there!"

Robert let go of me. I knew what he was thinking, and when he turned around and started running, *I* grabbed *him*.

"No! No!"

He'd have run straight in, just like I would have. He was struggling, and finally

71

he shoved me away from him. But Mr. Hammond grabbed him and knocked him clear to the ground. Emmie squeezed me so tight it hurt, but I didn't even know when she'd grabbed me again. Willy and Frank and Sam Hammond were all running over by the barn, running around the back side because the crashed-in front was all on fire. Robert broke away from Mr. Hammond and went running over there too.

Right then I thought I was going to die. I thought of Mom at home, and I thought I was going to die. Rorey turned and looked at me, her face like a ghost's in the crazy light of the fire. I met her eyes for just a minute, the pounding in my head seeming like it could come clear through my skull, but I had to turn away. She wasn't even helping. She wasn't doing anything at all. And it was all her fault.

"Here!" Franky started yelling. "Here!"

I leaped and ran, barely aware of leaving Emmie and her father behind me.

Around the back, just past the only barn door still standing, Berty lay on the ground in a crumpled heap. Willy stayed by him, but Robert and Franky and Sam were all inside the doorway, working furiously throwing back splintered boards and pulling at a pair of arms sticking out from what looked like part of the loft that must have fell when the other section came down.

"Daddy!"

I knew they were in danger. Every one of them was in danger. The smoke was awful bad, and the flames were spreading toward them now. Willy moved Berty farther away. But I stood frozen.

Finally they had Dad unpinned. They dragged him out to the grass, and he was so still I thought I'd choke inside.

"Dad!" Robert was shaking him. "Dad!"

"You dumb fool!" Sam Hammond yelled over at Berty. "What'd you go in for?"

Berty just coughed and coughed. He didn't even try to talk.

Then Daddy coughed too. And I busted apart and cried. I ran up and hugged at him and cried. He was alive. *Thank you, God!*

"Get off him." Robert pulled at me. "Get off him, Sarah. He's bad hurt."

I sat up, staring down at my father, somehow expecting him to get up and say that Robert was wrong, that he was really fine. But he just lay there, looking gray and black and broken.

I'd blamed Rorey. But I should never

have made such a stupid promise. If I'd told on her, if I'd only had the sense to do something about it right away, maybe none of this would've happened. Maybe Daddy would be okay.

It was really my fault.

5

Julia

Thelma was frantic not knowing what was taking place at the other farm. I could scarcely keep her in bed. She wanted so badly to get up and go over there, to find out if everybody was okay. I had to tell her two or three times how little sense that made. She shouldn't be going anywhere.

Little Rosemary was lying there so peaceful, but Georgie was fussy in Katie's arms so I started singing, trying to calm my own nerves and settle him back toward sleep. Finally Thelma was trying to relax again too.

"I wish I had your faith," she said.

There wasn't much I could say to that. So many times I'd wished for more faith. Like Emma Graham had known; she'd been so amazing. Or like Samuel, who'd changed so much since we'd come here. He was a saintly man, true, and all the neighbors knew it. They came to him for help with things, knowing he wouldn't ever turn them away.

Rosemary still wasn't sucking much, but she did a little, and went to sleep in her mommy's arms. Katie took Georgie back upstairs for me. And I made Thelma a cup of shepherd's purse tea with a little red raspberry mixed in. That would be good for her right now. But I wanted coffee. Strong and black.

I was sitting in the kitchen alone for a minute, just sipping the coffee and thinking, when I finally heard a vehicle coming up the lane. My first feeling was wild relief. Fire must not have been bad for them to have it under control already. I jumped to my feet, expecting my family and Sam Hammond to come straight in the door.

I'd heard the vehicle stopping. But now I was sure I was hearing it move right on again. Who in the world could that have been?

I was on my way to look out when Delores Pratt came bounding in the back door without knocking.

"Julia, honey!" she exclaimed, almost running into me. "Richard just dropped me off. We seen the flames over toward Hammonds', and he went to see if he could help. God be with 'em! Your men over there? Thelma all right?"

"Yes, they went," I told her quickly. "Thelma's fine. Just worried for all the rest. And you're a grandma again."

She set her bag down on the table with a thump. "Whew! You manage all right?"

"I — I think so."

"Poor dears. You're a-worryin' too." She took my hand and pulled me into the other room with Thelma. She started in praying out loud for the safety of the whole Hammond family.

And Samuel, I added in my mind, not knowing why. *God save my Samuel.*

6

Sarah

Robert wanted to put Daddy in the truck right away and start off for the hospital. Sam Hammond brought a couple of blankets from the house almost before I realized he had gone to get them. He said that if they rolled Daddy onto a blanket and then picked him up, blanket and all, it would make the moving easier on him.

I couldn't stand it. I stood there with my fists tight shut, wishing this was just a dream. When they started moving Dad, rolling him just a little to get the blanket under him, he lifted his arm and got hold of the edge of Robert's shirt.

"Bert," he said with a choked kind of voice. And then he started coughing again. He didn't sound too good, but he was awake, and that made me feel better. I started crying all over again.

"He's okay, Dad. He got out," Robert

said, still sounding awfully worried.

Daddy pushed Sam Hammond back just a little, trying to sit up. But he moved real slow, and I could tell he was hurting somewhere. Robert could tell too.

"Maybe you hadn't oughta move, Dad. We'll get you to the truck."

"I think I'm all right," he said, but his voice wasn't steady enough to convince me. He looked so small. And I was used to Daddy being big and strong.

Suddenly Willy yelled, and we all turned to see him pointing to the house. The embers had kept on flying in that direction with nobody there to do a thing about it. One corner of wood shingle was caught on fire, the thin line of smoke trailing away almost horizontal. Scads more of those dreadful sparks kept landing, making the roof and porch look like gatherings of crazy-shaped fireflies.

Mr. Hammond and Willy and Kirk went running over there. Sam Hammond and Robert and Franky all hesitated, not wanting to leave Daddy and Bert so close to the burning barn. Quick as anything, Sam and Robert had Dad and that blanket up and moved clear over to the back of the truck. Franky brought Bert, half carrying him and struggling because Bert couldn't seem to hold his weight just right on his left foot and Franky was always dealing with a pretty bad limp himself. Emmie took my hand again and grabbed on to my blouse besides. She was scared and no wonder, the poor little kid.

"Samuel all right?" Mr. Hammond hollered to us.

"Yeah," Daddy answered him. "I'm all right."

"Then we need your help over here, boys!" Mr. Hammond hollered again. "Sam! Frank!"

Just about then, somebody I thought looked like Thelma's brother came driving up to lend a hand. The roof of the house was a mess. The porch too, with embers everywhere. And now the goat fence was burning, and the pigsty. I wondered if anybody was praying for the wind to stop being so cruel.

"Save the house," Daddy told Sam and Robert. "Go on."

They went because he'd ordered them too. But not before Robert insisted I not leave Daddy's side. He should've known I wouldn't have anyhow.

Franky stood for a minute, looking from Bert to my father. "Are you sure you're all right?" he asked either one, or maybe both.

Berty nodded, coughing again.

"Go on," Daddy told him, holding himself up against the truck rail. "Go on."

Franky went. And I guess it took all of them drawing bucket after bucket out of the well, passing them hand over hand, and then dousing that roof and porch time after time, beating at embers with boots and blankets and bucket after bucket after bucket.

Then Mr. Hammond just stopped. "You can let it go, boys," he said, sounding weary enough to drop. But they didn't let it go.

Emmie climbed up beside Bert, who gave her a hug and then told me he was sorry for going in. I didn't say anything to him. I just sat there by Daddy, holding on to him tight, feeling him slowly sag heavier. Finally he let me help him ease down to lie flat on the rough wood of the truck bed.

"Where are you hurt, Daddy?" I begged him to tell me, wishing the older boys hadn't taken him so much at his word when he told them he was all right. Maybe Mr. Hammond was right. Maybe they should let the house go. Anything just to get Daddy away from here and to a doctor. Or at least to Mom. She would know what to do.

"It's all right, Sarah," Daddy told me, but I could barely hear him over the fire and the yells, even when I leaned close.

Emmie was still holding on to Bert, but at least he was sitting up. She was crying, I knew she was. And I couldn't blame her. I was crying too. Holding Daddy's head, watching the endless dance of sparks, I felt like the night would never end. The last of the barn fell down, but I don't know if anybody but me even turned at the awful crash. Again I wondered where Lester Turrey was, or if he'd been here at all. Rorey was gone now; I didn't know where she went. Maybe she was helping somewhere out of my vision, but I couldn't say for sure.

One of the embers landed on Kirk's shirt, and Franky doused him just in time. They were keeping ahead, sort of, but it was like trying to catch confetti, the contrary wind kept sending up so many sparks. A wonder somebody else's clothes didn't catch. Or their hair.

"They might lose the house, Daddy," I said. He didn't answer me. I looked down at him, not sure if he was awake now or not. "Dad?"

" 'Least the sparks isn't comin' at us," little Emmie said. "Is our house gonna burn up?"

I couldn't answer her. Daddy's sudden stillness was scaring me. "Robert!"

Somebody else came driving up in a truck. I wasn't sure my brother heard me. So I yelled again. "Robert!"

He turned his head, and then he came running. Whoever it was that just got here came running too. Barrett Post, the schoolteacher's brother-in-law. "I don't think he's as okay as he said," I told them as soon as they were close. "Something's wrong."

"Dad?" Robert called, touching Daddy's arm and sounding every bit as afraid as I felt. "Dad?"

"What happened?" Mr. Post was asking, looking awful stern.

Neither of us answered. We both waited, hoping Daddy would respond.

"We've got to get him to a doctor," Robert said solemnly.

Suddenly it was hard for me to breathe.

"Where's he hurt?" Mr. Post asked.

"Don't really know," Robert admitted. "He was savin' Bert out of the barn. Part of it fell in 'fore they got out. But he came around. He said he was okay. But now . . ."

I'd never seen Mr. Post look so grim. He climbed right up on the truck beside me. I didn't move. I was still holding Daddy's head.

"Samuel?" He leaned way down, listening, I knew, for his heart or his breath. Then he looked over at Robert again. "You say he got out on his own?"

"No, sir. He was pinned pretty bad. And he might've been hit in the head. He wasn't conscious when we first pulled him out."

"Can you drive?"

Robert said he could. And suddenly Mr. Hammond was there by the truck too, telling Emmie and Bert to jump down.

But Emmie was crying even more than before.

"No," I told her father. "Berty's hurt too. And Emmie ought to stay with me. Not here."

"Sarah's thinkin' right," Mr. Post declared. "We'll take care a' this, George. Jus' do what you can to save your house."

Mr. Hammond backed away, not really wanting to, I could tell. In the fire's eerie light he looked pale and forsaken. Robert made Bert and Emmie scoot farther toward the front, and then he went to start the truck.

Harry and Kirk were suddenly yelling. Me and Mr. Post turned our heads at the same time. "Good Lord," he said under his breath.

I wished we could all be dreaming. Sparks had caught a haystack and were spreading across the ground into the trees and toward the cornfield.

Mr. Post jumped out of the truck. "Robert!" he yelled. "You go on out a' here! Get your mama and find the doctor! I gotta see if there's any stoppin' this, 'fore we burn up the whole countryside."

It'd never occurred to me to wonder how old Mr. Post might be, but he looked really ancient then. "I'm sorry, Sarah," he said in a hurry. "You be brave and stay with your papa. It'll be all right."

I watched him run to his truck for a shovel. Everybody else was fighting sparks wherever they could. *They're gonna lose the house,* I thought with a sick feeling. *And the field too, and who knows what all else.*

At least the wind wasn't blowing toward our house. At least that should be safe. But looking down at Daddy, I didn't feel much comfort.

With a sudden jerk we started moving. Robert hurried faster than the truck ought to go, and we left the awful chaos behind us.

"Sarah?" Emmie called. "Why'd God make this happen?"

"It wasn't God," I answered her. But that was all I could say.

I sat there for a minute, feeling the wind on my wet cheeks and thinking of Daddy carrying me on his shoulders the way he used to do.

Suddenly I remembered hearing somewhere that people who get hurt need to be kept extra warm. I didn't have nothing else to cover him with, so I took off my sweater and stretched it across his chest as best I could.

"Please wake up," I whispered.

I knew we weren't far from home. It shouldn't take long to get there. But it seemed like forever, even with how fast Robert was driving.

"You okay, Bert?" I yelled, 'cause he had gotten quiet too.

"I think so," he answered softly. "It's just my ankle. I think I turned it. But Mr. Wortham — I'm awful sorry . . ."

I couldn't say anything at all. I couldn't blame Berty. I should've stopped him from going in. I should've been quicker. But more than that, I should've told on Rorey before any of this ever got started.

"Is Mr. Wortham gonna die?" Emmie asked.

"No!" I yelled at her. "No, he's not, and

don't you say it again! He'll be just fine. You'll see."

Emmie and Bert looked at me, and neither of them said a word. I knew I shouldn't have yelled. And I knew I should probably say something now to make them feel better. Only I couldn't think what.

Daddy moved just a little, and I held tight to his hand. *Please, God,* I begged inside my head. *Please, please, let him wake up and be okay.*

"Pumpkin . . ."

Daddy's voice was low just as we were turning down our lane. And I got excited. I could hardly believe my prayer would get answered so fast as that.

"Oh, Daddy!" I smiled and squeezed his hand, glad to be hearing him call me "pumpkin" again, just like when I was a little kid. I thought he'd sit up, but he just looked at me. And I guessed that was enough for right then.

He was coughing some, and Emmie scooted closer. Robert drove us up between the barn and the house and then stopped the truck and came flying around to the back. "How is he?"

Daddy tried to sit up. Using my arm to pull against, he got halfway, and Robert jumped up beside us. "Maybe you oughta

87

lay still, Dad. I'll get Mom."

But Daddy wouldn't hear it. "I'm all right, son. I just want to get in the house."

Light from the oil lamps spread across the yard as the back door opened, and I could see Mom standing there looking out, surely wondering who it was and why we were back so soon. She would know the fire wasn't spent. Anyone could tell that by the glow in the sky, in the wrong place to be the sunrise.

"Samuel?" she called.

"Right here," he answered her, sitting forward despite Robert's protest.

Mom must've thought it strange that none of us were hurrying toward the house. She came running.

"He's hurt, Mom," Robert told her before she even got close.

"I think I'm all right," Daddy said again. "Just help me inside."

"But, Dad —" Robert started to say, just as Mom got to the truck.

"What is it? What's happened?"

"Juli, I'm all right —"

"Part of the barn fell," I tried to explain. "He was in there getting Berty out."

For a minute Mom just stood there. "Oh . . . Lord, have mercy . . . oh, Samuel." She climbed right up in the truck and started hugging on him, and then she saw Berty and hugged him too. "Thank God you're both . . . you're all right, aren't you?"

For a second, nobody said anything.

"It's not bad, Juli," Daddy told her. "It could've been worse."

"He wasn't awake when we pulled him out, Mom," Robert said. "And we were pretty worried when he —"

"Just help me into the house," Dad interrupted. "I just need to rest a while."

"I'll go fetch the doctor," Robert persisted.

"No," Dad told him. "Not now. I'm all right. Go help George." He started scooting toward the back of the truck. I went with him.

"What about Bert?" Mom asked. "Are you all right, Bert?"

"Yeah," he answered her. "It's just my ankle twisted. But I'm sure glad Mr. Wortham pushed me out. I couldn't find the door. And I'm awful sorry . . ."

Mom reached to help Dad as he got to the open back end.

"Dad," Robert persisted. "I'm not so sure you oughta be —"

"Help us inside, Rob," Dad insisted. "Then hurry back over there. They need you. It's bad enough that I can't —"

"Mom!" Robert protested again. "We need the doctor."

"We left word for him to come when he can, to look at the baby," Dad said, taking a deep breath. "He can see to me and Berty then. You've got to help them with the fire."

Robert looked to Mom again, and she nodded her head.

"Help me to a chair, Juli," Dad said. "Robert, help Bert. Then go. Please."

When Dad first got his feet on the ground, he stopped for a minute. I could feel him taking another deep breath. Mom put her arm around him, and he put his arm over her shoulder. I jumped down to his other side.

"You sure you're all right, Samuel?" Mom asked.

He said he was, but I wondered too. At least nothing was broken, or he wouldn't be standing up. That's what I figured, anyway.

But we moved slowly. Dad was walking but kind of leaning on Mom, and that made me worry. *Is he okay, God? I thought he was okay.*

Berty tried walking on his own and couldn't quite manage it, so he ended up

90

leaning on Robert. Emmie took hold of the tail of my blouse and came right alongside us as I heard what sounded like a rumble of thunder off in the distance.

"This'uns a bad night," she said softly.

"Yeah," I told her. "But just like Dad said, it could've been worse."

That thought had my stomach in flip-flops. Daddy could've died. He very nearly did, or so it had seemed. And Berty could have died too. *"Lord have mercy,"* Mom had said. He must have had mercy. On Daddy and Bert, for sure.

But suddenly I couldn't help wondering what the Lord thought of Rorey if she or Lester Turrey had somehow set that blaze. I wondered what he thought of me too, foolish friend that I was, promising to keep mum at such a horrible cost.

Forgive me, I whispered, too quiet for anybody to hear.

Tell your father that, something strange and ugly in my head jumped right back at me. *He's* not *okay. And it's all your fault.*

7

Julia

Samuel was doing his best, not wanting any of us to worry, I could tell that. But I could also tell that he was weakened, and he wasn't bearing full weight on one leg.

I was glad for Delores to meet us on the porch as we were coming up the steps. "Oh, Lordy be," she said. "Goodness gracious." But that was all she said. She held the door for us and then hurried to turn around the nearest kitchen chair for us to set him in. Then she quick got a chair for Berty too.

"What's happened?" Thelma called out, coming into the kitchen with baby Rosemary in her arms.

"Just what are you doin' up?" her mother demanded.

"Was it the house?" Thelma kept on. "Did everybody get out?"

"The barn," Samuel managed to say.

"They're all right."

"Imey's lost," Bert said sadly.

"Oh, Berty," Thelma answered him. "Better the calf than one of you all."

The room seemed almost chaotic then, with Thelma trying to comfort Berty, and Delores trying to shoo her back to the bedroom and look at Berty's ankle at the same time. Sarah and Emma Grace got up close as I was trying to check Samuel over, and then Katie came from upstairs looking dreadful worried.

"Is Georgie asleep?" I asked her.

"Yes."

"Good. Bring in fresh water and set some on to heat, will you please?"

Katie went running out, and I remembered Robert still standing in the doorway, just looking at us all. "How bad is the fire?" I asked him.

"Spreading, Mom. Looked like it might take the field."

"Go!" Samuel demanded. "Go help them!"

For just a moment our son hesitated, and then with another glance at me he turned and disappeared. "Thank you, Robby!" I called after him. "Please be careful!"

I looked down at Samuel. "He's just worried about you."

Samuel shook his head. "Can't take time for that. I ought to be over there —"

"No. You ought to be lying down. Can I move you to the bed?"

He shook his head again. "Thelma," he said. And I knew what he meant. We'd given Thelma and the newborn our room for the night.

"Go ahead and put him in there," Thelma said quickly. "I'm gonna rock the baby, and I can do that in the sitting room. Then we can just stay there, on your davenport. But can I be helping first?"

"No. Not tonight," her mother answered. "Go set yourself down. Go on."

Katie was back in before long, wiping at tears with one arm and carrying a bucket with the other. She put the water on without asking any questions, and I turned my eyes to little Emma Grace standing there watching me.

"Sarah, take Emmie to your room and see if you can get her to sleep up there with Georgie."

"I don' wanna sleep," the little girl protested.

"It's night," I told her. "Time for you to be asleep. Don't you worry. Everybody'll be all right."

Sarah didn't want to go either, I knew

that. She was standing about as close to her father as she could get. But she was good to mind me and take the little girl upstairs. And almost immediately I was glad that they were gone, because Samuel was looking paler.

"Are you sure you're all right?" I asked him again.

"Yeah," he said, but his voice sounded kind of strange. He took another deep breath, and it seemed to take extra effort.

"Samuel, you have to tell me what's wrong. Where do you hurt?" I knelt beside him and put my arm around his shoulder, feeling my heart suddenly pounding faster. What was it Robert had said? That he hadn't been awake? I should've paid him more attention. That could mean a head injury. Robert was right to worry, if that was the case.

Samuel reached his hand to me. "Juli — it's going to be okay."

"Does it hurt you to breathe?"

"Some. I'm just bruised, that's all."

Katie was standing there by the stove looking at us. I felt bad to have all the kids scared like this, but nothing could be done about it. "Help me get him to the bed," I asked her, and she came running to my side. Maybe we shouldn't have sent Robert on. The Hammonds certainly needed help, far more help than they had, with the fire going wild, but it might have been better to send Robert looking for the doctor. Now we were left without the truck.

"I'm all right," Samuel said again. Katie got on one side of him, and with me on the other we helped him out of the chair. But it was slow progress to the bed. Despite what he said, he seemed weaker than before.

We finally got him settled down, and Katie hurried to light the lamp and the pair of candles sitting on the dresser. Then she was right back at our side.

"Samuel?" I said. "Tell me everywhere you hurt."

"My head."

Those simple words made me feel sick to my stomach. "Is that the worst?"

He was quiet for a moment. "Yeah."

I thought back to the time, several years ago, when he'd fallen through the pond ice and struck his head on one of the wooden beams that served as a dock. He'd been unconscious then too. Quite a while. But he'd come around and been all right. I wondered if it mattered with a head injury that there had been another one some time before. *Lord, help.*

"Where else?" I pushed him. "Samuel, I've got to do what I can. I've got to know."

He nodded. Slowly. "My side," he said, seeming to have trouble getting the words out. "My leg."

Looking down at my husband, I wondered where I should look first. He was so filthy with soot that I wasn't sure I could even find anything.

"Katie, bring me some water and a cloth."

She went, but maybe I shouldn't have sent her out so soon. She looked scared, worse than Robert, seeing all this. And we weren't even taking the time to give her a word of comfort.

Samuel moved his right arm against his side. "Juli, I'm sorry," he said so softly.

"Stop," I told him. "You have nothing to be sorry about. Do you hear? You saved that boy's life."

I kissed his smudged cheek, unable to stop a sudden rush of tears. "Close your eyes and rest. Please, Samuel. We need you better."

"Is Bert all right?"

For a brief, awful moment, I wondered if he didn't remember Berty coming in the house with us, and before that telling us it was only his ankle that was hurt. But I decided Samuel was surely just looking for an assurance that Berty was being taken care of too. "Yes, honey. Delores is seeing about his ankle. He'll be just fine. Thank God you got him out."

He seemed to relax a little. Katie came rushing back with a bowl in her hands and a couple of towels over her arm. I started washing Samuel's face just as gently as I could.

"His leg is bleeding, Mom."

Katie's words, so quietly spoken, jarred me nonetheless. Why hadn't I noticed?

I examined the leg more closely. It didn't look to be bad. But I couldn't tell for sure. I had to get my sewing scissors and cut some of the trouser out of the way to get a look. He had a gash, bleeding slowly, with plenty of blood drying around it.

"Oh, Samuel." I knew that leg would need attention, but I was more worried about his head. I grabbed one of the towels and wrapped it around the leg wound. "Hold this, Katie," I said. "Keep it nice and tight."

She nodded and obeyed me stiffly. "Is he gonna be all right?"

"Yes," I told her. "Say a prayer, but don't you worry."

I knew she was terrified. Sarah too. And Emmie, the poor child. I reached my arm over Katie's shoulder for a quick squeeze. Robert was scared too, I knew, and right in the middle of everything. *Lord, bless him. He's having to be such a man tonight. Keep him safe.*

"Samuel, I need to see your head," I told him, hurrying to the business at hand. "I may lift it just a little, so I can feel the back. You just stay relaxed, and let *me* do it, all right? Don't try to move."

He was still. He didn't answer me a word, but his eyes were open, watching. Katie had tears trailing down her cheeks, but she was doing what I told her, holding that towel tight against his leg. I picked up the bowl of water again. I knew it wasn't very warm. What Katie'd put on to heat hadn't had time to get hot. But the cool would probably feel good on his head. I hoped so.

Something had hit him; that was clear to me. On the back of his head I felt quite a lump beneath a small but jagged cut with dried blood caked over it. A wonder he hadn't bled more.

I wished the doctor were here already to ask about this. But it worried me, knowing there was very little even a doctor could do for a head injury. Dr. Howell had told us that before. I began to pray that nothing was serious, and nothing broken.

"How do you feel now?"

"Sore."

I kissed him again, remembering his tender caress of such a short time ago. *Lord, help him. Heal him quickly.*

I let Kate bathe his forehead for a minute, which Samuel seemed to welcome.

I could hear Delores in the kitchen talking, probably to Bert, but I couldn't quite make out what she was saying.

"Let me see your side," I said, carefully unbuttoning Samuel's shirt. But I couldn't see any injury there. I couldn't feel anything either, but my touch hurt him. I could tell, even though he didn't say so.

Feeling numb, I went to get another cloth and bowl. Delores looked up as I entered the kitchen. "How is he?"

"I don't know yet."

She was setting Bert's foot down to soak in a mixing bowl full of water. She glanced up at me again with concern on her face. "Do you need to sit down for a minute?"

"No. No, not at all. There's too much to do." I grabbed a clean cloth, scooped some water out of the kettle into another bowl, and then threw a kitchen towel over my shoulder. "How's Thelma?"

"Still rockin' the baby. Don't you worry 'bout her. She's got a strong constitution about her, that one. She'll be fine bein' up this soon. And I'll see that she don't overdo."

I nodded. It was all I could manage before hurrying back into the bedroom. Samuel's eyes were closed. That bothered me at first, even though I'd told him to rest. What if he was unconscious? What if something was seriously wrong?

But he opened his eyes as I neared the bed. "Juli, all of you need to get some sleep."

"There's no way we can sleep with you and Berty hurt! And that fire going on. We're not even half started cleaning you up."

"I should be helping," he said. His voice sounded weak.

"I don't want to hear such nonsense. The only way you're to help is to stay still while I see to you. I want to get your shirt all the way off and wash you up and see if there's anywhere else —"

"I love you." His words were quick and soft, stopping me in midsentence.

I just stared, wishing I could hold him till forever and make all the hurt go away.

"Oh, Sammy, I love you too. I'm so glad you're all right."

As soon as I said it, the cruel doubts started beating my insides. Was he all right? I'd once heard about a man who'd been hit with a chunk of rock inside a cave. He thought he was fine. Everybody thought he was fine. He just went home, and the next day they found him dead in his bed.

I couldn't say anything else. And Samuel didn't either. He closed his eyes again as I bathed the back of his head. Katie went to get fresh water and came back as I was taking the towel off his leg.

"Can you get his boots off for me, Katie?"

She nodded, looking grim. "Do they know how the fire started?"

"I don't know, honey. I doubt it."

"It's so good he isn't burned."

"Yes," I said, feeling a little sick inside. "Thank God for that."

I took the sewing scissors to Samuel's pant leg again and cut the rest of it completely off from midthigh so I could really see the wound and not have to bandage over or under the dirty denim. Katie struggled with the boots and then brought in another oil lamp from the sitting room. I folded one of the cool cloths and left it against the back of Samuel's head and then turned my attention again to his leg.

Once we had the blood cleaned away, I could see that he'd have a lot of bruising on that leg. The gash was at least four inches long, and deep. It would require stitches. And I knew I ought to be putting something on to help it right away.

"Katie, go and see if the water's hot. And set out the comfrey and plantain from the cupboard if you can find them."

She went out quickly, and I felt over the rest of that leg and the other one. "God's grace that nothing seems to be broken," I said.

Samuel didn't answer. His head was turned just a little to one side, his eyes still closed. *Let him be sleeping, Lord,* I prayed. *Just let it be a nice, restful sleep.*

But I wasn't sure how he could sleep at a time like this, any more than I could, if he was really all right. A weight pressed hard against my stomach. What if there was nothing that could be done? What if he didn't wake up?

"Mom? How is he?"

Sarah's words jarred me. I hadn't heard her coming down the stairs.

"It's all right, honey," I told her. "He's resting."

I sounded so phony to myself that I wondered if she knew. But she only stepped closer, looking at her father with cautious eyes.

"Is Emma Grace asleep?" I asked her.

"Yes. She didn't want to, but she was too tired to fight it long."

"Thank you, Sarah, for all you did."

She looked at me oddly, almost as if my words hurt her. "There wasn't much I could do, Mom. I hope I never see nothing so scary — never again."

She looked closely at her dad's leg with tears in her eyes, and then up at his face again. "Oh, Mom —" she stopped, not quite able to say anything else. And I was no better.

Suddenly, Katie called to me from the doorway. "Mom, the water's warm. Do you want me to set some aside with the herbs in it?"

"Sarah, help her, will you please? I need two tablespoons of the ground comfrey and plantain both to a quart of water nice and hot. Let it steep about five minutes. And I'll need some wide strips of clean cloth for bandaging. You can use the torn sheet I saved in the linen drawer. And bring a glass of water for when your father wakes up."

I saw the worry on both their faces and was sorry to be so abrupt. "I'm proud of you both," I added quickly. "You're being such a help."

They disappeared, and I was glad to be alone for a moment with just Samuel and God. "Thank you," I whispered. "That he's still with us. Just help him get better."

Out in the sitting room I could hear baby Rosemary crying, sweet and delicate. I could hear the voices in the kitchen too, and Whiskers outside barking at some critter. Then, over all that, I heard the rumble of thunder. I hoped that would mean rain. The summer had been so dry that everybody I knew was worried for their harvest. And now a brutal fire! Who knew how much it had already cost. Maybe the sky would pour down rain and stop the fire's raging before it got any worse.

It wasn't two minutes and I heard the patter of raindrops. I was so glad. So relieved. Water from heaven would quench that awful fire. But I couldn't help thinking that if the rain had only come sooner, if everything had already been dripping wet, maybe there'd have been no fire. And

Samuel would never have had to leave my side.

Soon it was pouring. I took the cloth from Samuel's head to wet and cool it again. I thought of everyone over at Hammonds', getting soaked now and surely glad of it. Let it pour! But too much mud would make our dirt roads bad. Too much mud would make it harder for the doctor to get here.

Samuel moved his hand slightly but didn't open his eyes, and I knew he wasn't awake. As I put the cloth back, I could feel myself trembling just a little. Lord only knew how close we'd come to losing him. I didn't want to think about that, but there was no way I could help it. I sat beside him on the bed, trying hard not to cry, wiping away the one tear that defied my wishes by slipping slowly down my cheek.

Why, Lord? I cried, staring out the window at the darkness. *Why did this have to happen? Samuel's been so good. And he's gone through so much in his life. It doesn't seem right. Samuel wouldn't agree, I know he wouldn't, but I would rather it have been me.*

The girls came back with a pile of cloth, a jar with the steeping herbs, and a glass of water, which Katie set on the nightstand that Samuel had made for us two winters before.

"The fire will be out now, won't it?" Sarah asked. "With all the rain?"

"Let's hope so."

"It should've rained sooner."

It surprised me, how much Sarah's feelings mirrored my own. Perhaps I should have told her that there is a time for everything and that God is in control, even when things are far out of our hands. But I didn't. I thought it might sound as hollow as I felt right then.

I soaked one strip of cloth in the plantain and comfrey water and then folded it carefully over the wound on Samuel's leg. Then I wrapped other strips over it and secured them as best I could. The longest strips went around his leg twice with room left to tie. I carefully bathed the rest of his leg with the herbed water and then covered him to the waist with a blanket.

"I wish we had ice," I said more to myself than to the girls. It would be good to set a piece of it against the back of Samuel's head.

"Do you think Mrs. Post might have some?" Katie asked me hopefully.

"Honey, I don't know."

"Do you want me to run over and see?"

Her willingness surprised me. Over a mile and a half. With no horse or vehicle. Through driving rain. At night. "Oh, honey, it's good of you to offer, but it would take you an awfully long time getting over there and back. If she did have some, it might melt before you got it here. Maybe we'd better just wait till Robert is back."

"Surely it'll be soon," Sarah added.

I soaked another cloth in the herb water. "I'll have to lift your head a little, Samuel," I whispered. "To get another bandage on you."

I wanted him to stir. Especially when I was laying the cloth against the back of his head and wrapping it to stay on. But he didn't open his eyes or make any sound at all.

You're scaring the girls, Samuel. I should've thought to send them out.

"Is there something more we can do?" Katie asked so quietly. Sarah just stood beside her looking pale. They were both exhausted, I could tell.

"No. It's almost morning. You should try to get some rest while you can. I expect it'll be a busy day coming on."

"But Robert'll be back soon," Sarah protested. "I want to wait."

"Help Delores get Berty settled some-where. If Robert's not here by then, you need to lie down for a while too, at least until you hear him come in."

"What about you, Mom?" Sarah asked.

"I'll stay right here with your father."

The girls went out reluctantly. I could hear them in the sitting room, smoothing what had been Robert's bedding for Berty on the floor. Delores was there too, talking about my old woven laundry basket being the perfect bassinet for baby Rosemary. Thelma might not be very comfortable on the old davenport Herman Meyer had given us, but I was glad she was willing to go there for Samuel's sake. After a while, things got quiet, and I knew the girls had obeyed me and gone upstairs.

Alone with Samuel, I moved the oil lamp closer and carefully pulled off his shirt, hoping to check every inch of him to make sure there wasn't something I'd missed.

I went for clean water, warmer this time, and began to bathe him carefully.

"Juli . . ."

His eyes opened slowly and focused on me, and I felt relief like a weight lifted off my back. "Oh, Samuel. How do you feel?"

"Been better." He gave me the barest

hint of a smile. But then he looked more serious. "You need some rest."

"I don't think —"

"Juli, please. Come here with me."

For a moment I just stood there. Come here with him? On the bed? Of course, it was *our* bed. But he was so . . . hurt.

With some effort he moved his right arm and patted the bed beside him. "Come on."

Somehow the look in his eyes convinced me. I set the water and cloth aside and sat down beside him just as close as I could, being extra careful not to jiggle the bed too much.

"I love you," he said again.

"I love you too, Samuel. More than all the world."

He closed his eyes, and my throat tightened, but then he opened them again. "Is Robert back? Is the fire out?"

"It started raining, honey. That ought to take the fire down. But Robert's not back yet."

"Lord be with them. It was bad, Juli."

"I know."

"I hope they saved the house."

"The most important thing is for everyone to be all right," I told him. "A house can be rebuilt."

He closed his eyes again.

"Samuel, will you take a drink?"

"I'll try."

Something about the way he said that made me afraid. I reached for the glass of water, watching him carefully. "Are you hurting a lot?" I asked him, hoping he would tell me it was getting better, or at least not any worse.

"Yeah," he said simply.

I tried to help him drink, but he didn't seem to want more than a sip. "I've got mullein and nettle, Samuel, that might help the pain. I could make a strong tea if you think you could manage it."

"I don't know."

"Is your head still the worst?"

"I don't know."

I clasped his hand. I wanted to lay my head on his shoulder, but I wasn't sure it wouldn't hurt him. I shouldn't have listened to him when they first came. I should've made him stay in the truck, and then brought out a lot of bedding to cushion him and had Robert drive us straight to Dr. Hall's hospital in Mcleansboro.

"I'm so tired, Juli."

"Well, you ought to be tired. It's been a hard night."

"If I sleep, will you wake me when Robert gets back?"

"Yes," I told him, wondering if he was aware of having slept already.

"Come here, Juli. Come closer."

I was already sitting on the bed right against him, holding his hand with both of mine. But I knew what he wanted. Carefully I eased down to lie beside him. I put my hand on his bare chest. His heart was racing, but his breaths were slow.

For a long time we lay like that. Once, Delores peeked in, but she went right back out. The house was so quiet. I hoped all the children were asleep.

I knew I should be doing something. Making mullein and nettle tea, at the very least. But I wasn't sure that anything would help Samuel more than just doing what he wanted, just staying right here. Soon the rhythm of his breathing changed, and I knew he was asleep. A good, hearty, restful sleep, I hoped. A normal sleep.

I kissed his cheek. Then I sat up slowly. He looked so peaceful. I hoped Robert and George and all the rest were peaceful by now. I hoped everything was all right.

In a few minutes, I went back to the kitchen, thinking that I might put on Samuel's medicine tea in case he'd take it when he woke up. I wasn't sure if I should finish what I'd started, washing him and looking him over, or just let him sleep a while first.

"You want coffee?" Delores asked me.

"Yes, thank you."

"How's he doin'?"

"I don't know." I stopped, feeling an uncomfortable churn of emotion inside me. "Oh, Delores, he's hurting, I know he is. I'm just not sure what to do . . ."

She came and hugged me, then she sat me in a chair. "Do you think he has bones broken?"

"Not that I could tell, but his head . . . I just don't know how bad . . ."

"Is he talking like himself?"

"Yes."

"Then he's gonna be fine. You jus' believe for that, honey."

I knew what she was saying. And she was surely right. But inside me the nagging doubts still lingered. What if he wasn't fine? Sometimes, with a head wound, it was just so hard to tell. And what about his side?

Delores set a cup of coffee in front of me, but I almost couldn't drink it. This night would change some things for George Hammond. That was clear. But what about us?

8

Sarah

Katie and me lay on the floor because Georgie and Emmie were on our bed. It was almost morning. I kept expecting to see light through the window, but it was still dark. I couldn't sleep for thinking about what had happened. And I guess I wasn't the only one. Katie rolled over after I thought she was already asleep and just stared at the ceiling for a while.

"What if Dad had died?" she asked me with something strange and trembly in her voice.

"He didn't," I answered crossly. "There's no use talking about something like that."

For the first time in a very long time it bothered me that she'd called him Dad. He wasn't her dad. He was only her cousin or something. Never mind that our family had taken her in when she was only six and he'd been a dad to her ever since. It upset me anyway.

"Sarah, I'm glad I wasn't there," she whispered. "I would've been scared half to pieces."

"Well, I was scared too. Anybody would be."

"Do you think he'll be all right?"

"Of course he will. Mom said so."

"I know. But she's more worried than she wants to let on. I think it's serious, getting knocked in the head like that."

Of course it was. Any fool knew that. I wanted her to shut up. I wanted to tell her to. But I couldn't be that mean. "Go to sleep. I don't want to talk about it."

She lay there quiet for a while, and I hoped she'd done what I said. Little Georgie giggled at something in his sleep. *He just doesn't know,* I thought. *There's nothing to laugh at tonight.*

"Do you think one of them went to check on the animals and spilled their lantern over?" Katie suddenly asked.

"How should I know?" I scolded. "I wasn't there when it started." She rolled over just a little to face me, but I didn't look her way. "I wish I had been," I said under my breath then, but she heard me.

"How could things have been different if

you were?" she asked. "There was no way we could know it was going to happen."

"At least I could've been watching." I felt a sudden tightness inside me, like somebody was squeezing as hard as they could on my stomach. *Dumb fool!* a voice in my head raged. *You could've done more than watch! You could've seen to it that Lester Turrey never came! It was probably him who spilled a lantern, after coming nearly two miles in the dark!*

"I don't think there was anything anybody could've done," Katie said softly. "We wouldn't have known what to watch for."

She didn't say anything else, and I was glad. I felt pretty miserable just lying there. *Why don't you tell her?* I kept thinking. *Why don't you go tell Mom? Why are you still keeping your stupid promise?*

I had no answer, but I couldn't seem to make myself say anything more. For a little while there wasn't a sound except the rain and Emma Grace's breathing. But then in the distance I thought I heard a truck. It got closer pretty quickly. I sat up.

"That's Robert," Katie said, getting up too. "I hope he has good news."

There won't be much of that, I thought. Even with the fire out. I knew the Hammonds had lost a lot, and that meant we'd have less too, 'cause we always shared everything.

Georgie'd rolled so much on the bed that he had one leg hanging over. I got up and pushed him farther up. Then I covered him and Emmie and headed for the stairs.

Maybe it didn't matter how the fire got started. Maybe it wouldn't matter if I never told what I knew about Rorey. If it was her fault, she'd probably already learned her lesson. And surely nobody would care about having someone to blame.

I hurried down the stairs. I wanted to hear Robert tell us the fire was out. I wanted to know how bad it had gotten after we had left. I could hear Katie behind me, but I didn't wait for her.

Robert was just coming in the back door as I got to the kitchen. I expected him to be alone, but he wasn't. I guess I should've known that Mr. Hammond might send his younger boys over here along with him. Franky and Harry. They spent a lot of time at our house anyway. But what about Rorey? She was younger than Franky.

"How's Dad?" Robert asked right away.

"Sleeping," Mom told him. She looked so tired. I wished I knew something to do about it. Robert looked tired too.

Drenched to the bone and muddy to boot. But nothing like Franky. Franky looked like he could fall over.

"Sit down," Mom told them all. "Let me get you something to eat. You've been working so hard. Is the fire out?"

"It looks out," Harry answered. "But Pa an' Willy an' Kirk are stayin' put just to be sure."

"Mom," Robert persisted. "Is he really okay? Is it really just sleep?"

Mom stopped in her tracks for a minute. She saw me in the doorway and glanced my way but turned quickly back to Robert. Franky was the only one to sit down.

"I believe it's good sleep," Mom said. "I believe he'll be all right. But once you've had a chance to sit a minute and get a bite or two, I'd thank you to go inquire after the doctor, in case he heard Delores was here and thinks we might not need him. It just serves us well to be cautious."

Robert took her very seriously. "I can go now, Mom. I don't have to wait."

"No. Let me at least get you a sandwich to take along. And maybe you ought to have company, to keep you awake. Would you be up to that, Franky?"

I knew Franky well enough to know that despite how he felt, he wasn't likely to tell her no. But before he got a chance to say anything, Robert was answering for him.

"No, Mom. Not Franky. I didn't even want to bring him here. I sure don't want him along no further. Besides, he's hurt."

"Hurt?" Mom jumped on that one word and was immediately at Franky's side. But I stared at my brother. It wasn't like Robert to sound so hard. Franky wasn't his best friend, that was true. But he *was* a friend. Practically a brother, for all the time Franky spent with our folks. Why wouldn't Robert want to bring him?

"What's happened?" Mom was questioning Franky. "Where are you hurt?"

"I'm all right," Franky answered her. But I knew he wasn't, and so did Mom. She noticed the filthy old hanky around his hand at the same time I did. She lifted his arm gently, but he started to pull away.

"Quit acting so tough," Robert said harshly. "Let 'em doctor you. You know that's why your pa sent you. That and getting you out of his sight for a while."

Mom looked really angry. "Robert John! No matter what kind of night we've had, you're not to speak like that! What has gotten into you?"

"It was his fault, Mom," Robert said, with something awfully raw in his voice.

119

"They lost the barn and a whole lot else, and the house is damaged, and we almost lost Dad —"

His words struck at me deep. "It — it doesn't have to be somebody's fault!" I cried without thinking.

"You don't know what their pa said," Robert answered me right back.

"Sarah's right," Mom interrupted. "There's no use pointing fingers. Accidents happen."

I couldn't believe how calm she sounded. I couldn't have said another word right then. But Franky? How could it be? Had he followed Rorey tonight too? Had he fought with Lester again? I wanted to ask him. I wanted to demand that he tell me, but I just stood there half choked.

Mom took hold of Franky's hand and asked him to let her see. She turned her eyes to me only for a second. "Sarah, get your brother and Harry a couple of sandwiches."

"Yes, Mom," I managed to answer her. I felt like I was shaking. I hoped nobody could tell.

"I could ride to the doctor with Robert," Katie suddenly offered. "I'm sure I'm not as tired as Harry or Frank." I hadn't even realized she was that close behind me.

Mom nodded. That was all. And for a minute I thought I should have offered, but I was glad I hadn't. I would rather stay here, because Daddy was here. I didn't want to be gone for a minute.

Another truck came hurrying up our lane, and I wasn't sure who to expect. Thelma's brother, maybe. Mrs. Pratt came in the room then, took one look at Franky's hand, and reached for some water.

"You get a nail in it, honey? Best soak it some to draw out the poison."

Franky didn't say anything, only obediently stuck his hand down into the water. I wondered how much worse this night could get. Robert had said they'd lost a lot and the house was damaged. How bad was it?

Harry moved to the door and opened it before whoever it was had a chance to knock. Thelma's brother Richard came in from the porch, followed closely by Mr. Post.

"How's Samuel?" Mr. Post asked right away.

"He's sleeping, Barrett," Mom said softly. "I'm glad you both are here. I was going to send Robert for the doctor, but I'd feel better about it if one of you went along."

I expected Robert to say something about that. But he didn't. Neither did Katie, though if Mr. Post or Richard went, it wasn't likely she'd need to.

"Is he in the bed?" Mr. Post asked.

"Yes," Mom answered him.

"You mind if I go in and see him a minute?"

Mom shook her head. She looked so tired. But she got up and went with him. I wanted to go too, but she'd given me a job. Delores was seeing to Franky. I had to hurry up and make those sandwiches, and it'd be the right thing to feed Mr. Post and Richard Pratt something too, since they'd been helping. And Franky, if he could eat right now. Mom had only been looking at his one hand. But now Mrs. Pratt was looking over both of them.

"I think you got burns on this other hand," she told him. "Not bad, but it hurts, don't it?"

I didn't hear his answer; I was hurrying to lift the cellar door in the pantry off the kitchen. But I saw his face before I took off down the steps. A nail in his hand, Mrs. Pratt had said. And burns. I wondered if any of that happened while he was helping pull my daddy out of the rubble.

But there was no time to think of it. I

needed the butter from the cool pit. And there were three or four hard-boiled eggs left from what Mom had cooked up to send to school with us last morning. I'd make egg sandwiches. So I'd need some pickles off the shelf too.

Katie came with me, even though I didn't ask her to. But she knew what I was about.

"Do you think we ought to open a jar of green beans?" she asked me. "Or some blackberry preserves?"

"I'm not taking the time to cook any beans," I told her. "We need something they can take right along with them on the way to the doctor so we don't slow 'em down any. But I don't know why they don't just go. They could eat when they get back."

"Mom knows they must be hungry after fighting the fire all night," she said as she caught up to me at the bottom of the cellar steps. "Wouldn't you be?"

"No. I'm not a bit hungry, and I don't think staying over there would have made me hungry, either."

"Sarah —"

"You get the preserves and some pickles. I'm going to get the butter and eggs and a little milk. It's a good thing Lizbeth brought us some extra bread."

Katie didn't say another word, and neither did I. I just hurried as fast as I could, pulling the basket of perishable food up from Emma Graham's old cool pit in the corner of the cellar room. Mom was glad to have the cool pit. Even though times were not as hard for us as they'd been when we first came to Mrs. Graham's house, we still couldn't afford an icebox. Maybe we'd never get one.

We hurried back up the stairs, and Katie started cutting bread while I peeled the eggs. Then she was chopping pickles while I mashed eggs in milk with some pepper and sugar. Soon we had some passable egg salad, and I started spreading it on bread.

Richard was in the other room with his sister and the baby. Mom and Mr. Post came back in the kitchen pretty soon, and she got him a drink of water. I wished they would talk about Dad a little, but they didn't. They didn't say anything at all, and it bothered me terrible.

Then Richard came back in the room, and Mr. Post moved for the door.

"We best be goin'," he said. "Richard, your mama's gonna be here a while. You mind takin' Robert in to see about Dr. Howell? I'm gonna go over t' home and

fetch Mrs. Wortham a chunk or two a' ice
outta what's left in the icebox, an' I hope
it'll do some good."

"All right," Richard said. I knew him to
be almost twenty-three, but right then he
looked older, and paler, than I'd ever seen
him. "You ready, Robert?"

"Wait a minute," Mrs. Pratt interrupted.
"Where's Thelma's Sam? If the fire's out,
why ain't he come back?"

"He didn't wanna leave Pa just yet,"
Franky said quietly. "Even with Willy an'
Kirk there."

"I guess you can imagine George takin'
things hard," Mr. Post added. "He don't
seem too strong right about now. I left 'em
my truck, 'case they have need. I 'spect
they'll all be over once there ain't nothin'
left smokin'. An' I don't reckon it'll be too
long; only the rain died back 'fore they
could be all sure."

I handed Robert and Richard the first
egg sandwiches. Katie was spreading
blackberry preserves on four pieces of
bread, one after another. I grabbed two of
them, smacked them together, and handed
them to Mr. Post.

"We'll hurry, Mom," Robert said.

"Just drive careful," she told him. "Tell
the doctor everybody seems to be doing all

right. We just need him to take a look. Don't be worrying, please."

They left. Quick. Without any more talk, and I was glad. Mr. Post took our truck, and I knew it wouldn't take him long to get to his place and back.

"Did Daddy wake up?" I dared to ask.

"No, honey," Mom said. "But it's barely daylight. He needs to be resting. So do the rest of you."

Her words were sure, but her eyes weren't. She was as scared for Daddy as I was. I dropped the fork I'd been using, and it hit my shoe and clanged on the floor.

"You want a sandwich, Harry?" I managed to say.

"Yes, if you don't mind."

Katie picked up the fork for me and then squeezed my hand. "How about you, Franky?" she asked in a soft voice.

"No," he said barely loud enough to hear. "I couldn't eat nothin'."

9

Julia

It was a relief to have Robert and Richard off for the doctor, though I hated to worry the kids that way. The morning was dawning cloudy with a rumble of thunder lingering in the distance, but the rain had stopped. I was glad for the sake of the roads, though I hoped it'd been enough rain so that the fire couldn't spark up again.

I went to check on Thelma in the sitting room. She was sleeping peacefully on the old davenport with baby Rosemary looking like a tiny angel all bundled up in the laundry basket beside her. Berty was sleeping too, coughing just a little, his foot propped up on a pillow Delores had brought him. His foot had swelled a bit, I could see that. He would benefit from some ice too, or he might have if it had gotten here sooner. I would be glad to get it just the same.

Samuel worried me far more. I went and kissed him before going back to the kitchen. I knew he really did need to sleep, but still I hoped he would wake, just so I'd know that he could. But he didn't, and I had to tell myself that rest was a powerful medicine, the best in the world according to Grandma Pearl.

Franky wouldn't say much. I came back to his side, though Delores surely wouldn't need much help bandaging the puncture wound on his hand. I didn't realize until I looked again that he had burns too, not bad but visible over part of the other hand.

"What you got to draw the bad blood outta that?" Delores asked me.

I brought her some of the comfrey and plantain water, but Franky didn't want to soak his hand again. He just wanted to get up and be done. So I only washed the wound with it a bit. Delores said it would be all right to leave his hands open to the air a while. I was relieved to see that the burn didn't bother him much and that he could move both his hands.

But he didn't seem like himself. He wouldn't drink any of the mullein and nettle tea I'd made just before they got here. He was impatient with us, shaking his head and telling us not to fuss over him

128

anymore. As soon as he got the chance, he got up and walked outside.

"I think he's feelin' awful bad about the fire," Katie said.

"He oughta," Harry replied immediately.

Sarah looked pale as a ghost.

"I don't want to hear any words about blame," I told them. "You know as well as I do that accidents can happen to anybody."

"Yeah," Harry said with a scowl. "But Pa says Franky's as clumsy as an ox an' purty near as stupid in some things. He didn't have no business bein' up."

Sarah turned and went upstairs.

"Anybody want something else to eat?" Katie asked, giving her attention to the things on the counter.

I almost went outside to speak to Franky. Lord knew that he could use some words of peace. But baby Rosemary woke with a wail, and Berty woke up too and called for me. Delores and I went to see to them as Katie made Harry another sandwich.

Poor Bert had dreamed he was trapped in the barn, he and Samuel, and they couldn't get out. I calmed him the best I could and got him a drink of water. I wished he would go back to sleep, but I knew he wouldn't with the light beginning to peek through the sitting room windows.

Wouldn't be long before Georgie was up too, and Emmie Grace. We had a houseful again, and it would get even more full and stay that way if George and the rest of his family had to live with us for a while until their house was repaired. I wondered how badly it was damaged and what it would take to make it livable again, but I hadn't wanted to ask in the middle of everything else. There would be time for that later.

I began to consider what the doctor would think. Surely he'd be home by now from wherever he'd been. And hopefully he'd had a chance to rest. Three people injured. And a baby born. He'd probably shake his head at us and wonder how in the world such things could happen all in one night. I wondered myself.

I gave Bert a reassuring hug and then went to wet the cloth that I'd left lying on Samuel's head. I kissed Samuel's cheek, hoping again that he'd wake and look at me. But he didn't stir.

Heavenly Father, still my heart. Give me confidence that he's only resting as he needs to, and that he'll wake and be all right.

Little feet came bounding down the stairs; I knew it was Emmie. She peeked in the bedroom at me.

"Shhh," I told her. "Mr. Wortham is sleeping, and I think Thelma's trying to as well."

"Oh," she replied with a smile. "Can I see the baby?"

"If you're quiet," I told her, but she disappeared before I got the words out.

I marveled at Emmie this morning. She'd been so scared last night, and no wonder. Seeing the fire, and her brother and my husband hurt. But this morning she seemed to have no worries at all. I guess she was just confident that we'd helped them, God had healed them, and they would be fine now.

I looked toward the sitting room before heading back to the kitchen and saw Emmie squatted down beside the rocking chair where Delores was rocking the baby.

Berty was sitting up, staring out the window. I expect he was feeling bad about the fire too. And about Samuel.

"I guess we'll have to do chores before long," Katie said quietly as I entered the kitchen.

"Yes," I acknowledged. "And I would appreciate your help. But Harry, you ought to get some sleep. Go up to Robert's room. He won't mind."

"Just don't send Franky up," he said

coldly. "I bet Robert would mind that. He's real upset with him on account of Mr. Wortham."

"Mr. Wortham is going to be just fine," I answered a little too curtly. "And I'll have to have another talk with Robert when he gets back."

"Maybe you oughta talk to Pa too," Harry said in a softer voice. "He's even madder than Robert."

Harry went upstairs then, and Katie went to feed the chickens and gather eggs. I knew she had a hard time milking, so I wouldn't ask her to do that. Or Sarah either. I would just do it myself.

As I headed out the door with a milk pail in my hands, I looked around for Franky. If his father was as upset as Harry said, he'd probably railed on the boy some before sending him over here. Poor Franky. He would've felt bad enough even without being scolded.

I looked but didn't see him anywhere. I'd expected him to be under the apple tree like last night, but he wasn't. For the first time it occurred to me that that was the same spot Samuel chose when he just had to think. But where else might Franky be?

The woodshop. That was Franky's favorite place. Samuel's too, sometimes. They'd made so many beautiful things there. Kitchen chairs. Cedar chests. So many nice things to remember.

And sad things too. Seven winters past, they'd made two caskets. One for Emma Graham and one for Franky's mother. Samuel had expected to do the work alone, but as young as he was, Franky had wanted to help. And ever since then, Franky and Samuel had been very close. Close enough to ignite Robert's jealousy at times.

I opened the door slowly, leaving the milk pail outside. Franky was sitting in the corner at one end of their homemade workbench. He didn't look up.

"Franky? Aren't you tired? We'll make you a bed where you can get some sleep."

"No. I wanna stay out here."

"He'll be all right. It wasn't your fault."

He looked at me then. "Are you sure?"

I wasn't certain what he was asking me. "Franky —"

"If he was doin' real good, there wouldn't be no hurry goin' for the doctor. Bert ain't that bad. An' the baby's all right or you woulda sent Sam or somebody over to Mcleansboro earlier. I can tell you're worryin', Mrs. Wortham. I can tell somethin' ain't right."

"But it's not your fault, no matter what happened."

"I know." He sighed. "I just don't know if anybody else'll ever know. They won't listen to me."

I stood for a moment. "Franky, what do you mean?"

"I didn't start no fire. Don't know how it started. But they won't listen to me."

I stared at him for a minute. Why on earth would his father blame him then? Why would Robert blame him?

"I guess people'll think what they want to," he said. "Can't change that. But it was botherin' me, you thinkin' it too. I wanted to ask you 'bout Mr. Wortham. I wanted to know if there's anythin' I can do, but I didn't wanna . . . I didn't wanna bother you if you thought . . ."

"Oh, Franky." I leaned forward to give him a hug. He started to draw back, but I wouldn't let him. I just held him for a minute. He shook a little in my arms, and when he pulled away, he had to lower his head and wipe at his eyes.

"Is he gonna die?"

"No." I wanted to tell him of course not and why. I wanted to assure him with plenty of confident words, but right then I couldn't find any.

"I was awful scared, Mrs. Wortham. I don' know what we'd do without Mr. Wortham. Pa always needs him. Awful worse now, even. But that ain't all. He's just . . . he's just the best that anybody ever been to me." He looked up, and even in the dim light I could see the turmoil in his silvery eyes. "E'cept you, Mrs. Wortham," he added, lowering his head again. "I wish sometimes I could help you half as much as you been helpin' me."

"Maybe you don't see what a help you are to us," I told him. "You are always a willing worker, something you know I appreciate."

He didn't look up.

"They'll find out the truth soon enough," I tried to encourage him. "They won't keep blaming you."

"I ain't so sure."

I didn't know how to address that at the moment. So I put my hand on his shoulder. "Do you want to see him?"

He raised his head with a hopeful expression. "Can I? It wouldn't cause no problem?"

"No. No problem. Come on."

He limped beside me back toward the house. I was about to ask him how his injuries happened when we heard the truck coming back. Whiskers went to meet it in joyful anticipation of Samuel as usual, but I knew it was Barrett Post, hopefully with ice for Samuel's head and Bert's ankle. Barrett pulled up almost beside us and stopped, holding up a burlap bag.

"Louise wanted to come," he said. "But I told her you had Delores here already, an' you had greater need a' some other kind a' help for now. She's cookin' you up a feast for the midday, Mrs. Wortham, seein's you've got so many here to feed."

"Thank you. And thank her." I took the burlap bag as he was getting out of the truck. But I was thinking of Robert and Richard. *I hope they haven't had trouble finding that doctor. I hope he's not already been called somewhere else.*

Franky followed me toward the house, though his limp was worse. Mr. Post passed him by easily enough. In the kitchen, I banged the ice down hard against the table and broke off a chunk separate to wrap in a dish towel. Then I hurried the bag into the sitting room. I was glad to find Thelma nursing the baby. I gave the bag to Delores and asked her to hold it against Bert's ankle as long as he could stand. Then I went straight to Samuel's side with the towel.

I knew the back of his head had swollen.

Not badly but enough that my touch could tell. Hopefully the ice would help. I squeezed the towel as gently as I could between the pillow and his head, trying not to disturb him but at the same time almost hoping he'd open his eyes at the movement or the cold.

"Samuel?" Mr. Post called. "You got mornin' waitin' for you."

Samuel didn't respond at all. My legs felt like butter, I was suddenly so weak.

But then I heard a quiet voice in the room, speaking peaceful words of faith.

"He that dwelleth in the secret place a' the most High shall abide under the shadow of the Almighty. I will say of the Lord, He is my refuge an' my fortress: my God; in him will I trust . . ."

At the first instant, I didn't realize who was speaking. It could almost have been an angel, sent by God to give me strength. But it was Franky, head bowed and shoulders quivering, his hands dangling awkwardly in front of him.

One tiny trickle of blood oozed from his wounded palm. Somewhere I'd read or I'd heard something from the Bible that now leaped into my mind: *They of my own house have turned up their heel against me . . .*

I didn't know what it meant or why I was thinking of it now. I only knew that for a split second the bowed figure before me hadn't seemed like Franky.

It made me shake. Turning back to Samuel, I still was shaking.

But Franky didn't look up, didn't stop for a moment his prayerful recitation.

"He shall cover thee with his feathers, and under his wings shal' thou trust: his truth shall be thy shield an' buckler. Thou shal' not be afraid."

How foolish for George or anyone else to blame Franky for the fire, whether or not they had some cause to think it. I prayed for all the Hammonds then, and my own children. This situation was hard enough already, and I hoped it wouldn't get harder, with bad feelings and accusation on top of the strain of Samuel's injury and the financial burden such loss was bound to create for George. I thought Sarah's words very wise. *It doesn't have to be somebody's fault.* But my own son, among others, had been quick to find someone to blame. God help us. God especially help George to see what his words, his actions, could do.

Behind me, Franky continued his quiet recitation. Hearing him speak day to day and knowing how he still struggled to read, I found it was easy to forget how good his memory was, and how flawlessly he could repeat the words he heard our pastor say. Samuel didn't wake or even move a muscle. But hearing the Ninety-first Psalm in the quiet of that room gave me peace.

"Because thou has' made the Lord, which is my refuge, even the most High, thy habitation; there shall no evil befall thee . . ."

10

Sarah

Emmie'd said last night was a bad night. Well, this was starting out to be a pretty bad day too. I kind of felt like screaming, if it would've helped anything at all. Daddy was just lying there downstairs in his bed. I wasn't sure if he could get up if he did wake. And now Robert and Harry were accusing Franky of setting that fire.

Maybe it *was* Franky. Maybe he'd gone and fought with Lester, and they'd overturned a lantern. Or maybe he'd fought with Rorey. She would fight. She'd been in fights before. And Franky'd been in one just yesterday.

Why couldn't he have just told on her? Maybe none of this would've happened if he would have just told his pa whatever he'd found Rorey up to.

I looked over at Georgie on the bed, knowing it wouldn't be long before he woke up. Especially after Harry came up to Robert's room the way he did, with no particular effort to be quiet. I knew I should go back downstairs pretty soon. We'd have to get breakfast for everybody who didn't have sandwiches, and there was plenty more besides that to do. Mom would be occupied with Bert and Frank and Thelma's new baby. Not to mention Dad.

Lord, heal my daddy. Wake him up. I couldn't think of anything else to pray. I couldn't think of anything more scary than having him lying there so still.

But another voice was nagging me, chasing away my prayers and making me feel guilty for even praying them.

It's your fault. It's your fault! And nothing will be right until you tell.

I knew I had to go back downstairs. I should tell Mom what I knew about Rorey first thing. But for a minute I stood looking at myself in the little wall mirror, wondering what Rorey might be thinking right now. Was she worrying about my dad and her brothers? Was she praying for them?

Down inside I really didn't care what Robert or Harry said. Because even if Franky had started the fire, it probably had something to do with Rorey, who shouldn't have been up, and Lester, who shouldn't have been coming over. Then it wouldn't be Franky's fault, would it? It was Rorey's fault. Surely it was. Rorey should've known better. At thirteen, she was too young for a boyfriend. But old enough to know it.

It wasn't my fault. All I'd done was promise not to tell. And that's what friends do. Who could expect me to do anything different? A promise is a promise, and Rorey would expect me to keep it. Of course she would. Even now.

Mom was being strong. And I knew I'd better get that way too, even though I was afraid I'd cry again if I went downstairs. But maybe Daddy was waking up right now. Maybe he'd smile that glad-to-see-my-pumpkin smile again. And then sit up and have breakfast and be just fine.

I could hope so. I could maybe even expect it, except I was afraid of feeling worse if it didn't happen.

I looked out the window and saw Katie coming back to the house with a basket of eggs. Why couldn't I be like Katie? Katie was always doing the things she was supposed to be doing. She was never in on any of Rorey's trouble.

I remembered Rorey refusing to take Katie along two winters ago when she wanted to go sledding in back of the school. We'd crashed into the outhouse and broken the door, and then I wished I hadn't gone either. And Rorey had never wanted to play beauty shop with Katie when we were little, so Katie wasn't the one who got in trouble for having cut-up hair. Rorey never would tell Katie her secrets.

I used to think I was the lucky one for being Rorey's best friend. Not anymore.

Georgie stirred on the bed with a little chuckle and rolled enough for his legs to plop over the side again. I scooted him, not wanting him to fall. And he opened his eyes and looked at me with a merry smile.

"Sarwah," he told me. "I stay-ed at your house."

"Yes. You did. Do you need to hurry down to the outhouse?"

"We gots a pot unner the bed at my house."

"I know. But we usually use those only if somebody's sick."

"Mommy sick?" He suddenly frowned.

"No. She's fine. And you have a baby sister. Remember?"

"Dat baby?"

"Yeah. You wanna go see her?"

"Me baby." He pointed to his chest and

looked at me kind of sideways, as if he were challenging me to disagree.

"You were. You still are. Sort of. But you're a big brother now too."

"Carry me?"

"Oh, Georgie."

But he wasn't very big. I knew I could, so I did, and we went downstairs together.

Mom and Mr. Post were standing in the bedroom doorway as I got to the base of the stairs. I didn't say anything because I didn't want to interrupt.

"He's always been strong," Mr. Post was saying. " 'Fore we know it, he'll be up helpin' George get on his feet again."

Mom just nodded, looking back into the room.

"I told those boys to let the pastor know if they get the chance. I wouldn't be surprised if he was to come right out here. It'd be like him."

Mom didn't say anything. I hoped the pastor did come. I hoped he brought his wife, because she was Mom's best friend. Delores was good, but nobody talked and laughed with Mom the way Juanita Jones did. She oughta be here because it would make Mom feel better.

"Down! Down!" Georgie suddenly protested, his eyes turned to the sitting room, where we could see his mother on the davenport. I put him down, and he scooted away.

"Need me to do the milkin' for ya?" Mr. Post was asking. "Gonna be a full day for you, seems like."

"Yes, thank you," Mom told him. "I'd appreciate that."

Mr. Post didn't look how he usually did. Gray and serious in a way I didn't like. Mom told him where the milk pail was and thanked him again, and he went outside.

Tell. I felt the prompting inside me. *Now. Tell Mom about Rorey and her boyfriend.*

I was close to doing it. I might have done it. But Emmie came running at us all of a sudden.

"Can I he'p make breakfast?" she begged. "Is Pa comin' over? Did they go to bed at our house?"

"I expect he'll be over eventually," Mom answered. "But I doubt they went to bed."

Mom looked so tired herself. I wanted to help her so she could rest. "Mom, Katie and me can make breakfast. You could sit down or something."

"Thank you, but you girls weren't upstairs long enough to catch even forty winks. You ought to go back —"

"We can take a nap later. Honest, we can

make breakfast. Emmie can help."

Emma Grace jumped up and down. "Yeah! It'll be fun! An' we can carry some right to Mr. Wortham an' anybody else that don't wanna get up an' come to the table."

Mom nodded, but she had an odd sort of look on her face. I figured maybe Emmie saying that might have hurt her a little. But Emmie didn't know any better.

"Thank you," Mom finally said. "That's very kind. It would be a blessing if you girls would make breakfast."

She turned and walked back toward Daddy in the bedroom. And I went in the kitchen with Emmie pulling on my hand. I wondered what was the matter with that little girl anyhow, that she didn't take a bit of consideration over what had happened. She didn't even ask if they still had a house. I guessed they did, from what Robert had said, but it was probably not in very good shape.

Katie was standing at the counter already, wearing an apron and looking in one of Mom's cookbooks. "Let's make pancakes," she suggested. "I remember how to make the syrup, and that's one thing we can add to and stretch no matter who all shows up."

There wasn't a thing wrong with her deciding for that or saying so, but I was suddenly mad again. "A bunch of cornmeal mush would only take one big pot," I told her, not very kindly.

She answered as calmly as she ever did. "Well, all right, if you think it'd be easier. But Dad doesn't like mush very much."

Dummy! I wanted to tell her. *Do you see Dad sitting at the table, asking for breakfast?*

"I'm kind of hoping when he wakes up he'll be hungry," she went on, as though she'd heard my thoughts. "Maybe I'm just being silly, but I wanted to make one of his favorites, just in case."

I stood there for a minute as Emmie jumped up on a chair and asked to help again. Why did Katie have to be so perfect? That was such a nice way to think, a nice way to try to trust. And I wasn't being very nice. At least not to her. "Okay, then," I managed to answer. "We can make the pancakes."

She was looking at me kind of straight. "Remember what you told me. Mom said he'd be all right."

I didn't want to answer her a word. I didn't even want to stay in the kitchen right then because I felt like such a cross-patch compared to Katie. But I'd promised Mom, and it wouldn't be right to leave Katie to cook alone with Emmie right in the middle of things. "I'll measure the flour," I told her. "How big a batch do you think we'll need?"

"Maybe triple," she said. "If the rest of the Hammonds get here. What do you think?"

We started in, filling the bread bowl with pancake batter before long.

"I bet Rorey'll be over soon," Katie told me at one point.

I didn't answer. But I couldn't quit thinking about Rorey and how she'd looked in the crazy light of that fire. She hadn't made any effort to approach me last night. Even when everybody else had run to find Daddy and Berty, she'd stayed back. And I wasn't anxious for her to come walking in now in time for pancakes.

11

Julia

Franky stood as still as stone beside the bed, his psalm finished. I walked up beside him, thinking that it might be time to move the ice to Samuel's leg for a few minutes and then back before it melted. Or maybe I should use more of the plantain and comfrey as a wash for his leg again and the back of his head.

I might've been all right with Samuel sleeping long. I think I would've been, except that I knew there was no way I could've kept on sleeping if someone had pushed ice behind my head. I thought of his mother suddenly. Would she want to know what was going on? How would she react?

"Samuel," I said softly, "I'm going to be moving the ice just a little and washing the area with some of the herb again."

Maybe it was silly to talk out loud, but I

wanted him to hear me. I didn't expect him to open his eyes. But he did. He looked first at me, then at Franky, and I felt like I could breathe again.

"Oh, Sammy."

"Juli . . . I'm thirsty . . ."

I smiled, delighted to find him "talking like himself," as Delores put it, and asking for something. I grabbed the glass of water off the nightstand and did my best to help him sip at it carefully.

"I made nettle and mullein tea, Samuel. It might help the pain if you think you can manage it."

"Yeah. I'll try."

Excited as a child, I ran to the kitchen for a cup of the medicine tea I'd left at the back of the stove to stay warm.

"Thank the Lord," I told the girls as I rushed past them. "Your dad's awake."

Kate smiled. Sarah dropped what she was doing and followed me back into the bedroom.

Samuel didn't say anything when we came in. I gave him the tea right away, and he took two or three sips in a row before stopping and looking up at me.

"Thank you," he said.

I set the cup down and gingerly gave him a hug. "How are you feeling?"

150

He looked over at Sarah and Franky. I thought maybe he didn't want to tell me with them standing there. But slowly he spoke, looking at them. "Don't worry. I'm all right. Just tired."

Sarah smiled. "Gonna be hungry soon?"

I knew the hope in her voice. Samuel did too. "Maybe so, pumpkin," he answered her quietly.

"We're making pancakes for you," Sarah went on with a sparkle in her eyes. "You want a spoon of vanilla in the syrup?"

"Sure," he told her. "That'd be great."

"Okay. We'll have it ready pretty quick." She gave me a little hug and then rushed up to kiss her father's cheek before leaving for the kitchen again. I knew Samuel had calmed her fears just that easily. I only hoped he really would be hungry.

Only Franky stood there beside me now. I knew the relief in him too.

"Don't worry 'bout them orders we got comin' due, Mr. Wortham," he said. "I'll take care a' the sandin' on Mrs. Calloway's cedar chest today an' see that she's happy with it. I'll start the Porters' rockin' chair too, so you don't have to be thinkin' on none a' that."

"Thank you," Samuel whispered. "You're a good partner."

I wondered how much work Franky could do with his hands the way they were. But I had no doubt he'd try. I thought of Robert and Richard again and hoped they'd be back quickly with the doctor.

"Mr. Post is milkin'," Franky continued. "But I'll make sure all your animals got feed an' water since Robert ain't here. Anythin' else you want done, you jus' let me know."

"Franky, are you sure your hands are all right?" I asked.

"Nothin' but a scratch or two," he answered me, though he absolutely knew that I knew better. "Nothin' to stop a body from gettin' a few things done."

I wondered at him. Perhaps he wasn't wanting Samuel to know he'd been hurt. So I only nodded. "Make sure you get some breakfast," I told him. "I'll let you know when the doctor gets here."

"I'm glad you're seemin' all right, Mr. Wortham," he said and turned to the door. For a moment he hesitated.

"Thank you, Frank," Samuel told him.

Franky didn't say anything more. He just went to see about the animals like he'd promised.

"I'm sorry if I had people worried," Samuel told me as soon as we were alone.

"We just care so much about you. Everybody's wanting you to be fine."

"I will be," he said.

"You're still hurting, though, aren't you?"

He managed a bit of a smile. "What can we expect? I guess the barn fell on me."

"Oh, Sammy." I could just about laugh and cry at the same time. I gave him a kiss, and he wanted me right up next to him again. It wasn't long before Sarah, Katie, and little Emmie all came in together bringing Samuel a handsome-looking plate of pancakes and a glass of milk.

"You want some too, Mom?" Sarah asked me.

"Not right now, honey."

Samuel looked at the food and then at the girls. "Everybody else fed?" he asked them.

"No. You're first."

"Well . . . doesn't seem right to make them wait. You wouldn't mind going on and getting everybody else's breakfast, would you?"

They probably did mind a little, hoping to be with him. But they didn't argue. And when they were gone, Samuel looked at me with his dark eyes clouded with care. "Help me eat this, will you?" he asked. "I don't want them to be disappointed."

I set the plate on the side of the bed and took his hand. "Tell me, Samuel, please. Where are you hurting most now? Is your side still bothering you? How does your head feel? Are you really all right?"

"Too many questions." He sighed. "Juli, I don't know. I just hurt. All over."

I took a deep breath. "I'm expecting the doctor before long."

He shook his head. "Don't worry. Please."

"I don't know how you think I could help it."

He looked at me, trying to smile again, and squeezed my hand. "Well, at least I still know who you are."

"Samuel, that's not funny."

"Something to thank God for. Right? It's okay. I'm gonna be okay."

I couldn't help it then. I didn't want to cry in front of him, but I did, hugging his neck and hoping it didn't hurt him. "I'm so glad you risked your life," I told him. "But I hope to God you never have to do it again."

He only held me, for a long time. When I finally moved a little I accidentally set my hand right in the middle of that plate of pancakes. We both looked down at my squishy fingers dripping with syrup. He laughed. And it was a beautiful sound.

I had to go to the kitchen to wash up a bit. Emmie thought I was pretty funny, making a mess of my own. I wasn't usually so clumsy. I guess Sarah and Katie thought it was funny too.

When I went back into the bedroom, Samuel had me help him sit up a little. He tried to eat, but he could only manage a few bites before he had to lie back down. Dizzy, he told me. And not hungry, either. I finished what he didn't eat because he wanted me to.

"Has George been over?" he asked me.

"No. But I expect him and all the rest. I'm not sure they can stay at home. Robert said the house was damaged. Do you think we can manage them here?"

"We've done it before."

I nodded. Sure, we'd had all the Hammond kids here plenty of times. But not like this. Our house was like some sort of nursing station already. I wasn't sure how well I'd deal with more. But I had little time for wondering. We could hear somebody pulling up in a vehicle outside and Barrett Post's voice greeting them.

"Go on," Samuel told me.

I didn't want to leave his side, no matter who it was. But I did.

I could have hugged that Mcleansboro

doctor, Right in front of Mr. Post and Franky. There he stood, beside his old car with his big black bag in hand.

"Heard you were having a new baby out here," he called to me. "I was sorry not to make it last night. Made sure to find a way to get here this morning."

"Bless you," I told him with my heart suddenly thumping faster. I wouldn't have had to send Robert for Dr. Howell, if only we'd been patient.

"Mr. Post was telling me the baby's just the beginning, with the fire and all."

"Yes. Yes, please come in."

I ushered him straight to the house to see Samuel. I thought maybe Franky would follow us. He knew I would want the doctor to look at his hands. But he didn't follow, only turned around toward the woodshop again.

"Guess your home became something of a hospital last night, Mrs. Wortham," Dr. Hall was saying. "You must be exhausted."

"I suppose we should've tried bringing everybody in to you — it's just . . ." I looked at him and almost broke down in sobs. "Oh, I don't know . . ."

"It's all right. I don't mind coming out. I know you've had a hard time of it."

He heard the baby in the sitting room

and glanced in that direction, but I urged him toward Samuel again, and Delores agreed with me.

"Take a look at Mr. Wortham first," she told the doctor. "He give us all quite a scare."

Samuel was still awake when we came in, and I was grateful for that. He greeted Dr. Hall by name, which I'm sure the doctor would understand as a good thing. Sarah came in behind us and wanted to watch, but the doctor told me it might be better if she didn't.

"You can come back soon as he's done, pumpkin," Samuel said to help her feel better. But she was none too happy about being asked to go out.

Dr. Hall was thorough. He took his time looking Samuel over, arms and legs, chest and back. In the daylight I could see so many bruises and scratches I hadn't seen before. It looked just like what Samuel had said, that the barn had fallen on him. I knew it to be a miracle that he'd survived.

"Well, Samuel," Dr. Hall said quietly. "I'm pleasantly surprised not to find you dealing with obvious broken bones. Only thing I'm wondering about in that way is your ribs here." He pointed to Samuel's right side. "You've got some bad bruising

157

in this area, and you seem awfully tender."

Samuel nodded. I took a deep breath, but it came hard. Broken ribs? How much of a problem might that be? And what could be done?

"It's a little hard to know for sure," the doctor continued, "unless we put you under an X-ray picture machine. I don't blame you for not coming into town, though. With your head injury, the bumpy roads wouldn't have done you any good."

That scared me. Terrible. What about the head injury? I wanted to ask how bad it was, but I couldn't seem to get a word out. Thank God we hadn't let Sarah stay in the room. I just stood there and watched, twisting my apron between my fingers. *Dear God, let him be all right. Let it be that the doctor's only being cautious and it's not really all that bad. Please, God.*

Dr. Hall spent some time looking in Samuel's eyes and ears with some kind of magnifier and an even longer time looking over the obvious wound on the back of his head and then asking a whole series of questions, some of which didn't seem relevant at all.

Finally the doctor turned and looked at me. "Was he unconscious?"

"Yes. For a while. When it first happened. And then later. He seemed to be sleeping, but I wasn't sure if it was normal sleep."

Samuel glanced over at me with something strange in his eyes.

The doctor frowned and did some more looking, feeling over Samuel's head with his hand. I could tell it hurt. Finally, the doctor spoke to me again. "Could have been much worse. I'd say you have a lot to be thankful for that your husband's still here."

"I know," I managed to say, hoping he'd go ahead and say more. And he did.

"His eyes are fine. His thinking's fine. No fluid in his ears at all. Structure of the skull feels fine despite some swelling in the skin. I don't expect any skull fracture. Bit of a miracle, I'd say."

I smiled.

"Still, a whack on the head's nothing to mess around with, especially when he's lost consciousness. He been dizzy or nauseous at all?"

"Yes," I said. "And hurting too."

"You'd about have to expect that. I'd say he's got a concussion. Have to be careful for a while, till we know the swelling's gone, and pray there's none on the inside."

"On the inside?" Those words hit me

hard. "What would that be like?"

He turned away from Samuel to face me. "Mrs. Wortham, I wasn't meaning to alarm you. There's no reason at all to expect —"

"Expect what? What could happen?" I thought of the man from the cave, the man who'd been hit with the rock and then died in his bed.

The doctor looked uncomfortable. "We should expect him to just be getting better —"

"But if there's a chance . . ." I stammered, "if there's a chance of complications, I want to know."

He sighed. "Mrs. Wortham, don't be worrying yourself. There's always a chance, but —"

"Tell me. Please tell me what could happen."

He sighed again. "It's a tricky thing," he said, turning his eyes back toward Samuel. "We just can't predict something like this very well. I'm sure he's fine. But in some cases there can be bleeding or swelling inside. You can't tell it looking at the outside, and it doesn't always show in the X-ray pictures we can get, because it's gradual. If it happens, it can cause problems. Loss of memory, or function, or worse. But we've no reason to think —"

My heart was pounding in my throat. "Could he die?"

Dr. Hall shook his head. "Mrs. Wortham, there's no cause for such alarm. I don't believe we have any such problem here."

"Can we know for sure?"

"I wish I could say so. Soon they'll have machines, and we'll be able to tell anything you want to know. For now, the best thing to do is relax and make sure he gets plenty of rest. I saw you had ice on his head. That's a good thing. Get more if you can. Keep him still. There's not much more you can do, unless you want to move him to town, but I'm not sure that would be to any real benefit. He should recover fine at home."

"What about his ribs?"

"I'll wrap them tightly. That's another reason he shouldn't be up moving around. They should heal on their own all right. You can expect it to be painful, though. And four to six weeks, probably, before he's full on the mend."

Surely he must be wrong about it taking so long! Surely there must be some way to help him more quickly. I knew I shouldn't worry, but it was pouring over me like water. Could broken ribs create bleeding and swelling inside too? Should I ask? How could we know?

"I'm sorry if this seems like bad news, Mrs. Wortham," the doctor told me. "But I believe he'll come out fine. You've got plenty to be grateful for, that he's doing this well. And with him sitting here talking to us, I don't expect any complications."

"Yes," I told him. "Thank you."

He looked at Samuel's leg and told me I'd done a fine job bandaging it. I'd thought it would need stitches, but he said it was already closing on its own and he believed it'd do all right.

"Maybe I'd best take a look at the others while I'm here," he said then. "I'll come back in to Mr. Wortham again before I go."

I knew it could have been so much worse, and I was probably just irrational for worrying over what might be. But still I felt numb inside. It was hard to move, showing Dr. Hall into the sitting room toward Berty and baby Rosemary. Sarah and Katie both came up beside me, and I hugged them, telling them not to worry, that the doctor said we had plenty to be thankful for.

"Go get Franky," I told them. "I want to make sure the doctor looks at his hands."

Thelma was sitting up on the old davenport, happy to talk to the doctor. I was relieved there'd be no difficult news with her.

She seemed to be fine, just like her mother had said. The doctor said so too, and congratulated me on doing so well.

"Fine baby you got here," he said, lifting Rosemary into his arms. "She nursing well for you?"

"Took the breast twice already this morning," Delores told him like the proud grandmother she was.

It didn't take the doctor long to look the baby over and pronounce her healthy. "Congratulations to you," he told Thelma. "Where's the father?"

Thelma looked down for a moment. "Over with his pa. They lost their barn last night, and we don't know what all else. They're making sure the flames don't kick back up. And I think Pa Hammond's having a hard time of it."

"I understand. Quite a night you've all been through." He turned his attention to Berty. "Let me take a look at you, young man."

Bert didn't look up. "It's only just my ankle. An' . . . an' I reckon I deserve that much."

"Oh, Bert —" I started to say.

"Why?" the doctor asked him.

"Because I run in after Imey, my calf, that's why. An' I shoulda knowed better. I

163

shoulda knowed I couldn't save her, an' it weren't worth it to try. I near got Mr. Wortham killed. He was the one rushed in there an' got me out."

The doctor glanced up at me for a second, and then back to the boy. "Well, a lesson learned, I'd say."

Bert nodded. "I'm just awful sorry, that's all. I ain't never felt so bad over nothin'."

"Let me see that ankle?"

Bert looked at me, but then he assented, stretching his leg out in front of him. It was kind of puffy and pink, but the doctor wasn't worried.

"Can you put weight on it?"

"A little. It hurts, though."

Dr. Hall didn't take long looking it over. "Got you a bad sprain, I'd say. And angels watching out for you. Could have died going in a burning structure. Don't ever do it again."

"No, sir, I won't."

"You'll have to stay off of that ankle a few days. Soak it morning and night. If you're not on it by next week, have your pa bring you in. But I think it'll be fine."

The doctor patted Bert's shoulder, then turned to me. "Well, Mrs. Wortham. You had one busy night. Any more?"

"Yes. One. Bert's brother Franky has a

burn on one hand and what looks like a nail puncture on the other. He was fighting the fire. And he helped pull my Samuel out. Can't keep him from working today, though. I sent the girls for him."

"Well, where is he? I can go to him."

He did. We were started on the way when Sarah and Katie came back, telling me Franky wouldn't come. "He says he don't need a doctor, that his pa'll be mad," Katie said.

I was immediately stirred almost to anger over the idea. Surely George wouldn't be angry over his son seeing the doctor. Not if he had a lick of sense about him.

I took Dr. Hall straight to the woodshop, and there was Franky sanding away on the beautiful hope chest he and Samuel had been working on earlier in the week. He didn't stop when we came in. He didn't even look up. I'd never known Franky to be stubborn before, but I thought that was what I was seeing in the set of his jaw. Until I came closer and saw the tears in his eyes.

"Franky, let Dr. Hall look at your hands, please."

He didn't even stop what he was doing. "I'm all right."

The doctor reached forward and took the sanding board right out of his hands. "I already know you're a brave young man. It doesn't hurt to let me look."

Not having much choice, Franky consented. The burn on his left hand wasn't bad, but the doctor spent some time looking at the nail puncture. "You're gonna have this infected if you don't take care," he said. "If you've got to work, it'll have to be bandaged. Let me clean it out for you first."

We went to the well. I got washcloths and a towel, and Dr. Hall cleaned him up and took a bottle of something called Landin's Disinfectant and poured it over the puncture. I could see that the skin all around the wound was red. The doctor put Baxter's Wound Cream on the burn and the puncture wound, and handed me the rest of the jar. Then he bandaged both hands. Franky wasn't very happy with that, I could tell.

"It's been a while since I've seen any of you," Dr. Hall remarked, looking into Franky's face. "You the one had the broken leg some years back?"

"Yes, sir," Franky acknowledged.

"Doing all right with it?"

Franky didn't answer.

"He still has some limp," I said gently, though I expected Franky probably would've preferred me to keep quiet.

"Well," the doctor said with a sigh, addressing Franky as though he'd been the one to speak. "I hate to hear that. But it was a bad break, no question of that. I still wish your pa had let you stay in the hospital longer. Might have helped. Can't say for sure now." He glanced over at me. "Their mother's been gone a long time now, hasn't she?"

"Yes. Seven years."

He nodded. "I'd appreciate it if you or Mrs. Pratt would see that Bert soaks his ankle. And this young man needs to keep the bandages on except for twice a day to put on some more of the ointment I'm leaving with you. In a couple of days you can leave the wounds open to the air a while. I'll try to be back to take another look and see about Samuel then too."

I thought he was finished, but he was still eyeing Franky pretty straight. He reached his hand up to touch Franky's bruised cheek. "Did this happen fighting the fire too?"

"No, sir," Franky answered. "That was earlier."

"What happened?"

It took Franky a moment to answer. I knew he didn't want to. "I was in a fight, sir."

"Well, let's hope you've managed to learn a lesson about that sort of thing. Put a cool cloth on it if it bothers you."

I knew Dr. Hall would be going soon. He still had patients at the hospital in Mcleansboro. But he started back toward the house to see Samuel again first.

"Do you think we should bring him to your hospital?" I asked him, even though I knew what he'd already said.

He shook his head. "I wouldn't be doing much different for him than what you can do here. And I can't say that he ought to be moved right now, Mrs. Wortham. Better him staying as still as possible. I'll be out to check on him as much as I can or send Nurse McCulley."

"But you said you could take X-ray pictures."

"You're right. We could. But with the head and the ribs, there's not much we could do if we did see that they're broken."

"Should we have brought him last night?" I continued to question.

"Hard to know those things. But don't worry. I'm thinking he'll get along all right."

I wasn't sure whether to be relieved or not. I wasn't even sure if I was hearing good news or bad. "But what if he does bleed or swell inside?" I asked him plainly, glad there were no children close enough to hear.

He stopped on the porch and turned to me with a sigh. "Mrs. Wortham, the best thing you can do is pray and believe for the best. We've got no cause to expect more problems."

That should've been enough for me. In ordinary times, it would've been. But my heart was still racing along, afraid for the husband I loved more than life itself. "We weren't expecting the problems we've already had," I told him. "If he were to have trouble, I just want to know what we could do."

He took a deep breath. I could tell he really didn't want to say more. There was such softness in his eyes. "I'm not a surgeon, Mrs. Wortham. If he were to have complications, we could try to get him to one. But the best thing we can do is believe he won't need more help. You know I'll do everything I can. And I'll move him if you want me to. But it would only make him uncomfortable."

I stood on the porch step and took a

deep breath, willing myself to do what he said and believe for the best. Why was I having such trouble with that?

"Please don't worry. It's a wonderful sign, him talking to us the way he did. There's no reason to expect anything but a full recovery."

He went walking on in, and I mustered myself to follow.

Samuel was still awake. Dr. Hall applied a generous amount of the wound cream to a square of cotton, laid that against the back of Samuel's head, and bandaged it in place. He did the same with his leg, telling me again that he thought it would do fine without stitches and that I'd done well with what I'd done before he got there. He said he'd leave a bottle of Chandler's Aspirin Tablets along with the cream for the wounds, since I didn't have any in the house. I helped him pull a wide cloth band underneath Samuel's middle in order to wrap his ribs. Samuel was still hurting, I could tell, especially with the movement and the contact, but he didn't say a word.

"Let your friends and family take care of the farm," the doctor cautioned him. "I want you to stay in this bed."

"How long?" There was a determination in Samuel when he asked it that I was glad to see. Of course, I didn't want him in a hurry to get up, but I was glad he was thinking on it.

"A couple of days, for starters," the doctor answered. "I'll be back to see you, and we'll talk about it then."

Samuel looked at me.

"We'll manage fine with you in bed," I told him. "Don't you worry about that."

"All right," he agreed.

"It was good of you, saving that boy," the doctor said. He held out his hand, and Samuel shook it. "I've got other patients waiting." He turned toward the door. I asked him what we owed him for his trouble.

"I'll not be charging you in this," he told me. "Looks like you folks have had more trouble than what it was to me coming out here. But next time, I might take a meal."

"We could feed you now," I offered.

"No. But thank you. I've got to get back." He turned to go, and I followed. He stopped again by the back door.

"Mrs. Wortham, get some rest. Don't be worrying, and don't wear yourself down seeing to everybody else."

"Yes," I said simply.

"If Mr. Hammond has any questions about those boys of his, you just send him over to talk to me."

"Yes, sir. Thank you again."

"Three times a day change your husband's bandages and put on more of the cream. At least twice for that bigger boy. More if he gets the bandages wet or dirty."

I nodded, and he smiled. "You did fine, Mrs. Wortham. You'd make a fine nurse. And a midwife. Could use more of those in these parts."

I didn't know how to respond to that, so I didn't say anything at all. I didn't want anything more to do with midwifery. Or nursing injuries either.

He walked away and got in his old car. A 1910 Model A like we used to have back in Pennsylvania. Dr. Hall kept it shiny. I stood on the porch, watching him pull away down our long lane. *Thank you, God, that he came. Bless him.*

"Mom?" Sarah called out to me. "I think Daddy's gone to sleep again."

For a moment, the words shook me, but I took a deep breath and decided not to fret. "It's all right, honey. The doctor said he'd need a lot of rest."

I thanked Barrett Post for doing the milking and asked him if there was any way he could bring me more ice. He looked so tired that I felt bad for asking. But he didn't seem to mind. He carried the milk in for me and then he was gone. *Lord, bless him too.*

Inside the house, Thelma was singing to the baby. I looked across the timber and wondered what was still going on over at the Hammonds' that was keeping young Sam from coming back to his wife and newborn. I wondered if the fire had flared back up or if George had somehow gone to pieces over all they'd lost. He'd been doing better than before. Though times were still hard, at least the Hammonds had gotten so they were no worse off than the rest of the struggling folks in our area.

And now this.

I was about to go back in the house, but I saw Franky over at the well. He must not have known I was watching. He took a drink, and then slow and deliberate, he started pulling the bandage off his right hand.

"Franky!" I hollered immediately. "Leave that bandage be! You heard what the doctor said."

He stopped what he was doing and looked up. I came closer. He was looking so awful with yesterday's bruises on his tired face.

"I don't wanna go 'round wrapped up

like it's real bad or somethin', 'cause it ain't," he told me with determination.

"That's good, Franky. I'm glad it's not worse. But if we want it to heal up, we'd better do what we're told, don't you think?"

His silvery eyes were deep and solemn. "I don't want nobody lookin' at me an' thinkin' I'm wantin' 'em to look."

Such a notion would never have occurred to me. "Why would anybody do that? Franky, you can't help it that you were hurt."

He lowered his head. "Not everybody thinks like you."

I hardly knew how to respond. "If anyone looks at you funny, they've got problems of their own that are not your concern. And it's just for a couple of days. The doctor said you could give it open air then, and I think you should heed him. Please? To keep the medicine in and the dirt and sawdust out."

He just stood looking down at his hands.

"For your right hand especially. It could get infected if you try to work without protecting it. And you need it getting well quickly, not getting worse."

"All right." He sighed, suddenly looking like he was carrying a new weight. "I'll do what you say."

I didn't really understand what was bothering him about it. He headed back to the woodshop, and I turned to the house. Franky did a lot of thinking, I knew that. He was always turning things over in his mind. But I couldn't remember him being sullen like this before or concerned about the way somebody looked at him or thought of him. Maybe it was because his father was blaming him for the fire.

Sarah was waiting for me when I got to the porch. "You think Franky could have done it?" she asked me.

"No," I said immediately, not at all pleased to be hearing such nonsense again. "I don't know what happened. But it wasn't Franky. He would tell me if it was. You know that, don't you, Sarah?"

Something in her eyes changed. Suddenly she looked scared. She glanced around quickly and then back at me but didn't quite meet my eyes. "Mom —"

She was about to say something, but Georgie came running out of the house, waving a pancake in his little fist. I reached and grabbed him before he could go flying down the porch steps.

Delores was right behind him. "Come back here, you little hooligan!" she called to her grandson. "You're supposed to be sittin' an' eatin' that, not runnin' out to play with the dog!"

"Whiskers like pannycake?" Georgie asked me. His grandmother whisked him out of my arms.

"You're not gonna feed those fine pancakes to no dog! Now come back inside an' finish your breakfast!"

I smiled, glad to see some of the shenanigans that were more common fare around here. But Sarah was looking pale.

"Somebody's coming," she said.

I hadn't heard anyone, but she was right. Down the road, we could see a truck coming our way. It wasn't long before I knew it was Richard Pratt's, and I wished we could have gotten some word to him and Robert that they needn't trouble Dr. Howell any further. I hated for the elderly gentleman to come all the way out here when Dr. Hall had already come and gone. But maybe they hadn't found him. Maybe he was busy again this morning. I went out to meet them, to tell them right away that everything was all right. Sarah, Delores, and Georgie all followed me.

There was no other vehicle behind the boys. And I could soon tell that there was no one else with them in the truck. For a moment I considered the possibility that

the two doctors might have talked by telephone before Dr. Hall ever left Mcleansboro. That way Dr. Howell would know he
didn't have to come out. But that wasn't
very likely.

Dr. Howell was just busy. Too busy for a
man his age. He didn't get around so well
anymore. But he sure got called on a
lot.

"Mom!" Robert yelled as they pulled in.
"Was it Dr. Hall we saw?"

"Yes. He was just here."

He looked so relieved. "What'd he say?
Is Dad all right? We were thinking we'd
have to go get him, but Richard thought
that was him up at the turn —"

"Dr. Howell's with someone else again
then?" I asked, glad they hadn't dragged
him out here.

"No, Mom," Robert said. And I knew by
his eyes that something was wrong.

"He's gone," Richard said quietly.

"Gone where?" Delores asked. "If he
ain't with a patient . . ."

Both boys looked grim. Richard cleared
his throat and tried to explain. "His
neighbor told us he was over to the elder
Mrs. Porter's house last night to listen to
her lungs, an' he just collapsed on their
porch. He was gone before they could do

anythin' at all. They think it was his heart jus' givin' up."

Beside me, Sarah reached for my hand. "You mean . . . you mean Dr. Howell is dead?"

"I guess the Lord called him home," Delores said with a sigh. "He certainly is deservin' of his eternal rest."

I was glad Delores was receiving the news so calmly. I was feeling a little unsteady. Why did bad things just keep piling on top of each other? Dr. Howell had been our friend ever since we came here, when he used to come and check on dear old Emma Graham. He'd been a blessing. I didn't know what to say.

"Mom, how is Dad?" Robert persisted.

"Resting again," I managed to tell him. "And Dr. Hall said we can expect him to be just fine."

"We sent Charlie Hunter to tell the pastor what happened," Richard told me. "He said Ben an' Lizbeth was over to Mrs. Porter's an' he'll go an' tell them too."

I nodded. Pastor would surely come. Ben and Lizbeth too, once they could get away. The elder Mrs. Porter was Ben's grandmother, and I hoped she was all right. A dreadful shock that must have been, to lose the doctor in such a way. And she'd been growing weaker and weaker of late.

"You gonna stay here tonight or go on over to Sam and Thelma's?" Richard asked his mother.

"I'll be talkin' that over with Sam when he gets back. Thelma's plenty strong enough to travel, and we're needin' to get outta Mrs. Wortham's hair —"

"You're fine here if you want to stay another night or two," I said quickly. "The doctor did tell Thelma not to do too much too soon."

We all went inside. The girls fed Richard all he'd eat, and he held the baby a while before he left. Robert was quiet. He didn't really want to eat. He just wanted to sit with his father, and I sat with him, watching Samuel sleep again. He looked so different with the doctor's big bandage around his head. I was glad most of the bruises were not visible for my son to see.

"How bad is he busted up, Mom?" Robert asked me. "I know you don't want to say, but it's not like I'm a little kid. What else did the doctor say? Don't you think I oughta know?"

"He has a concussion, Robert," I said with a sigh. "Maybe broken ribs. But he'll mend. He's doing all right. He's just to stay in bed a while, at least till the doctor's back to see him in a couple of days."

So many times I'd seen Robert's clear green eyes looking into mine, but this time was different. He was still my little boy. In a way, he always would be. But now the look on his face was more like a man than I'd ever seen in him, moved deep to his heart but still so strong.

"I thought he was gone, Mom, for a while. An' I didn't know what we'd do."

I hugged my son, feeling his near-grown muscles tense with worry. "He'll be all right," I whispered to him. "He'll be just fine."

I looked up to see Sarah standing in the doorway, and I wasn't sure how long she'd been there. She didn't have a word to say. Both of my children seemed numb, not really wanting to do anything.

But Katie stayed in motion. Maybe keeping her hands busy helped her. She gave out as many pancakes as she could, washed up all the dishes, and then started making a batch of muffins, because they were quick, she said, and we were low on bread.

I wanted all of them to go and take a nap, but they weren't minded that way. Berty had slept, and Harry was still sleeping, but they were the only ones. Delores suggested I lie down for a while, but I wouldn't have felt right about that unless Samuel woke and wanted me at his side again.

About 10:00 in the morning, George came. Young Sam brought him in the truck with Rorey and William. I was glad to see animals in the back. At least some of the stock had survived. Mostly goats. A couple of pigs. I wondered about the cows, the two horses that pulled George's wagon, and for the first time, the wagon itself. Had they lost that too?

"Can we put the stock over here, Mrs. Wortham?" Sam Hammond called to me.

"Yes, of course."

"Ever'body doin' all right?" George yelled.

I nodded. "They're all right."

Robert came out to help Willy and Sam unload the animals and get them all situated in our barn lot. Rorey started for the house. She looked exhausted but not near as dirty as her brothers. She stopped on the porch anyway, to wash at our basin. Sarah came out just as Rorey was about to go in. For a moment they were face-to-face. I expected a hug or something, it had been such a traumatic night. But strangely enough, the girls who had been the best of friends since we came here only side-stepped one another and went on without a word.

12

Sarah

Rorey wasn't sooty like her brothers. Rorey wasn't half the mess Franky was when he first got here. I wondered if she'd helped at all or just stood there like a dunce the whole time, the way she had when I'd seen her.

And Lester Turrey wasn't around. I walked out across the yard, thinking of Lester pulling my braids in the school yard. And pushing Katie into a mud puddle. He was just plain mean. He'd always been mean.

He was probably the one who started that fire. It made my heart beat faster just thinking about it. *He's the one who should've been hurt.*

I knew Bert was feeling bad over my daddy. And Franky was dealing with plenty enough too. I wondered if Rorey was feeling guilty. And how much did she have to feel guilty about?

"Everything all right?" Mom asked me.

I nodded, not wanting to say out loud what I really felt. *Everything's not all right at all.*

I wished I could've told Mom about Lester and Rorey when I'd had the chance. I couldn't now with everybody around. So I'd just have to wait till Mom was alone again to tell her what Rorey'd been planning. And I didn't think I'd feel bad to do it. Even though Rorey'd probably never trust me with a secret again.

"Kirk'll be over in a little while with Tulip," Willy was saying. "We had to put Teddy down. He was bad hurt."

Tulip and Teddy were Mr. Hammond's horses. I wondered if he could do the farmwork with only one, or if they could afford to get another. Probably not, from what I could see. "What about the cows?" I asked him.

"We found Dolly an' her calf. Guess we lost the rest."

"Where'd you leave Dolly?" Robert asked him.

"Tied up over t' home. Pa said they'd be all right for a while. I'll go back over an' get 'em."

"Eat something first," Mom told him.

I wondered why she was so quick to think of that. Seemed like it was always that way. Whenever anything bad happened, somebody was always checking to make sure everybody ate. We'd brought food when Phyllis Meyer's mother was so sick. And people had brought food out here when Emma Graham and Rorey's mama died. But I didn't like remembering that. Most things had been good since then.

"I'll go with you after Dolly," Robert told Willy.

"We still got a house," Mr. Hammond was telling my mother. "Gotta fix the roof now and a wall on the west side. It's purty bad where the fire caught it."

"Is there loss on the inside?" Mom asked him.

"Perty smoky. Most things is all right, though. The boys worked awful hard to save it. I'd a' give it up. I didn't have the strength."

I saw Sam Hammond look over at his father with something pained in his eyes. I wondered what had happened over there after we left. I think all the Hammond kids, except maybe Emmie or Bert, understood that their pa had problems sometimes. He wasn't like my dad. He kind of fell apart when times got tough.

Sam told my mom in a quiet voice that most of his pa's crop and some of ours was gone. The fire had spread into two fields and a stand of timber. Plus all the hay, the smokehouse, and the machine shed. I already knew about the goat pen and the pigsty that had been closest to the barn, so that meant there wasn't nothing left standing at the Hammond place but the house and the woodshed. And maybe the chicken coop.

"Who knows how bad it'd been if the rain hadn't come when it did," Sam added. "That was God's gift."

Mom only nodded. And I thought the same thing I'd thought before. Why couldn't the rain have come sooner?

Kirk brought the horse before long. I'd hardly ever seen Tulip without Teddy, and I kind of felt sorry for her. Maybe she'd be lonely. But Kirk was awful good to her. He loved horses, and I knew he was sad about the loss of Teddy.

We had some more to feed now. Katie was right. It was easy to keep adding to the batter to keep the pancakes coming. I was amazed at how much Willy and Kirk could eat. And their pa. I was surprised he could eat at all. Rorey couldn't. Not more than a few bites.

Daddy slept a long time. That bothered me, even though we were all pretty tired. Mom kept telling me he'd be okay, that the doctor believed it too. I guessed he must have, or he wouldn't have left without taking Dad to the hospital with him. But I still hated the thought of Dad lying there in bed with a head concussion and busted-up ribs. I couldn't be mad at Berty, though. It wasn't really his fault. He was only thinking to save Imey. I should've been able to stop him.

Rorey wasn't saying much to me. She only shook her head when I asked if she wanted milk. She wasn't really saying much to anybody. I wondered what she was thinking. Maybe that it was all her fault.

Mom and Delores Pratt prayed about Dad. He woke up again for a while, and I thought he sounded tired but some better. I wished he'd get up, but Mom said he wasn't supposed to try. He didn't seem to like that any better than I did.

"It doesn't seem right to stay in bed," he told us.

"Dr. Hall came all the way out here," Mom argued. "The least we can do is mind his advice."

"It'll do you good to rest until you're mended, Samuel," Mrs. Pratt maintained.

He didn't answer.

"Can I get you something to drink?" Mom asked.

"Yeah. Thanks."

Mom gave him some more of her medicine tea. It was probably a nasty flavor, but Dad drank it down without saying anything. Mom was glad he'd finished it all.

Mr. Hammond came in. I knew he wanted to see Dad and make sure he was okay, but I didn't want to be there when they talked. I don't know why.

I went and helped Katie clean up the new bunch of breakfast dishes. Then I went walking outside. What I needed was some way to look busy and get clear away from everybody. So I decided to work in the garden. I could pick what few tomatoes were left and see what else I could find. Most of the garden had been done in by the summer's heat. We had a few things left over, and we'd planted some fall crops to come on late. But it'd been too dry for any of that to do very well. Until last night. Maybe the rain *had* been a gift of God, if it wasn't too late.

Only two squash were left on vines too shriveled to do them any good. I was leaned over picking them when Rorey came out of the house. I knew she was looking for me. I didn't want to talk to her. I wasn't sure what I'd say. I wasn't even sure why she'd want to talk now, after saying so little to me just a few minutes before. But I could see that she did want to talk, now that nobody else was around. She was charging my way.

"That was the worst fire I ever seen," she said once she got close. I saw her look one way, then the other, checking to see if anybody was in sight, but I didn't say anything at all, just set the squash at the end of one row and started to pull weeds out of the bed where we'd planted more late lettuce. Only four or five plants came up, and they didn't look good anymore. Maybe the rain would help.

"Lester didn't come." Rorey said the words quickly, as though she was afraid somebody else would sneak up and hear. "He didn't even come, Sarah. You didn't say nothin' to nobody, did you?"

I just looked at her. Why did she care about that so much, after people had got hurt? Why wasn't she telling me she hoped my dad would be just fine?

"You didn't, did you?" she pushed.

"No," I said, hoping only one word

wouldn't betray the anger I was suddenly feeling. *No, I didn't tell!* I screamed inside my head. *But I should, you selfish thing!*

"I watched for him," she went on. "But he must've known Franky was gonna be watchin' too. Maybe when they fought yesterday Franky told him he'd watch. You think so, Sarah?" She paused, waiting for my answer.

"How would I know?" I turned my eyes back to the lettuce bed. *Go away,* I told her in my mind. *Leave me alone.*

"Anyway, I seen Franky go out there. I seen him go in the barn. And that's when the fire started. That's when everybody heard Franky yellin' an' wakin' people up. He was in the barn for a while, an' I saw the smoke. It musta been his doin'."

"I don't think he's said that," I told her.

"You shouldn't care what he says," she answered right back. "He might try to blame Lester or anything, just to keep his own self out of trouble."

I just stared at her for a minute. I might have replied somehow, I don't know what. But her pa came out the back door of the house right then. I was hoping he was just getting some air, going to check on his animals or something. I didn't want him coming over and talking to us right then, that was for sure.

He glanced our way a minute, and I felt kind of swirly-sick inside, thinking he might somehow yell at Rorey for some kind of an explanation or at me for not saying something sooner.

But what he did next was far worse. He turned his eyes toward the woodshop door, took two or three steps closer, and then hollered as loud as he could for Franky.

Oh no, I thought. *He's going to blame Franky just like Robert did. He's going to rail on him right now.*

I was glad Mr. Hammond hadn't come over and talked to us. I was glad he hadn't heard what Rorey had just got done telling me. But maybe he'd already heard. Maybe she'd started that kind of talk in the night, before we even got over to the fire.

"Franky!" Mr. Hammond bellowed again, and I felt something tighten inside of me. Rorey walked away. I don't know why, but she went straight back in the house. She was out of sight before Franky came out of the woodshop. Usually Franky was quick when somebody called. But not this time, and I didn't blame him. He had what looked like a new-carved chair rocker in his bandaged hand, and he looked his pa straight in the eye.

For a moment they were both silent. Franky spoke first. "You need me for somethin'?" he said kind of quiet. "I got me an' Mr. Wortham's orders to fill."

I guess it was the wrong thing to say. Mr. Hammond looked like he could shoot sparks right out of his ears. "Franklin Drew Hammond, I know 'bout your dad-blame orders! That don't mean you ain't got the time if I call you, you hear me?"

I didn't remember ever hearing Franky's whole name shouted out like that, so I knew this was bad.

"Yes, Pa," Franky said, standing as still as he could.

I prayed just a little. Maybe Mr. Hammond wouldn't be too hard on him. If he *had* started the fire like Rorey had said, it was surely just an accident. But maybe she didn't really know how it all happened. She hadn't actually seen the fire start. Had she?

The awful swirly feeling was growing in my stomach, and words jumped in my head sudden. *How do you know you can trust what she tells you?*

No! I argued with myself. *She wouldn't lie. Not to me! Would she?*

Mr. Hammond was talking, and his

voice sounded low and mean. "I told you to tell Mr. and Mrs. Wortham you was sorry. But you didn't, did you?"

"I'm sorry he got hurt," Franky said, starting to turn away.

"That's not what I said!"

Franky faced his pa again, and I thought him brave for looking straight in those angry eyes. "We're all sorry, Pa," he said. "Ain't nobody would've wanted such things to —"

Mr. Hammond jumped forward, grabbed the chair piece in Franky's hand, and threw it hard on the ground. I was scared. Kirk came up, but he didn't interfere. I thought about getting Mom. I'd never seen Mr. Hammond beat his kids or nothing like that. But I'd never seen him look like he was looking at Franky now.

"I ain't havin' it! I ain't havin' you lie to me —"

"I didn't set the fire, Pa," Franky stammered. "An' I ain't —"

"I never said you'd do it of a purpose, boy! But you's the clumsiest —"

Franky tried to get away, but his pa grabbed him by both arms. "I tol' you to 'pologize! Not come over here an' get yourself all babied by the doctor! Look at you! Fixed up like you got somethin' broke on you! Gettin' attention on yerself so they wouldn't go blamin' you — ain't that it?"

I almost couldn't stand hearing all this. I'd never seen Franky angry. But there was something strange in his eyes, and it scared me as much as his father's behavior. I started for the house. I had to get Mom. She'd know what to do.

Before I got there, Franky broke away from his father. He turned back to the shop for a second but started off toward the timber instead.

"Don't you turn your back on me!" Mr. Hammond yelled.

But Franky didn't stop. He couldn't run good with his limp, but he was moving pretty fast. I half expected Kirk to chase him. But he didn't. Their pa didn't either.

"Go on, then!" Mr. Hammond yelled. "Get! I ain't got no more to say to you anyhow! You done cost us more'n we can even figger."

I didn't get to the porch. Mom was coming out, and coming out fast. Maybe Rorey'd fetched her. That was my first thought. But then I knew she hadn't. She wouldn't. Mom had come on her own, after hearing all the ruckus.

"How can you yell at him so?" she demanded. "Loud enough for the world to hear, and you're not even thinking what that boy's going through!"

"I don't much care —"

"You need to care! You need to stop and look at yourself. Franky wouldn't hurt a fly! He would no more lie to you than the man in the moon. Why can't you see —"

"It's you that don't see, Mrs. Wortham."

I couldn't listen to no more arguing. I might've run into the house, but Robert was standing in the doorway looking fierce.

Robert. He ought to be Franky's friend. But he was believing Mr. Hammond. I knew he was. And believing Rorey too. They were all believing Rorey. Suddenly I knew it. She'd started this blaming. She'd turned attention away from herself. I was suddenly so mad I could hardly see straight.

Instead of the house, I went running for the woods after Franky. Somebody ought to tell him that his word meant more than dust in the breeze. Mom would. I knew she would. Eventually. But Mr. Hammond had her attention now.

I wondered if I'd find him. I didn't know how far he'd go. His pa wasn't even giving him a chance. His pa wasn't even thinking. Or listening.

I went around a wild rosebush and saw

Franky up ahead of me, sitting under a pin oak and staring into the trees. He didn't look up when I stopped in front of him. I didn't know what he'd think of me following him. I wasn't sure what to say, but I knew I ought to say something.

"Are you all right?" I finally asked.

He still didn't look at me. "Yeah. Why wouldn't I be? What are you doin' here?"

"I didn't think your pa was being fair. He don't know what happened."

Franky sounded mad. "What difference does it make to you? You don't know neither."

Almost I said I did. But he was right. Just because I knew Rorey had planned to be in the barn didn't mean she caused the fire. I didn't know what to say. I thought maybe Lester had done it, and I figured Rorey knew the truth. But she was my very best friend. I couldn't just come out and blame her until I found out for sure. "All kinds of things can happen," I said. "Your pa didn't have to blame you."

"He knew I was awake. I guess it stands to reason in his mind."

"Why were you awake?"

"Heard a noise. Was goin' out to check when I seen the fire."

I stood quiet for a minute. "That's all?

You don't know how it started?"

He suddenly looked even angrier. "If I did, don't you think I'd tell somebody? Not that they'd listen."

Rorey had said Franky would try to blame Lester. Rorey didn't know him very well, it didn't seem like.

"You oughta go back," I told him. "They'll be wonderin' about you."

He shook his head. "Your mama, maybe. But she'd be the only one."

He stood up and started walking away. I wasn't sure what to say. He looked so awful sad. I wanted to tell him that his pa and all his brothers cared a lot and would wonder too, but I wasn't sure that was true. They didn't act like it sometimes. "Lizbeth'll be coming out probably," I called after him. "She'd worry if you wasn't around."

He was walking away and not talking very loud. So I could hardly hear his answer. "Can't go far. Got orders to fill. Nowhere to go, anyhow."

For a minute I watched his back. He was a couple of years older than me but not any bigger. I'd never really thought of him as older, because he wasn't like his brothers, or Robert either. He wasn't tall. With his limp, he never seemed quite as sturdy as them. And he wasn't out of the elementary primer yet.

But he had a job with my dad. And it suddenly didn't seem right to keep calling him Franky like he was still a little boy.

"Frank?" I called after him. "Where are you going?"

He stopped and glanced back. "I don't know. Just away for a minute. Why are you followin' me?"

Again, I wasn't sure what to say. He didn't wait, so I had to run to catch up to him.

"I told you why," I said when I got close enough. "It wasn't fair. Your pa ought to listen to you. If you say you didn't start no fire, that oughta be good enough —"

"Yeah, well it's not. Not when it's me talkin'."

"That's not right."

"Maybe not. But that don't change nothin'." He turned and looked at me with something fiery hard in his eyes. "You watch. Pretty soon the whole countryside'll know 'bout this. They'll think I set the fire an' now I'm jus' lyin' about it. Too clumsy to get things right and too much a coward to own up. You watch, Sarah Jean. There won't nobody trust me 'fore long."

He was the only one besides my mother

who ever called me Sarah Jean. It might've bothered me some other time, but it didn't then. I wanted to tell him that what other people thought didn't matter. It wouldn't, to some kids. But it did to Franky. A lot. He wasn't much of a kid anymore. Not really. And stuff like trust was important to him. Real important.

That's when I noticed he was looking pale. "Maybe you don't unnerstand," he told me. "I'm used to bein' a laughin'stock, havin' lessons read to me 'cause I can't read 'em for myself. But at least folks figured I was honest an' good with my hands. I won't never live this down! 'Specially with your pa so bad hurt . . ."

He sat down, seeming to sink right in front of me. Clear to the ground, but not just that. He looked terrible small all of a sudden. I sat down too, just so I wouldn't feel like I was towering over him.

I thought I better say something. "Frank," I started to say but stopped when I saw the turmoil in his eyes.

"Pa don't believe me," he said. "Why would anybody else? And there ain't nothin' I can do about it."

I swallowed hard, thinking of Rorey. Had she lied? Or had she just seen Franky awake and assumed it was his fault? I didn't want to think that she'd cause all this trouble on purpose, but there was no doubt in me about Franky. He wouldn't lie about this. Not for hundreds of thousands of dollars.

"Maybe your pa'll change his mind," I suggested. "He's got to think on it some. There's no reason for him not to believe you."

Franky shook his head. "I guess he don't need a reason."

I wondered if he knew what Rorey'd said. I couldn't help but think on it more. She said she'd seen him go into the barn. But he hadn't said that. So I asked him straight out. "Did you go in, Frank? Did you go in the barn, before the others woke up?"

He stared at me so stormy, his strange-colored eyes looking like thunderclouds. "What difference does it make to you?"

"I — I'm just trying to understand."

He sighed, and I realized what he must be thinking. That I didn't believe him either.

"I seen the fire," he said real slow. "I yelled for Pa an' the rest. But I didn't wait. I run to save what animals I could. But the fire was already goin'. I led the horses, but Teddy got 'way from me, jumpin' kinda wild. They was scared, all of 'em. I unlatched what gates I could to let everythin' else go out, but I couldn't get 'em all. Didn't think there was time to go back in. I shoulda kep' watch on Berty, shoulda figured he'd do somethin' like he did. He loves them cows. I'm sorry what happened to your pa. But it was God's grace for 'em to live. It was smokin' awful bad . . ."

He got up. He just stood for a minute. Then he started limping away again, toward the pond.

What he'd done started sinking into me. He'd risked his life to save what he could of his father's livelihood. Then he pretty much risked himself all over again, helping to save my dad. And his pa didn't even care. Wouldn't even hear it.

"Frank!" I called after him again. "I believe you."

He stopped. He turned just a little. He didn't smile. But I thought I might have seen just a little less weight pressing him down.

13

Julia

I almost wished I could hog-tie that George Hammond and make him listen. How in the world could he treat his son so badly? I didn't care who started the fire. Even if Franky had been the one, that was no excuse for such yelling and carrying on. It was just an accident.

George went walking into the barn to check on his surviving horse. I let him go, though he should have been following Franky into the timber to apologize. He'd always been too hard on Franky.

I was glad Sarah had gone. It surprised me a little because she didn't usually say much to any of the Hammond boys. They were just Rorey's brothers to her, never gaining any special attention. Her sense of justice must have been aroused. Maybe she was as mad about it as I was.

"Mom, do you want me to call Sarah

back?" Robert suddenly asked me. "No sense her running off too. All he's gonna do is pout."

I turned and looked at my son, almost speechless. Why was everyone tearing Franky down today? Why wouldn't they give him a chance?

"I ought to send you after the both of them," I said. "You need to think about this, Robert. You need to consider whether it's right to condemn someone with no evidence at all."

"There *is* evidence. Besides his pa's word. There's a witness, Mom."

"What witness?"

"Rorey. She seen him. He set the fire. Going in the barn with a lantern. That's how it happened. And it almost got Dad killed. So I don't think nobody's being too hard on him."

For a moment I couldn't answer him. If the question came down to Rorey's word or Franky's, which would be believed?

"Robert, you know I can't prove right now what happened. Does it really matter? It was an accident either way."

"It matters, Mom. Because he won't own up. It ain't so hard, forgivin' an accident, but he's tryin' to lie his way out. An' that makes him no more'n a yellow-bellied coward. I think that's what's got his pa so riled."

"Rorey could be mistaken."

"He was up, Mom. He said that himself. He was in the barn. There ain't no other way."

I looked at my son, thinking of him in the woodshop with Franky a couple of Christmases back. They'd worked so hard together on a little truck for Berty. I'd thought that would be the beginning of a greater friendship between them. "Franky is no liar, Robert. You should know that."

He shook his head at me. "I don't know nothing right now."

He walked away. And I felt like screaming. Yesterday I thought our lives were coming along so very well as we gathered for a birthday feast. How could we so soon be shaken into pieces?

I almost headed to the woods myself after Franky and Sarah, but little Georgie was yelling over something, baby Rosemary was fussy, and somebody else was driving up our lane. They'd be all right, I decided. Sarah and Franky both had good enough heads on their shoulders. Maybe they'd talk it out and come to the sensible conclusion that other people's unpleasant attitudes didn't matter to a hill of beans.

It was the pastor coming. My spirits lifted a bit just recognizing his car. And when I noticed that Juanita was with him, I felt even better. She was a blessing to have around. She made herself helpful in so many ways. Just as good, George would surely listen to the pastor, even if he wouldn't listen to anyone else.

I walked to meet them, thanking God for giving us their friendship. Juanita waved before the car even stopped.

"How is everyone?" Pastor called as he parked beside the rosebush.

It was hard not to answer with a flood of tears. "Samuel's hurt, and George has run Franky off, blaming him for the fire."

"Run him off?"

"He just . . . he just took off into the woods. Sarah followed him."

Pastor looked awfully stricken as he got out of the car. "Do you think I should follow them?"

"Yes . . . no. I don't know. I think they'll come back. I think it'll be all right."

Juanita came up beside me and took my hand. "How is Samuel?"

I wasn't going to cry. Not a bit of it. But it suddenly came pouring out of me like somebody'd opened a gate for it. Juanita put her arms around me, and I tried to stop. "He's . . . he's all right. We might have lost him, but Dr. Hall says he'll be all right."

"What can we do?" Pastor asked me. "Tell me what you need first."

"A . . . a prayer. Please. Just a prayer that everything comes out all right."

He obliged me, right on the spot. Holding my hand and Juanita's, he prayed low and fervent, and I felt a little better. "Thank you," I whispered when he was finished. "Thank you so much for coming."

"Do you think I should try to find Franky?"

I shook my head. "He'll come back. He and Sarah both. It might do more good for you to talk to George."

I told him everything that had happened, about the baby coming and the injuries in the fire and the accusations against Franky. He listened grimly without a word.

"Many are the afflictions of the righteous," Juanita said. "But the Lord delivereth him from them all."

I knew she was quoting Scripture, and it made me think of Franky in Samuel's room such a short time ago, quoting that beautiful psalm and giving me peace. *Lord, help him. Help his father see that it can do no good to cast blame.*

"Where is George?" Pastor asked.

"Still in the barn, I think."

He started in that direction, and Juanita walked me to the house with her arm around my shoulder. "Is it a good time to see Samuel?" she asked.

"I — I think he's gone back to sleep, but you can come and see."

"Have you managed to get any rest?"

I stopped and looked at her. I wanted to tell her I had, but I didn't really think she'd believe me. So I said nothing at all.

"I didn't think so. Julia, I think you need to have a seat and put your feet up. This has all been too much."

"No," I said, not even knowing why I was arguing with her. "It has not been too much. The Lord said he would never give us more than we can bear. I remember your husband told us that in a sermon once."

"You're right. The good Lord doesn't. But that old devil sure tries to. And he was hittin' hard out here last night and today too. You're going to have to rest, Juli. I don't know when I've seen you so worn down."

Again I didn't even try to answer her. I hadn't expected that she'd say anything at all about me.

We went on walking, up the porch steps and into the house, through the kitchen and to Samuel's side.

"The Lord has his hand on Samuel," Juanita said quietly. "He had his hand on this whole situation.—That no one was killed, Juli, it's a blessing of God."

Of course I knew she was right. One part of me did. But still I bristled inside at those words. *This has nothing to do with the hand of God,* another part of me said. *If his hand was with us, then why did it have to happen at all?*

Tears filled my eyes. I didn't want to be so ungrateful. Without the Lord's protection, things might have been so much worse. I knew that. I knew how much of a miracle it was to have Samuel still with me. I knew we were blessed. *Thank you, Jesus,* I said in my mind. *Thank you for Samuel, and Berty, and everyone else being safe and sound. Help me be more grateful. Help me to rejoice.*

Juanita handed me her handkerchief. I hadn't even noticed that my cheeks were wet. "I don't understand," I struggled to say. "Samuel is such a good man. Why did this have to happen to him?"

"I don't think anyone has the answer to that question," she said. "Much as we'd like to. But you know, he showed a real Christlike heart risking himself for Bert that way. And you said he'd be all right. We'll just believe that."

I nodded. I reached and took Samuel's hand. I was glad for Juanita to be here, because in front of her I didn't feel a need to try to hide the tears.

"He looks peaceful," she said.

I had to agree. Even with the bandage on his head and all the hidden bruises, Samuel looked peaceful, lying there sleeping so quietly. But it didn't last for long.

Something in his face changed. He rolled just a little, and I saw the pain in his features, even though he didn't open his eyes.

"Samuel?" I whispered. "Are you all right?"

"M-mother?"

Suddenly my throat was constricting. Didn't he know me? Even with his eyes closed? Juanita came up closer. She held my hand as I held Samuel's.

"Samuel, it's me," I said. "Julia."

Slowly he opened his eyes. He looked up at me, but he seemed uncertain. "Is . . . Mother . . . all right?"

I couldn't imagine why he was asking that, what he was thinking. I swallowed down a nasty lump of something. "I — I don't know. It's been months since we talked to her. But she was fine then."

"I must've been dreaming."

I took a breath, feeling the relief in me as though it were pushing aside a weight. "Maybe so," I told him. "Do you want to tell me about it?"

He frowned and looked so thoughtful. "Not sure I can. I was just . . . just worried about my mother."

"She'd be worried about *you* if she knew what happened."

His deep eyes looked at me in question. "You think so?"

"How could she not, Sammy? She's your mother."

He seemed less than convinced. "Yeah. I know. But you know my mother."

Indeed I did. And she had not exactly been an easy person to deal with. Certainly not easy for Samuel to live with when he was young. Still, she would care about something like this, surely. I wondered that I hadn't thought more about that. Perhaps I should try to get word to her. "Do you want me to have someone drive to Dearing and call her?" I asked.

"No. No, I'll call her. When I get to town."

I had to smile at that. When I get to town. Just like a normal day. Samuel, in his own mind, would be up and at 'em before any of us needed to take time to send word in his stead. Thank God.

"All right," I told him. "Are you hungry?"

"No." He turned his eyes to Juanita for a moment and smiled. "Mrs. Jones. Good of you to come. Is your husband here?"

"Talking to George," I started to say, but my words were interrupted by a giant crash in the kitchen, followed by a chain reaction of smaller thumping crashes, one after another.

"Boomie!" came little Georgie's merry toddler voice. "Boomie!"

"Excuse me," I said to Juanita.

I leaned to kiss Samuel's cheek quickly and went for the kitchen. But Delores had gotten to the little fellow before I could.

"So sorry, Julia," she said. "He got plum out of my sight. Did he wake Samuel?"

"No, he was already awake. And I should've tied that cupboard shut long ago. Georgie and I have dealt with this before."

The little fellow laughed up at me. "Boomie," he whispered and melted into giggles.

"Yes, indeed," I said. "Time to put the

211

boomie baking pans back into the cupboard, though, Georgie. You want to help?"

"We'll get it, Julia," Delores assured me. "And Georgie sure enough will help, won't you, Georgie?"

Pans were scattered across the floor clear to the table. The two of them made an awful lot of noise putting everything back again, which of course was a delight to Georgie. That boy loved noise. Maybe he'd work on a train someday. Or play percussion for a symphony.

I left them and went back to Samuel's room. Willy and Robert had gone to bring Dolly and her calf to our pasture. A mercy that George had a surviving milk cow. And a calf. I supposed he'd lost the other three. He wouldn't be selling milk to the Posts and the Wainwrights for a while, unfortunately.

When Samuel saw me come back in, he asked if I'd help him sit up. "I'm not sure," I told him. "The doctor said you weren't to be moving around."

"I won't go anywhere," he promised. "Just up a little."

I felt good that he wanted to. That he was confident and feeling well enough. I used my pillow and a rolled blanket to set on top of his pillow to prop him up. Still, I could tell the moving was painful for him. He didn't say anything, but it was plain on his face.

"Did you get any sleep?" he asked me.

"No. Too many people here. Too much to do. I can't sleep in the daytime anyway."

He shook his head. "But here I am."

"Sammy, that's different. You're supposed to rest."

"Doesn't mean I like it."

Juanita smiled.

"I ought to be helping George sift through the rubble and getting things cleaned up over there," he continued.

"Don't you even think it," I blurted out. "George isn't even considering that yet. They'll get to it soon enough, but that's not your job."

He mumbled something low about helping his neighbor, and I shook my head. "You've done more for George than any of us could count. It's somebody else's turn this time around."

I knew he had a perfect answer to that. I could tell by the way he looked at me. But he didn't speak it. He just leaned his head back into the pillows and closed his eyes for a second.

"Hurting?" I asked him.

"My ribs. Maybe Dr. Hall was right about them."

"Maybe you shouldn't be sitting up."

"Feels better for my head though." He took my hand. "It was throbbing kind of crazy lying flat."

All the words the doctor had said about swelling in the brain rolled through my mind, tearing away at the relief I'd felt. I tried to push the thoughts away, but they wouldn't go, and suddenly I was feeling queasy inside. Juanita must have noticed.

"Julia, are you all right?"

"I'm fine," I told them. Glancing out the window, I could see the pastor with George walking in the yard. Maybe he was talking some sense into him. But maybe I should still go after Sarah and Franky. Weren't they back yet?

Emma Grace came looking for me to ask if she could get the Crayolas down from the cupboard to make a picture. I told her she could and went to fetch her some paper. Thelma was napping on the old davenport in the sitting room. Sam Hammond was sitting over by the window with Bert, his infant daughter nestled in the crook of one arm. Little Georgie had left the kitchen to try peeking at them from the stairway rails, but nobody seemed to be paying him much mind.

"Want to color a picture?" I asked him.

Merrily, he nodded. "Color!" he sang out, jumping down from the stairs with more daring than a two-year-old should muster.

"Settle down," his father told him. "Or you'll wake your mama."

Georgie knew that was no invitation. I could see the understanding behind his impish little grin as he stood stock-still turning it over in his mind. But then he went racing on toward the davenport like it was the greatest idea he'd had all day. I had no doubt that he would have jumped his boisterous little self on Thelma full and hard if I hadn't grabbed hold of him just in time.

"Oh no, you don't," I scolded. "You let your mama rest. It's hard work birthing a baby."

He shrugged his little shoulders. "Dat baby don't do nothin'."

"She will. Just give her time."

I took his little hand and led him to the kitchen table, where Emma Grace was already sorting the Crayolas into what she called rainbow order. "Teacher showed us at the school," she said proudly.

"That's very bright of you to remember,"

I replied, meaning every word.

Delores was peeling a washbowl full of potatoes, and Katie was beside her, cutting what few carrots we had left into sticks. I wondered why they'd bother. Surely nobody would want any dinner. Not any time soon, at least. We'd barely finished the rounds of breakfast, and I couldn't picture any of us having much appetite anyway.

"Better to keep the hands busy," Delores told me. "Besides, I'm gonna make a tater casserole with these, an' that'll take a while bakin'. Didn't want you havin' to think on food for this bunch."

I almost told her that Louise Post was making something. But I didn't. Delores was just trying to help. I didn't know how long she'd be here, or Sam and Thelma either, but I figured I'd let her do what she thought we needed as long as she was around.

I set Georgie down in the chair next to Emmie and gave them both some paper. "Share the Crayolas," I told the eager little boy. "Be careful with them, and no chewing on them. All right?"

His little head pumped up and down as he made a fist around one Crayola and started marking the page with long, deliberate black streaks.

Emmie started with green, drawing little stems and leaves at the base of her paper. I started to leave them, but then my eye caught the door of the baking pan cupboard, open just a crack. A real temptation, I knew, and Georgie was never at one thing for very long. I took an old apron, poked it through the cupboard handle and the one next to it, and tied them securely together. Georgie was too busy making giant black swirls across his paper to notice.

Ben and Lizbeth came pulling up in their old car before I got myself out of the kitchen. They were terribly worried for all of us, that was plain right away. From the doorway, I could see Lizbeth rush to give her father a hug, and then she started toward me. Sarah was over by the garden again, and I was glad to see her. I hoped Franky had come back too.

"Oh, Mrs. Wortham," Lizbeth called, and for the first time since she'd gotten married, I didn't feel all that glad to see her. All the Hammonds, all the people, were suddenly an unwelcome distraction. Maybe I'd feel better about things if everybody left us alone for a while. Just Samuel and me and our kids, until he was up on his feet again and I knew for sure he was really fine.

Lizbeth didn't hug me right away, even though it wouldn't have been that unusual for her. She seemed to know I was feeling a little numb. She took both my hands and squeezed them tight.

"Mrs. Wortham, I'm sorry for what all happened. How is Mr. Wortham?"

"He's . . . he's all right. Restless to get up, and that's a good sign, I expect."

"Yes, that's good. Is there anything we can do?"

Take your family, I felt like telling her. *Take every one of them home with you, or else to their house to fix whatever needs fixing. Just get them away for a while.*

But I didn't say a word of it. I didn't even answer her question.

"You look exhausted," she went on. "Come in and sit down. I bet you didn't get a wink of sleep."

She led me in. Ben stayed outside talking to Kirk. Pastor started for the woodshop, so I figured Franky must have come back and gone straight in there. George should be going with the pastor to apologize, or at least to say something civil. But he didn't go.

We were hardly in the house for two minutes when Barrett and Louise drove up too. I knew to expect them. I'd asked

Barrett for more ice. And he'd told me plain that Louise was fixing things to bring over later. But still, more people, more bustle. I was grateful that they cared, but I didn't like it anyway.

The Posts came carrying in more dishes than were reasonably necessary, and after getting ice on Samuel's head and Bert's foot again, I retreated back to Samuel's room, not wanting to be in the middle of everything. Juanita left us alone and shut the door behind her when she went out. *Bless that woman, Lord. She's got sense that comes straight from you.*

"Come here, Juli," Sammy said so softly it was almost a whisper. "Come up here and rest."

I snuggled beside him. I lay my head against his shoulder, and he pulled me close.

"Does it hurt, me leaning on you?" I asked.

"No."

I closed my eyes, just for a minute. Things got quieter. I don't know how long I stayed like that. But it seemed like only a moment, and Grandma Pearl was walking along beside me, pointing out the bee balms and a clump of trillium in the Pennsylvania woods.

But then I heard what was surely Harry clomping down the stairs, and I jumped awake with a start. How could I sleep at a time like this?

I got up to help Delores and Louise in the kitchen. They were wrapping up a lot of the food to send over to the Hammond house. George and Kirk and a good many of the others, including Lizbeth and Ben, were about to head over, looking to salvage what they could from the barn rubble and see what they could do for the house.

"Franky'll be stayin' to work on them orders him an' Samuel've got," George told me.

I nodded. I wanted to ask about his talk with Pastor and Pastor's talk with Franky, but I didn't. "Where's Rorey?" I did ask, realizing I hadn't seen her for quite a while.

"I b'lieve she went on over there," he said. "Prob'ly openin' the house, and settin' things out t' air. Don't know what I'd do without that girl. I tell you, Mrs. Wortham, since Lizbeth got married, she's been holdin' things together."

For a moment I wasn't sure what to say. Rorey certainly didn't display any great diligence at my house. "That's nice," I finally told him. "All of your children do their part."

"Gonna need ever'body to get back on m' feet," he went on. "Just when it was startin' to look like we was doin' okay, now we's worse off than ever."

"It'll come out all right," I told him. "You'll see."

"That's the kinda thing you always say."

He went in to see Samuel again, and the pastor went in too. I left the three men alone and went outside.

Sarah looked up at me from the garden, dropped a handful of henbit, and started in my direction. I came down off the porch and met her on the stone walk Emma Graham had put in so long ago.

"Mom . . ."

She looked so tall. So much a young woman with her apron on and her hair back. And her face so plainly mirroring the worries of the day.

"Mom, I guess Frank's going to be all right, but he's taking it awful hard about being blamed, and it's not fair —"

"I know it, honey."

"Mom, there's something about Rorey . . ."

"Yes. I heard what she was saying, and I'd like a chance to talk to her, but I guess she's gone back home already."

"But, Mom —"

I didn't get a chance to hear whatever she was about to tell me. Emmie was suddenly hollering at us from the barn lot. I hadn't even known she was outside.

"Mama! Mama! Come quick!"

Emmie was standing with her feet on the bottom rail of the fence, looking over at her father's goats. I couldn't imagine what could be wrong, but there was distress plain enough in her voice, and Sarah and I both hurried to her side.

"Looky!" she cried. "Janie May's hurt! Look at 'er! Her leg's real bad!"

I'm sure it looked bad to a seven-year-old in the middle of an already trying day, but I knew the young goat's jagged cut on a hindquarter was not all that serious. Nobody'd noticed it before, and she was walking on it fine.

"Thanks for letting us know," I told the girl. "But it really isn't bad. All she needs is a little bag balm and a bandage. You might even be able to take care of that yourself."

"Really?"

"With a little help. You'll help her, won't you, Sarah?"

Sarah gave me a funny look, I'm not sure why. But she went to get the balm and a rag of some kind.

"Ain't nobody else gonna get hurt, is there, Mama?" Emmie asked me.

"I don't think so. We've had more than enough for one day."

She looked at me with her big eyes full of questions. It took her a minute to speak again, perhaps because she was trying to decide which of the questions to ask first. "Why's everybody mad at Franky?"

"Not everybody is. Nobody will be, once they've had time to cool off and think about all this. Fires happen sometimes. Bad as it is, there's no sense trying to blame anyone for what was surely an accident —"

"But it ain't only about the fire," she maintained. "Rorey was mad at Franky yesterday. She said he was a puritan, only she said it kinda ugly, an' I don't even know what it means. An' I think she musta said he was a sourpuss too, 'cause prob'ly Sarah didn't think a' that herself."

What in the world could this be about? I remembered Franky looking over at Rorey when he came home all beat up last night, but neither of them had said anything. "Emma Grace, can you tell me what's going on?"

"I ain't for sure. I only heard Sarah an' Rorey talkin'. An' they didn't want me to hear 'cause they sent me to get Bessie's blanket an' she didn't even need it right then."

"Last night? Before you all went home?"

"Yeah," she affirmed, nodding her little head up and down. "An' the very oddest thing is when Rorey said Franky was mad at her for talkin' to Lester Turrey. An' I never did see him come over, not even once. You think she made that up?"

"No, Emmie, I'm sure she didn't."

"Well, then, when did she see him? He don't go to our school, nor even to church."

"I'm not sure. But thank you for telling me."

"I was jus' wonderin' 'bout this, that's all." She turned her eyes back to the goats.

"It is something to wonder about," I agreed, thinking Emma Grace a very bright girl for her age, regardless of what others might say.

Sarah was coming back to us, the bag balm and a cloth all in one hand. I looked at her and wondered if I should ask her right now about this strange conversation with Rorey. She'd been wanting to tell me something just a few minutes back. And it might well be more than repeating what Rorey had said about the fire.

But I thought of Franky alone in the

woodshop. I was sure it must have helped him to have Sarah follow him into the woods, and then to have Pastor come in and see him. But I thought of that fight yesterday and how he'd looked, and him refusing to tell me what had happened.

"Sarah, would you mind taking care of the goat while I speak to Franky a minute? We can talk when I'm through."

She nodded, but she seemed different. Tense. *Lord, what in the world is going on? Probably better not to get into it any further in front of Emma Grace.* I left them to bandage up the goat's leg and went to see Franky.

The door creaked as I gently pushed it open. Franky was carving out a chair leg. He looked up at me but didn't stop his work.

"I'm doin' all right, Mrs. Wortham," he said. "You don't gotta check on me."

"Your hands aren't hurting you too bad then?"

"No, ma'am. Not too bad."

"What about your other bruises?"

"Tell the truth, it's been easy t' forget about 'em, what with ever'thin' else goin' on."

"I can expect." I set a scrap board across a keg of nails and seated myself near him.

"Franky, I want to talk about yesterday. Was it Lester Turrey who fought you?"

He stopped what he was doing and looked up just long enough for me to see the surprise on his face. But there was no surprise in his voice. He tried his best to sound as though this particular subject meant nothing at all to him. "Why would you be askin' somethin' like that?"

"Because I think it's time you told me what happened. I can understand you not going to your father right now. Sometimes I know he's not all that anxious to hear what you have to say, Lord knows why. But that doesn't mean you can't tell me or Samuel whatever it is. And your father too, eventually. I'm sure he'll change his mind if he hasn't already and be more willing to listen —"

"Can't count on that, Mrs. Wortham. Pa ain't gonna change a whole lot. You oughta see that by now."

"Maybe you're right. But you still need to tell us whatever this is with Rorey and Lester Turrey. Why would she be upset with you? And why would he want to fight?"

He kept his eyes away. "I never said it was him."

"But it was, wasn't it?"

"Who tol' you all this? How can you know this stuff?"

"I was just talking to Emma Grace. She's a lot brighter than what some people give her credit for. And like you, she remembers what she hears."

"An' what was that?"

"That you weren't happy with Rorey talking to Lester, and that Rorey was upset with you about it."

He turned his eyes back to the chair. "Don't know how she come to hear that, but it ain't nothin' to talk about."

"Why not? If Rorey's trying to meet with Lester, don't you think your father should know?"

He stopped. He put down his tool and faced me. "It weren't but once, an' she made me promise not to tell."

"Franky, why would you promise something like that?"

"Because she started cryin', beggin' me not to mess up how peaceful things has been at home. She said she already decided not to see him no more, so me tellin' would just get her in trouble over nothin'."

"When was it that she saw him?"

"Week ago tonight, perty late."

"After dark, without your father knowing?"

"Yes, ma'am. I heard her go outside, an' I followed her, 'cause I wanted to know what she was doin' in the middle a' the night. That's what Lester fought at me for yesterday. He said I didn't have no business followin' her around, my sister or not."

"You could have told us."

"Nope. 'Cause I promised her."

"Oh, Franky."

"Besides, Lester said if I tell anybody it was him who hit me, he'll jus' deny ever talkin' to her an' say he only tol' me he liked her a little an' I got mad an' hit at him over it. He'll say I started it, so then he had to bust me up."

"Do you really think anyone would believe him? It's not like you to start a fight."

"Pa would believe it. 'Specially if Rorey said she didn't never meet with him. Then Pa'd reason it all to be how Lester said it was." Franky sighed. "It weren't so much to promise not to tell Pa 'bout seein' her with Lester. He'd b'lieve her over me anyhow. But I wasn't s'posed to tell you neither. An' I didn't. Not all. You had it mostly figgered."

"Where did they meet?"

"Out by the Claybanks bridge. But she promised me she ain't gonna do it again."

It was my turn to sigh. "Do you think she knows that Lester fought you?"

"Prob'ly. Ain't sure how she's feelin' on that, though."

"You know I'll have to tell your father this."

"No, ma'am. Don't seem to me you'd have to. He'd only think I'm tryin' to get her in trouble after what she said 'bout me."

"Then you know what she's told about the fire?"

"Yes, ma'am." He turned back to his work, not offering to say another word.

"Franky, why would she accuse you?"

"I guess she seen me out there an' jus' figgered she knew what happened."

"Then you're saying it's a mistake."

He looked up at me with his strange silvery eyes awfully sad. "What else would it be?"

14

Sarah

It made me feel all strange inside for Mom to put off talking to me and go see Franky first. I shouldn't have wondered, since he'd run off into the woods and all. She'd want to check on him after that. Of course she would. But she knew I was wanting to say something about Rorey, and she was looking at me kind of different.

Janie May wouldn't stand still for us, and I had to hold her real tight with one hand and try to help Emmie bandage her with the other. Good thing this wasn't a billy. I didn't even know where their billy was. Maybe they'd lost him in the fire along with so much else.

"Is our animals yours now?" Emmie asked me.

"No more than they ever was."

"But they's over here now."

"Just for a while. Till your pa gets another barn and pen built back up."

"I don't think Pa knows how to build us a barn," she said sadly. "An' your pa can't help. He's still in bed."

"Yeah. I know."

Finally we got the little goat all fixed up. She hopped away from us and immediately started stretching her neck, trying to chew on that bandage. All that trouble to doctor her, and it wouldn't last ten minutes, I'd just about bet.

"What's a puritan?" Emmie suddenly asked.

"What?"

"A puritan. Yesterday Rorey said Franky was one, remember? Is it some kinda stupid guy?"

I shook my head, wishing she hadn't heard a word of all that. "No. Puritans weren't stupid. They were just . . . real strict. And real religious. Rorey just meant that Franky don't think like a kid sometimes, that he don't approve of shenanigans."

"Oh," she said, thinking it over. "That ain't so bad. Rorey won't even get in no trouble over sayin' somethin' like that. I wonder how come your mama didn't go ahead an' esplain when I tol' her I didn't know what it meant."

"You told Mom that Rorey said that?" My heart suddenly pounded harder. "What else did you tell her?" *What else did she hear? Oh, Lord! Now Mom'll think I was trying to hide stuff from her! Now Mom'll think I'm in on what Rorey's been doing.*

"I jus' wanted to know how come folks is mad at Franky. Rorey was even mad at him yesterday —"

"And you told Mom that?"

"Yeah." She looked at me with her eyes getting damp. "I'm sorry, Sarah. Was I not s'posed to?"

I sighed. "It's okay. We're not supposed to keep secrets from our folks anyway."

"I didn't know it was a secret."

"I know. It's okay."

"Will Rorey get in trouble?"

"I don't know. Maybe."

"Then she's gonna be real mad at me."

"She might be real mad at me too, before it's all done."

"Will you still play with me, even if Rorey gets mad?"

"Yes. I'll play with you."

She took my hand. Apparently, my promise was enough to make her feel better about the whole thing. She bounced a couple of steps, leading me over toward the corner where we could see Janie May a little better.

"She's gonna pull her bandage clear off!" Emmie exclaimed. "Don't she know it's there so she can get better?"

"Sometimes goats don't know no better than people what's good for them, Emmie."

Emmie Grace looked at me with her head tilted sideways. "That's kind of a funny thing t' say."

"Maybe so. But it's true."

Emmie's pa and most of her brothers were leaving to go back over to their farm. Emmie didn't ask to go with them, but she went racing over there to hug most every one of them good-bye. Mom came over too and told them to come back for supper and to stay the night if they needed to.

"I need to talk to you when you get the chance," Mom told Mr. Hammond, and that made me feel cold inside. *Rorey's gonna think I told on her, and it wasn't even me!*

"I ain't in no mood for more talkin', Mrs. Wortham," Rorey's father replied. "Ain't nothin' more to be said." He turned his back and started walking off through the timber. Kirk went with him, but Harry and Sam and Willy went with Pastor and

Robert in our truck and the pastor's car. Mr. and Mrs. Post were leaving too. Mrs. Pastor gave Mom a big hug and explained that they had to go and see Mrs. Howell. Seemed like everybody was leaving, except Thelma and her mother and the kids.

We could hear the baby crying inside. Emmie looked that way and then up at me. "I could sing to her," she offered.

"That's a good idea. I'm sure Thelma would like that."

She smiled and went running inside.

Mom just stood there watching Robert drive off with the Hammonds. I wondered if she thought Mr. Hammond was rude for talking to her the way he did. "Did Rorey leave already?" I asked her.

"I guess so. She's certainly making herself scarce lately, isn't she?"

I felt her eyes on me before I even looked. "Mom . . ."

"I know you were going to tell me, Sarah. I know it was Lester Turrey who beat up Frank. But I don't know why you waited."

I didn't know what to say. How much had Franky told her? "I wasn't for sure it was him," I said quietly, almost hoping Franky'd told on his sister and not just Lester.

"Did Rorey know?"

"She — she wasn't for sure either," I stammered. "She only figured it was prob'ly him." It was suddenly hard to talk. I was feeling all tight inside, remembering Rorey's urgent face. *Promise me, Sarah. Promise you won't tell!"*

"I understand she was upset with Franky. Over Lester, I suppose. She must really like the boy."

"I — I guess so. Kind of." I took a deep breath. At least Mom wasn't making this too hard. Maybe all I'd have to do was answer her questions. Maybe she already had everything figured out, so I could honestly say it wasn't me who told.

"Apparently she likes him enough to sneak out and see him without permission."

"Yeah." Franky'd told, all right. And I was glad, no matter how mad Rorey would be.

"Has she seen him more than once?"

Now was the perfect time to tell about Rorey's plans to meet Lester in the barn. It was right there in my mouth to say. I felt like I was choking on it, but it wouldn't come out. And what I said instead wasn't a lie, but it wasn't the whole truth either. "They met last week. She . . . she said he didn't come any other time."

"You're sure?"

I nodded my head while my heart thumped and screamed at me. *Why? Why aren't you telling?*

Because I wanted to believe her. She'd told me plain out Lester hadn't come. That he hadn't been there.

"Why didn't you tell me about this days ago?" Mom persisted.

"I only found out yesterday. After supper when we were talking. And . . . and I think she's kind of dumb to get a boyfriend when she's only thirteen."

"Then she wants to see him again?"

"I — I don't know. Maybe not." *That's no lie either,* I told myself. *After the fire and all, I don't really know what she's thinking. Maybe she's had time to consider how stupid it all is. Maybe she's even mad at Lester for not showing up.*

Mom was still looking at me. "Well, if Rorey doesn't care to see Lester again, why would Lester care enough to beat her brother up over it?"

"He's just mean, Mom! He's just plain mean! That's all it is. He likes to do stuff like that. He was the worst bully our school had, an' he never did like Frank. Maybe Rorey was just his excuse!"

I wanted to run. I wanted to run clear out in the woods like Franky'd done, only I hoped nobody'd follow *me*. Maybe I was afraid. Maybe I was afraid of Lester pulling my hair again, or throwing my lunch pail in the mud, or worse. Maybe I was even afraid of Rorey teasing me, hating me, turning her back on me.

Why couldn't I just come right out and tell Mom about last night? It wouldn't be my fault if people stopped pointing at Franky and blamed Rorey for the fire. Because maybe *she'd* been the one in the barn, waiting for her "boyfriend" to show up.

But I couldn't manage to say anything. I didn't really know what had happened. I needed to talk to Rorey again. I needed to know for sure if she was telling me the truth about everything before I told anybody otherwise. I was just trying to be fair. That was all.

"Sarah?"

"Yes, Mom?"

"I know it puts you in a difficult spot for me to ask you what your friend told you in confidence, but I'm sure you understand that something like this is too important to be kept from parents. Lester was hard on Franky, and Rorey is far too young to know what she's getting into, especially with an older boy with less than desirable behavior."

"I know."

"I want you to tell me, promptly, if you hear anything more about him coming around or her trying to see him. All right?"

"Yes."

"I'll have to tell Mr. Hammond, even if Franky won't. He needs to know who attacked his son and why. Don't you think so?"

"Yes. But what will Mr. Hammond do?"

"I don't know. But that's not up to us, is it?"

I stood quiet for a minute. Mr. Hammond had walked off, not wanting to listen. Maybe he would keep on not wanting to hear a word about it. He hadn't bothered to find out who fought at Franky, that was for sure. I didn't think he'd even asked.

"Mom, what if he doesn't care? He didn't act like he cared about Franky getting hurt. And Rorey said her mom was only thirteen when him and her got together. What if he doesn't even care?"

"Rorey thinks he will, or she wouldn't want it kept a secret."

"I guess not. But . . . but maybe she won't meet with Lester no more. I promise

I'll tell her all over again that she shouldn't."

"I'm sure you will. And I hope she has the sense to agree with you. But we still need to tell her father."

"We?"

She smiled, just a tiny bit. "I can do it, Sarah. I know he's difficult to talk to sometimes. Just make sure you come to one of us next time if this keeps up."

"I will, Mom."

"One more thing: did you call Franky a sourpuss?"

"No, ma'am," I said, knowing Emma Grace must have mentioned that. "I was just asking Rorey how come she did. I guess she's wanting to feel all grown up and not have no big brothers watching over her."

"She's blessed to have big brothers, especially ones who care."

"I know it. I think Frank's all right. Just different, that's all."

"You're a good girl, Sarah," she told me, turning back to the house. "Thank you."

I stood there, just watching my mother walk away. I knew she was going to check on Daddy again, thinking I'd told her everything. My stomach felt all scrunched sideways. What was the matter with me, anyway?

15

Julia

I'd thought it would be a relief to have so many gone, at least for a while, but now I only wondered what they would find over there and how George would manage after losing so much of his livestock and equipment.

When I came in, Delores was rocking the baby and Emmie was kneeling beside them singing a sweet little song. Probably one she made up. Kate was chasing down Georgie, trying to get him to quit jumping on the stairs. And Thelma was at the kitchen table with a cup of tea and a slice of the rhubarb cake Louise had brought.

"Are you hungry, Mrs. Wortham?" she asked.

"No, not at all."

"I'm not either, but Mama keeps pushin' me to eat somethin'. I can't hardly, though."

"Why not?"

"All this is botherin' me too much. My Sammy said it's gonna be a hard winter for you if your husband ain't full strength, plus the loss of the field crops and Pa Hammond's livestock makin' it pretty hard on them. He'd like to help his pa and you both, but I don't see how we can."

"Thelma, winter is two months from now —"

"Maybe less. Lot a' times, it turns cold in November, an' that ain't but a couple a' weeks away."

Why did she have to talk like this? As if my own head weren't giving me enough reminders. I hadn't let it concern me before. But today, the worries just kept creeping at me, over and over. It'd been an awful year for the gardens, and now most of what was left in the fields was gone. Such thoughts were plaguing me, surely as much as they were her. But I wouldn't speak my doubt.

"We'll get by. The Lord'll provide, Thelma. We've had hard times before. And I'm sure Samuel will be just fine soon enough. He's talking fine already and anxious to get out of that bed."

"Mama said he was sleepin' again. I reckon that's good, 'cause they say rest's a fine medicine, but I'm awful sorry all this had to happen. I can hardly b'lieve you've

241

stayed so calm. I think I'd be half frazzled."

I didn't say a word more to her. I walked to Samuel's room, hoping Thelma and her mother were wrong. Rest was a fine medicine, I knew it to be so. But I was still hoping to find Samuel awake, if for no other reason than to rest my heart with his sensible words. After all, if he was talking to me, if he was just being himself, I could feel sure that he was already all right. I walked in anxious, hoping to be greeted by his smile.

But he was sleeping again, just like she'd said. I knew better than to let it worry me. I knew I should just keep on thanking God that he was all right, but my heart felt heavy that he was lying so still. I didn't like it one bit. How could he sleep again, so soon, and really be okay?

"Samuel?"

I was feeling foolish for trying to disturb him, but at the same time praying he'd open his eyes. He didn't. Even when I called his name a second time. A tiny chunk of the ice was left in a bowl on the bedside table, and I picked it up with the dripping cloth it was wrapped in and laid it against his head.

He didn't move.

What were those words, that wonderful

psalm Franky had been quoting?

He that dwelleth in the secret place of the most High shall abide under the shadow of the Almighty.

Psalm 91. I remembered it now. But for some reason, when I tried to recall more of the words, they all jumbled in my mind with another psalm that was so familiar.

The Lord is my shepherd; I shall not want. He maketh me to lie down in green pastures: he leadeth me beside the still waters. He restoreth my soul . . .

Samuel didn't stir, not so much as an eyelash. And I wanted to have complete confidence that the Lord of the psalms would restore, give us still waters, and hide us under the shelter of his wings. But my own heart would not obey me. Despite all the confidence I wanted, all the faith I thought I should muster, I knew I was falling short.

What if the bruised ribs had made something bleed inside? What if something had swelled in his brain, and that was why he wasn't awake?

I felt like screaming at myself for worrying this way. It was senseless. It was just not right. But I was doing it anyway. I could feel it even as I tried my best to return my mind to Franky's psalm.

I will say of the Lord, he is my refuge and my fortress: my God; in him will I trust.

One day perhaps I would laugh at myself, or at least shake my head over having such a struggle. But at that moment it was hard. It was beyond me, like two giant hands tugging my mind in opposite directions.

Surely he shall deliver thee . . .

But what about all those things the doctor had said? Should we have taken him to the hospital after all?

He shall cover thee with his feathers . . .

But what if he can't wake up this time?

Thou shalt not be afraid . . .

I had to do something else. I had to put my mind to something. But Delores and Katie were taking care of Thelma and the little children. We had some baking done and plenty of food fixed, thanks to Louise. Berty was all right sitting with a book by the sitting room windows. Nothing was really pressing for my attention.

Besides, as much as my mind was warring about it, I still didn't want to leave Samuel's side, at least not for long. So I went and got paper from a box in the cupboard and a pen that the schoolteacher had given me once. I sat in the rocker at the corner of our bedroom and started

244

drafting a letter to Samuel's mother. I guess I just poured my thoughts down more than anything else.

Dear Joanna,

Samuel is in bed today. Last night he saved the neighbor boy out of their burning barn, but part of the structure collapsed and Samuel was injured. The doctor tells us he should recover, but he has a head injury, possibly broken ribs, and his right leg has a frightful gash. The rest of us have been worried, but we trust that the Lord will work all to the good. By the grace of God things are not worse, as no one was killed, and the boy is getting along all right with a sprained ankle. Samuel has been awake off and on, and once he asked about you. I felt that you would want to know. Please tell cousin Dewey what has happened if you have any opportunity. You are in our thoughts often.

Most sincerely,
Julia

I read the letter over and very nearly

crumpled it up to throw in the kindling box. It would take quite a few days to get it to Albany, New York. Surely Samuel would be up and ready to go to town for his telephone call by then, and he could tell his mother what he wanted to say better than I could. But I set the letter aside on the dresser anyway.

Suddenly Samuel said something about "goompus."

I spun around. He wasn't awake. He was muttering something in his sleep about "goompus" jumping downstairs. Good thing I remembered that name from the bedtime stories Samuel used to tell the children. "Goompus" was a funny little bird Samuel had made up long ago. I hadn't heard the name in years. It wasn't exactly a comfort to hear it now.

I could hear the back door opening. Sarah coming in the house.

"It's starting to rain," I heard her say, but I didn't hear if anyone answered her.

Wonderful, I thought. *We needed rain all summer, and it comes again now, when so much of the crop is lost and the rest is stuck in the field unharvested. And the Hammonds are over there needing to fix a roof! Why, Lord? Why now?*

I stopped myself quickly from such bitter

thoughts. Thank the good Lord for his rain. It had stopped the fire last night. So much more might have been lost!

Why couldn't I see the good in all this? No one was killed. Everybody would be all right. And God had intervened by sending his wonderful rain when the fire might have spread beyond anyone's control and swallowed up who knows how many acres or farmhouses. God was still faithful to us, just like always.

Suddenly I thought of dear old Emma Graham singing one of her favorite songs. I could almost hear some of the words in her sweet, clear voice.

"Pardon for sin and a peace that endureth. Thy own dear presence to cheer and to guide. Strength for today and bright hope for tomorrow. Blessings all mine, with ten thousand beside!"

How I needed strength for today! How I needed to rejoice in our bright hope for tomorrow! Always, always, God had taken care of us. When we had nothing at all but each other and three little bags of belongings, God had provided Emma Graham and this wonderful home for us. When dear Emma and Mrs. Hammond died on the same day and we thought our hearts would burst with the pain of it, God had given us his comfort and his light.

When George took up drink and didn't think he could bear to go on, when Samuel fell through the pond ice, when Katie came to us in the midst of accusation and hardship, in every incident, at every moment of our lives, God had been there to take care of us, to take care of it all. Surely he was here just the same now. Surely he would take care of Samuel and our present need. How could I doubt? How could I continue to question him?

"Great is Thy faithfulness! Great is Thy faithfulness! Morning by morning new mercies I see; all I have needed Thy hand hath provided, great is Thy faithfulness, Lord, unto me!"

No wonder Emma had loved that song. It spoke her heart, and could just as well be speaking mine.

Samuel moved just a little, turning his head to one side. I leaned over close and kissed his cheek. He didn't open his eyes. He didn't wake like I wanted him to, but it was all right. He would, when he'd rested all he needed to. I climbed up beside him, ever so gently. I lay my head against his arm, careful not to jar him. "Thank you, Jesus," I whispered, and my heart felt lighter. Soon I closed my eyes and I could feel the tension falling away.

The voices in the kitchen sounded miles distant. Strangely it seemed that Joanna, Samuel's mother, was walking toward us looking terribly old and more tired than I'd ever seen her. But I didn't see the cold, hard eyes I remembered so well. Instead, this Joanna's eyes were altogether different, like those of some other person. She came up to the bed with a big box and dumped its contents all over us. Piles and piles of letters.

16

Sarah

No doubt Mom needed the rest. But I wasn't sure what to think when I peeked in and found her and Dad both asleep together. I shushed Emmie quick and told her we'd better do something real quiet.

"I'll bet the little dumplin's needin' a nap," Mrs. Pratt said behind me. At first I thought she was talking about Georgie, but after being up in the middle of the night like she was, Emmie would benefit from a nap too.

"Maybe you should go upstairs an' lie down with her a while," Mrs. Pratt suggested.

It wasn't exactly an idea I favored much, but she was probably right. And surprisingly, Emmie didn't protest. She was tired, I could tell.

"You oughta get a nap in too, Berty," Thelma's mother continued. "Though you ain't supposed to be up them stairs on that ankle. Let me plump you a pillow right where you sit. Maybe Katie'd like to lie down too, with Georgie beside her."

I saw what Mrs. Pratt was doing. She was hoping all of us would sleep. Even Katie and me, old as we were. I'd lie down, all right. I'd do that much to help Emmie get a nap, just like I was sure Katie would do with Georgie, but I wasn't going to sleep. Franky was up working in the woodshop. Robert was with Willy and Rorey and all of the other Hammonds over to their place working hard. So I couldn't sleep. No way.

I'd heat the iron over the stove in a little while, that's what I'd do. I'd take a good look at everybody's church clothes and iron whatever needed it. After all, to-morrow was Sunday, and surely we'd be going to church, just like usual.

I'd make sure Daddy's best shirt was all crisp and neat and Mom's flowered dress was looking its best. And we'd go into that church building tomorrow looking swell and feeling like the most blessed people in the whole world. Because we were. Because of Daddy still being here, when it'd been so awful close, so awful scary that it still hurt to think about it.

Mom was still asleep when I came downstairs. I was going to peek in and see her, but Mrs. Pratt had just done that and motioned me away from the door.

"Let 'em have every moment a' rest they can possibly get," she told me. "Your mama'll be up soon enough."

Dad too, I thought, suddenly uncomfortable with the way her words had come out. Did she mean it to sound the way it had, like she was expecting Daddy not to get up? Surely he would, though the doctor had said to rest. Because I knew my dad. And he wasn't one to sit or lie around for long. He just wasn't. Hurt or not, he'd be out of that bed.

"Joanna must be some kin a' yours. That so?"

It took me a moment to figure who Mrs. Pratt was talking about. "Do you mean my grandma? Daddy's mom?" I couldn't imagine how Mrs. Pratt would know her.

"That must be it. I found a letter your mama wrote. Thought we could save her a bit a' time if you was to know where the envelopes and yer grandma's address is at."

"Well, yeah. I think so." I went to the cupboard where Mom kept such things. There was even an extra stamp in the envelope box. I wrote Grandma's address real careful, and our return address too. Then I read the letter.

For Mom to admit that we were worried came as a surprise. I thought that for her to say so in a letter, she'd have to be very, very worried indeed.

I guess I had been too. Right at first, when I thought Daddy was lost to us in the barn, and then when he didn't talk, and then all that ride home just fretting over how bad it might be. But now — now, we could relax, couldn't we? With him resting peaceful, eating good, and talking to us with a smile? He'd even teased Mom about her getting her hand in that plate of pancakes, however that had happened. He'd laughed about it. So surely he was okay.

"I suppose your mama'd appreciate it if one of the boys was to run to town and mail that for her, since the post's been by already," Mrs. Pratt said to me. "If she'd had it done, Richard could've taken it when he left."

"I don't guess there's any hurry," I said quietly.

"No hurry? You gotta send out word! This is your papa's mama, didn't you say? I didn't realize, 'cause a' your mama calling her Joanna and all. But —"

"My grandma's a little different," I tried

to explain. "She probably didn't want my mom to call her Mama or anything like that. And — and even a letter like this I don't s'pose she'll answer."

"Not answer?" Mrs. Pratt plopped down beside me. She was suddenly looking at me like I was some little lost fawn or something. "I'd think a letter like this'd make her hop a train an' come just as quick as she can! I'm surprised your mama didn't hurry someone to town to call her, after the close call your papa had. His mama's bound to want to be here to nurse him back to health. Don't you think?"

"I don't know," I told her. "I haven't seen Grandma since I was about four. I used to make her cards and stuff all the time, but she never did answer anything, even from me or Robert. She won't hardly even talk on the telephone to us when we get the chance. And she's never come here."

"Well, this is different than any ol' day!" Mrs. Pratt exclaimed with a huff. "This is her very own son's close brush with death!"

I looked at her, and after those words I just couldn't help myself. My eyes filled with tears, and I couldn't hold them in for all I tried. *Close brush with death! Oh,*

God, that sounds so horrible! But I know it's true! Mom knows it's true, and she's still worrying. That's what the letter means. She's still scared.

"Oh, honey, honey," Mrs. Pratt started carrying on. "I didn't mean to upset you. I've known folks so poor they couldn't afford not even a postage stamp! Don't you reckon that might be the problem, why you don't see nor hear from her?"

"No, ma'am." I sniffed.

She just looked at me. I was trying to stop sniveling, and for a moment I guess she didn't know what to say. But it didn't take her long to come up with something.

"I know just what we oughta do, honey."

She waited a minute for my answer, but I didn't say anything.

"We oughta pray, you an' me right now, for that grandma a' yours. Whatever it is causin' her to be so distant from her own kin — an' I ain't talkin' 'bout miles — the good Lord, he can take care a' that, don't you think?"

"Yes, ma'am," I said, though I had to push the words out of my mouth and they sounded weak, even to me.

"Does your grandma know the Lord, honey?"

"I — I don't think so, 'cause Daddy

prays about that sometimes. I know he wants her to."

"Well, then, there it is. That's exactly what we oughta pray on. Right now. That your grandma turn to the Lord. And that he touch her heart to come out here to see you after all this time. You'd like that, wouldn't you?"

I wasn't sure if she meant the praying or Grandma's visit, but it didn't really matter. "Yes, ma'am."

I tried to dry my eyes, knowing she didn't understand that it was Daddy I was crying for, not Grandma. Maybe if I got my nerve up I'd ask her to pray for him too, that everything would be okay so Mom wouldn't have to worry anymore.

She took both of my hands. She started praying right out loud that God send just the right message to Grandma's heart to turn her toward the things of God. And that she get in a car or on a train or something to make the trip to come out and see us.

"Your daddy needs her," she said when she was done praying. "No matter what things has been like between 'em, when folks get hurt bad, even grown men, they need their mama's comfort, I can tell you."

I didn't say anything to that. I figured

Daddy'd been so used to his mother not being around that he wouldn't think on it much. It was Mom's comfort he needed, and he was getting hers, so he'd do all right.

"Your mama's mama's dead, isn't she? I think I heard her tell that one time."

"Yes, ma'am."

"That's too bad, that is. No wonder all a' you took to Emma Graham so well when you first come out here. You was needin' her, I guess."

I smiled a little at that. It'd been a while since I'd thought about Emma Graham. She'd been my special friend, even though she was so old. I'd always remember that we had the same middle name, and she said that made us like sisters. I'd laughed at first, thinking about being a sister to a woman in her eighties when I was only five at the time. But now I understood a little better. Back then, I could talk to Emma about anything, and it wasn't because of our names. I missed her now. She'd be able to tell me why I wasn't telling on Rorey yet. She'd be able to tell what I was afraid of that was more important than telling my own mother the whole truth.

"You gonna add a note a' your own in the envelope?" Mrs. Pratt asked me.

I doubt I would've thought of that. But obediently, I took out a piece of paper and wrote down the first thing that came to mind.

Dear Grandma,
We love you and miss you.

I stopped. What else could I say to a woman I'd never really had a chance to know? Suddenly I remembered the days when Katie first came to us. Uncle Edward had brought her, and he'd been so scary. I knew Mom didn't like having him around, even if he was Daddy's brother, because he'd acted so downright mean. But even so, she'd come right out and told him that she loved him and God did too. It didn't look like it would make much difference, but by the time he left Uncle Edward had softened considerably. He even wrote to us sometimes still, and they were nice enough letters to read out loud.

I turned my eyes back to the page in front of me. This didn't have to be a long letter. Mom had already written the important stuff. There was just one more thing that needed to be said. I took pencil in hand again to write it.

God loves you too.

And then I signed my name. I folded my short little letter and stuck it in the envelope with Mom's. I could remember all the lacy heart valentines I used to make and the Christmas cards with stars and baby Jesus all over them in Crayola. I'd always hoped those things would make Grandma smile. And write back. Now, I wasn't concerned so much about that. *Just let her think, dear God,* I prayed. *Let her think about Daddy. And you.*

Katie was up. She came walking in the room, pushing her wavy hair behind one ear. Folks said I was the one who looked like Mom. She looked like Dad, just because she was kin of his family. I wondered if Grandma looked anything like Dad too. I couldn't remember, not her eyes or her hair or anything.

"What are you doing?" Katie asked me.

"Mom wrote a letter to Grandma. I just got the envelope ready and put a little letter in with it."

She glanced at the cuckoo clock on the wall. "Mr. Mueller's already been by here, but maybe we can catch him at the corner," she suggested. "He always goes by up there on his way back to Dearing, and it's almost time. If we hurry, it won't have to wait till Monday."

She was right. We knew Mr. Mueller's pattern pretty well by now.

"That's a fine notion," Mrs. Pratt agreed. "Why don't you two get to goin' with that?"

She hurried us out the door, none of us thinking to consider whether Mom'd really been ready to mail that letter. I'd just assumed so, because of what Mrs. Pratt had said. And I guess Katie assumed so because of me. It wasn't strange at all for Katie not to write something to stick in too. Because she had a different grandma. I'm not sure why, since she was related to Daddy's family. He never did explain that very well.

We hurried down the road together to get to the corner before Mr. Mueller's mail truck went by. I'm not sure why both of us went, except that Mrs. Pratt said to. And both of us were being just as obliging as we could be today, because of Daddy and everything that had happened.

I guess we were most of the time anyway, especially Katie. Katie didn't ever do anything wrong. She would've told Mom about Rorey and Lester even before going to bed last night.

"Katie," I suddenly asked, "are you still afraid of Lester Turrey?"

She looked at me like I'd dropped my senses alongside of the road. I guess it was a funny thing to ask right then, to somebody who didn't know nothing of what I knew.

"Well, no. Why should I be? We don't never see him anymore, now that he quit school. I sure don't miss him, if that's what you mean."

"If you did see him, would you be kind of upset?"

"I'd just watch. I'd watch real close, 'cause you never can tell with him when he might steal your books, or try to cut your braids off, or trip you for no good reason. But why? I don't think Teacher'd let him come back to school, even if he did want to."

"I just . . . I just wondered if that's the same as being afraid. I mean, not liking the way a person is and being really wary."

Katie kept walking just as fast, but she looked over at me funny just the same. "I don't guess it's the same. Not exactly. But what difference does it make? Who cares about Lester Turrey? He's got no reason to come around here."

"Yes, he does. He likes Rorey."

I couldn't have shocked her more if I'd told her the sky was falling. "You mean really likes her? Oh, Sarah, no. She doesn't like him, does she?"

"Don't tell nobody. She told me not to tell."

She was suddenly walking even faster. "How could she? He doesn't even treat his own family very well. You saw how he picked at his sister Rose. Oh, Sarah! If he tries to come around, you'll have to tell somebody! You'll have to! Rorey's not old enough for a boy like him. I woulda thought she was smart enough, but you know what I mean. There's no telling the kind of things he might think up. She could really get in trouble."

I just stared at her, trying to keep up. She would have told, all right. She would have told already and been right to do it. So why hadn't I?

Mr. Mueller always drove his mail truck out past our house and the Posts on his country route and then circled around past the Hammonds on his way back to Dearing. So we stood at the corner where he'd be going by, looking down the road for any sign.

"Think he was early?" I asked Katie.

"He's never early."

"Well, if he's late, we might be here a long time."

"It's about time for him now, I think. But he'll probably be late. I don't know how he could drive by Hammonds without stopping to see what happened. He'll probably talk to them a minute."

"Too bad him and Orville weren't around to help earlier."

"They were probably asleep. And the rain had the fire down before he would've started on his route."

"Mr. Post came."

"He lives closer. And there's a lot of trees around Muellers' house. Even if they woke up, they probably wouldn't see nothing from there. What's wrong, Sarah? Mr. Mueller couldn't help it if he didn't know."

"I know."

Katie stood clutching Mom's letter in her hand and looking at me so straight. "It really bothers you about Lester, doesn't it? Are *you* afraid of him? He was kind of awful to us last year, no denying that."

"I don't think I'm afraid," I said with a sigh. "But I am bothered."

"If Rorey told you not to tell anybody, then why are you telling me?"

At first I didn't know what to say. And then the words came rushing out. " 'Cause I'm tired of it! I'm tired of thinking about it and wishing I didn't have to. But Mom already knows that much. Franky told her."

"How did Franky know? I doubt Rorey'd tell him anything straight out. She always tells you stuff. But not anybody else."

"He saw 'em together, Katie. That's why he got busted up. Lester did it, probably so Franky'd be afraid to tell anybody or follow Rorey anymore. But I don't think he's afraid."

Katie's eyes were looking way down the road away from me. "I think Mr. Mueller's coming."

I just looked at her. She didn't have anything else to say? When I'd let her in on a secret that Rorey's pa didn't even know yet?

I don't know what I wanted from her. I wasn't even sure why I was talking to her about it. I guess I wanted it off my chest, even though I hadn't been able to tell her any more than I'd told Mom. Why didn't they know to ask me more? Maybe that's what I wanted. For one of them to ask me the right question, so all I'd have to do was nod my head and be done with it. But Katie wasn't asking anything. She just stared down the road, waving that letter in the air.

At first I didn't see Mr. Mueller coming. But he was. It wasn't long before he pulled right up to us and stopped on the road to take the letter.

"How's your pa, girls?" he asked, so I knew he must've talked to somebody at Hammonds or somewhere.

I expected Katie to answer, but she didn't. Only then did I realize that she was fighting back tears. Mr. Mueller handed her his hanky.

"It'll be all right," he told us. "I'm sure he'll be all right. I'll have my family prayin' for him."

"Thank you, Mr. Mueller," I managed to say, wondering what in the world had set Katie off so suddenly.

"Need word taken anywhere, other than this letter, I mean?"

"No, sir," I answered. "The doctor's been here, and the pastor. And the letter's to let my grandma know."

He nodded his head. "He's a brave man. A good man. I'm sure he'll come out fine. Don't you girls be worryin'."

"Thank you, sir," I told him again.

He drove off without getting his hanky back. I turned to Katie and just looked at her for a minute. I didn't know what to say. We were friends. We'd always been friends.

But I was just as close to Rorey, maybe even more. And suddenly it occurred to me that Katie didn't have anybody else to be close to, except my mom and dad.

"Are you scared, Katie? About Daddy?"

"So what if I am? You were too."

"But he's doing better. Isn't he?"

"I guess so. I sure hope so."

"Please don't cry."

She looked at me and wiped her eyes with Mr. Mueller's hanky, then scrunched it up in her hand.

"It's not just that."

"Well, then, what's wrong?"

She sniffed just a little. "Why do you like Rorey so much better than me?"

I know my mouth dropped open. And my insides suddenly felt funny and cold. "I don't. You're my friend too."

"Not the same. It's not the same way, Sarah."

I shook my head. "Why isn't it? What do you mean? I like you too."

"Rorey doesn't."

"She does some. And you know I do."

"Maybe so. But it's partly because Mom and Dad told you you have to. Otherwise you'd be off with her all the time. And it bothers me, not just for me, Sarah. You've got more sense than Rorey does. But she's

266

always been in charge. And I'm scared she's gonna get you in as much trouble as she gets her own self into before it's all done."

"Before what's done?" I mostly just stared at her, scarcely believing she'd be saying these things.

"I don't know! Sarah, I don't know! I just wish I understood things better. I wish I knew what Rorey has against me, and why you always want to do what she wants. You're so smart, Sarah. You're pretty too. You don't have to listen to her all the time! You don't have to —"

"I don't listen to her all the time!" I answered back. "Mostly we're too busy with chores and school to get in any kind of trouble, so I don't know what you're worried about, Katie Ann! And I do too like you, without anybody telling me to. You're like my sister. Don't you remember how excited I was when you got to stay?"

She looked down at the ground. "Rorey said you didn't stay excited. She said you and her didn't need me and that I don't really belong here."

I had to swallow a hard chunk of something in my throat. "When did she say that?"

"It doesn't matter. But you know, the

only one she hates as much as me is Franky, and I don't understand that at all. I know I came from somewhere else. But Franky's her own brother. It's not right, her having Lester beat him up."

"I didn't say it was her idea!"

"Why would he beat up her brother if it wasn't okay with her? If he likes her so much, he's gonna do stuff to make her like him back, won't he?"

"Oh, Katie."

"Well, don't you think so? Do you think Ben Porter would've come and beat up Franky when he was wanting Lizbeth to see more of him? Do you? She'd have tossed him away like a rotten potato."

"Katie —"

"So *you* don't have to worry about Lester, so long as you stay on Rorey's good side."

"She's not like that!"

"Are you sure?"

I stood there on the side of the road with my head pounding. How could she say something like this? Rorey couldn't have known Lester was going to fight Franky! She couldn't have!

And yet, she did know. She knew last night that it was Lester, when Franky first got home, before anyone else had said anything about it. Why hadn't she tried to stop it, if she'd known it might happen? Or at least warn Franky, if Lester wouldn't listen to her. But she didn't even tell Franky she was sorry about it.

Doubts jumbled around in my brain. Why was Rorey still talking about Lester after the fight, still making plans to meet him? If I had a boyfriend who beat up my brother, I didn't think I'd want to meet with him, unless it'd be to tell him I didn't like that kind of stuff. But that wasn't what Rorey'd been about at all.

Suddenly I was so hurt and upset or just plain mad that I hardly knew what to do with myself. How could Rorey say such things to Katie? Katie wouldn't lie to me. Katie was always doing the right thing.

"You do belong here," I told her, hoping she'd believe I really meant it. "I'm sorry. I never meant to leave you out. I always wanted you and me and Rorey to be a threesome. Remember?"

"Yeah, I know," she said. "But Rorey gets her way."

We were so quiet walking back to the house. I could feel something different stirring around inside me. I wanted to go and talk to Rorey. Right then. But I knew I'd have to wait. Probably until she came back over. Maybe tonight. But then I'd make her tell me exactly what happened with the fire, and why she was so mean to Katie, and what she had against Franky that she would let Lester beat him up. I would make her explain herself to me, and then I would go and tell Mom that she'd been planning to meet Lester in the barn. I'd say it and be done with it and let whatever happens just happen.

I didn't even care if I got in trouble for not saying something sooner. I especially didn't care if Rorey got in trouble. She should.

We were at the head of our driveway when I finally managed to ask Katie another question that was jumbling around inside me. "How come you're so good all the time? I mean, I want to be, but I don't do so well as you do."

She didn't even stop walking. "That's easy. I owe it to Mom and Dad."

For a minute I couldn't answer. But then I grabbed her hand before she could get too far ahead of me. "What do you mean, you owe them? You mean for taking care of you?"

"Don't you think so? They could've sent me off someplace. They could've even sent me away with Uncle Edward, and I don't know where I'd be then."

"Katie, they wanted you here! All of us wanted you here."

"But they didn't have to. That's all I'm saying."

"But you don't have to feel like you owe something —"

"So I could be lazy and cause trouble? Would that make any sense?"

"Well, no, but —"

"That's just the way I see it. I love your folks. They're mine now. I ought to show them I love them. Don't you think?"

"Well, we all should. Rorey should. Look at what all Mom and Dad have done for the Hammonds, ever since their mom died."

Katie turned toward the house. "I know."

"I promise not to follow Rorey's notions anymore, Katie."

"I'm not saying you have to do that. She might have a good one now and then."

"You know what I mean. I promise to be a better friend to you, and not leave you out or listen to Rorey when I know she's going in the wrong direction. You're right. She's got no business with Lester, and I've got no business keeping secrets about it."

Katie didn't say anything else. We went

back in the house together just as Emmie was coming down the stairs. I went and shushed her so she wouldn't wake up the baby or Georgie and Bert.

"Can we color again?" she asked.

I got out the Crayolas, and Katie sat down with her. Mrs. Pratt was carrying in water to heat. "There ain't many yet, but it's best to wash up what we got a' Rosemary's diapers 'fore your mama has to think about it. Them towels that's soaking too, I reckon."

I went and got the iron and put it on the stove. I didn't want Mom to have to think about our clothes for tomorrow. I didn't care if she didn't do anything at all except stay right there with Daddy. He'd like that. But he'd get up pretty soon too. And things would get back to the way they ought to be.

17

Julia

I woke with a start, thinking about Dr. Howell's passing. I felt like I should do something; I should make a cake or something to take to the family. I hopped up off that bed before I even half remembered how much my movement could jar Samuel. But he must have been already awake.

"Hey, now, where you going in such a hurry?" I turned and saw his smile. "I'm not such bad company as that, am I?" he asked, giving me a wink.

"Samuel, how long have you been awake?"

"I don't know. A little while. I was being careful not to wake you."

"You should have! I've got no business sleeping the day away. Especially when other people are here doing my work for me."

"Maybe they know I just wanted you with me."

"Oh, Sammy. Are you feeling better?"

"Yeah, I think so."

Those were beautiful words to hear. I leaned and kissed him, and he tried to pull me toward him. It hurt. I saw his grimace, though he tried not to show it.

"Your ribs?"

"They're letting me know they're still there," he said. "No problem."

"The doctor said not to be moving around too much."

"I don't know," he said. "Seems like the only thing staying in this bed will accomplish is me getting stiffer."

"You're not getting up! Not until the doctor comes back. He was very clear on that."

"Yeah. I know." He took a deep breath.

"Do you really feel ready?" I asked him, glad at the thought of it, despite my fervent caution.

"I want to," he said. "I'm just not sure —"

He stopped with the sudden knock on our door. The door opened just a crack, and Sarah peeked in. "Mom? Dad? I heard voices, and I thought it might be okay to come in and get your church clothes out of the closet. I want to check 'em over, just to see if they need any ironing. Robert's shirt sure did."

At first I couldn't respond, seeing her hopeful face. Church clothes? She was expecting all of us to get ourselves to church as usual tomorrow. "Oh, Sarah," I said, shaking my head. "We won't be able to go this week."

She looked at her father, and I could see the hope still in her eyes. She wanted him to be fine *now*. And I supposed he'd just been telling me he wanted the same thing.

"The doctor said I'm not to get up till he sees me again, pumpkin," Samuel told her gently.

"But you're feeling better, aren't you, Daddy?"

"Yeah. Better."

She beamed. "Then maybe it'd be all right. Maybe we could go. At least we can say maybe, right?"

"Honey —" I started to protest.

But she didn't wait to hear what I might say. "We better have the clothes ready just in case. Maybe the doctor will come back tonight and say it's okay."

She walked past us to the closet and took down my flowered dress and Samuel's best shirt and trousers.

Samuel stopped her. "Sarah . . ."

"Yes, Daddy?"

"If the doctor comes, that would be fine.

But I don't think he'll say it's okay."

She looked stricken. "Why, Daddy? You said you're feeling better. Is it your ribs? Is it because of broken ribs?"

"Partly," he told her, and I held my breath, sudden worries rushing at me again. But I shoved them away.

"Mostly it's just too soon," he went on. "Doctors always want you to have plenty of rest before getting back to normal activities. I expect he'll insist I stay right here for several days."

I looked at Samuel in surprise. It seemed exactly the opposite of what he was telling me he wanted.

"But don't worry, pumpkin," he continued. "I'll be all right. Doctors just like to leave time to be sure."

She nodded, her smile gone. "I think I'll iron your things anyway," she said. "Maybe after he talks to you, he'll change his mind." She turned her eyes to me. "Is it okay, Mom? Do you have anything else you want me to iron?"

"Honey, you don't have to iron at all."

"I want to."

She'd never wanted to before. It was definitely not her favorite job, not even Samuel's handkerchiefs, which were so simple to do. But she looked so earnest right now. "It's all right if you want to iron," I told her, "but I don't have more, unless there was something in the laundry that you folded and carried in last night. But we got that all put away, didn't we? Goodness, with the baby I'm not even sure. But we must have, because Rosemary was sleeping in the basket."

"Yeah. Me and Katie put everything away last night. And most of it was okay, I think."

She walked on out, taking my dress and Samuel's clothes with her.

"Those girls," I said to Samuel. "They're going nonstop. And Robert too. He went over to help George look through the remains of the barn and maybe get started on the house roof."

Samuel laid his head back real slow, and something about the way he did it made me stop talking. He closed his eyes. "We're blessed, Juli. They're good kids."

"Samuel," I said, suddenly feeling tense, "you were just talking about wanting to get up. Are you feeling worse again? Is there something you're not telling me?"

He opened his eyes to look at me. "Just dizzy all of a sudden. Maybe it's just too soon, like I told Sarah."

"You'd tell me, wouldn't you, if it was more than that?"

He was quiet for a moment. He turned his eyes toward the ceiling. "Julia, I still hurt. I guess that'll go on for a while. I'm feeling nauseous, but not too bad. But the dizziness — just in the last couple minutes — I don't think I could get up if I tried."

"Well, you're not going to try. There's absolutely no reason to. Not yet." I took his hand, knowing he hadn't really wanted to tell me about it.

"It'll pass," he said softly.

"I know."

"I dreamed my mother was here."

His words shocked me. I guess because I could remember dreaming the same thing.

"She was different. She said she wished she could go back to being young and I could be the little boy on her lap again, and this time she'd do things right."

I knew only God could convince Joanna to say something like that in reality. She'd never apologized for her drunkenness. Or for letting Samuel's father or her second husband mistreat her boys. I might have said something about that, but Samuel spoke again before I had the chance.

"She almost looked younger. And she was wearing big flowers in her hat." He smiled. "Hard to imagine, isn't it? She never did care much for flowers."

"Well, people can change," I said, thinking about the box of letters in my own dream. "We should continue to pray for her."

He nodded. "Sometimes I get tired, honey, thinking it won't ever do any good."

I only hugged him just a little, not sure what else to do.

"You know what she'd probably say right now?" he asked me. "She'd probably say I had no business dealing with the fire at all. I should leave that to the firemen."

"But getting firemen here would've taken far too long! Coming all the way from Dearing —"

"I know. But she'd still think I brought this on myself, trying to act like I know what I'm doing."

"Oh, Samuel —"

"I'll telephone her when I get to town. When I'm feeling better. But I don't think I want her to know until then."

I glanced over at the dresser, suddenly remembering the letter I'd written. I'd come close to throwing it away. Now I should for sure, after hearing what Samuel had to say. But it was gone. One of the girls must have moved it. I'd have to ask them about it later.

"Samuel, I think I ought to make Mabel Howell a cake or something. I'm sure her sons will be coming, and maybe other family too."

He was looking at me a little strangely, and I realized he didn't know what I was talking about. How could I be so forgetful?

"Oh, Samuel, I'm sorry. I hadn't told you. Dr. Howell passed away last night."

He was quiet, like he wasn't sure how to respond.

"I was thinking I could get Robert to take the cake over for me tonight sometime," I said.

Samuel nodded. "Make sure he expresses our condolences."

He was looking out the window. I followed his eyes and saw Franky coming out of the woodshop.

"It was a hard night," Samuel said. "I hope that's the end of it."

I wasn't sure how he meant that.

"Is Franky all right?" he asked.

For a moment I hesitated. "I'm sure his hands will heal up fine."

"Is there another problem?"

"No, I'm sure he'll be just fine."

I wasn't quite sure why I wasn't telling him about some of the others blaming Franky for the fire. Maybe I didn't want him getting his dander up when he looked so tired. Or maybe I was just hoping George would put a stop to the accusations now that Pastor had talked to him. At any rate, I didn't want to trouble Samuel with it now.

I watched him a minute, wondering about that dizziness and noticing that he seemed a little pale. "I should bring you some more water," I told him.

"No. Nothing right now. I don't think I could hold it."

"Do you think I should send someone to ask the doctor to come tonight like Sarah said?"

He looked at me, and though I could tell in his eyes the struggle with pain, there was a sparkle of mischief there too. "Why? You don't think the church choir can manage without us tomorrow?"

"You know as well as I do that Dr. Hall won't give you clearance to go! I'm worried for you, Samuel. I just thought it might be a good idea to have him look at you again."

I shouldn't have said that. Now he was worried too. For me.

"Juli, we know there are problems, just like he said before — the concussion and the ribs. But everything's going to be fine. So stop your worrying. Please."

"Can I do anything to help you?"

"Go make Mrs. Howell that cake. A nice big one."

I had to smile. But still I hesitated to leave his side. I didn't like hearing that he was dizzy. And nauseous. "Samuel —"

"Go on. The sooner you get it done, the sooner it can be cooling to take over there."

I went and started cutting apples for the raw apple cake recipe that Emma Graham had once shared with me. But I couldn't stop my mind from thinking about Samuel. He was so brave. So strong. Not wanting me to know how much he was hurting. Not wanting me to worry. Almost it made me worry more.

He hadn't tried to sit up on his own. Of course he knew he wasn't supposed to yet, but still, it was hardly like him not to try.

"Mom?"

I looked across the room to where Sarah was ironing and Katie was helping Emmie Grace put away the Crayolas. For some reason I wasn't sure which of them had spoken.

"Is Dad really okay?" It was Katie, her eyes looking so serious.

"Yes, honey," I said. "He says he'll be just fine."

"Think he's ready for some lunch?"

"No. Not yet."

All three girls looked up at me then, even Emma Grace. "I drew a picture of him," she said, turning the paper to show me. "See? He's helping my pa make a whole new barn. That'll be fun, won't it? Makin' a new barn?"

"It sure could be."

Little Georgie came toddling in from the sitting room. He stopped when he saw me and cocked his head with an unmistakable gleam in his eye. "Boomie," he whispered, just barely loud enough for me to hear him.

"Not this time," I told him.

He rushed over to the cupboard door and started tugging on the old apron I'd used to tie it shut. He glared up at me in indignant surprise and tried tugging at it some more.

"Uh! Uh! Boomie!" he protested.

"Fixed you, didn't I?"

For a minute he just stood there. Then he gave one last mighty yank, but it still wouldn't come loose. In frustration he turned and crawled under the table, plopping smack down with his little arms folded.

"I'm sorry, Georgie," I said, peeking

under the table. "But all the 'boomie' was getting tiresome."

He quickly scooted around so his back was to me. I turned my attention to cutting apples and left him alone. And pretty soon he peeked his little head at me and ventured out from under the table as I was reaching the molasses down from the cupboard. Then he wanted to help when I got Katie and Emmie Grace started chopping walnuts. It didn't take him long to lose interest in that. I thought he'd gone back in the other room, but just as I was dumping the second cup of flour into a mixing bowl, he was suddenly at my elbow.

Katie hollered, "Georgie, no!"

I turned to the side barely in time to see the molasses jar slide off the table and hit the floor with a crash. It didn't shatter, but the glass bottom popped out, and soon there was molasses oozing out in all directions.

Georgie looked up at me, his wide eyes uncertain. "Boomie?"

"No. Not boomie. Not good at all. Do you understand?"

"I don't think he meant to," Katie said quickly. "Maybe he just wanted to see what it was."

I looked at Georgie, and he looked at

me. "Dat oops," he finally said.

It took me much longer to clean up that mess than it should have. Emmie Grace, always eager to please, jumped down from the chair she was on to grab a dishrag and help me, but she accidentally knocked a bowl of walnuts off the table in the process. And then she got too close and got molasses spread across her shoe. Top and bottom, I'm not sure how.

"Dat messy," Georgie told me, shaking his head side to side.

"You're absolutely right it's messy," I answered him. "And if you weren't so little, I'd have you be the one to clean it up."

"Boomie," he told me, crossing his little arms.

"Mrs. Wortham!" Thelma called from the next room. "Is Georgie causing you trouble?"

I sighed. "Just a little spill."

Katie looked at me from the floor, where she was picking up the walnuts.

"Where did Thelma's mother go?" I asked her.

"She went outside just before you came in, to rinse Rosemary's diapers and some towels and hang 'em on the line."

"Well, bless her for that."

I thought I could hear Mrs. Pratt in the

285

yard, singing "When the Saints Come Marching In." I doubted she'd heard anything of what was going on.

Georgie leaned over and stuck two of his fingers in the molasses. I grabbed his hand and wiped it off with the damp dishcloth.

"Sarah," I said with another sigh, "are you almost done ironing?"

"Yeah. Do you need help?"

"Just grab a couple of wooden spoons and take Georgie outside, will you please? Let him boomie on the porch steps to his heart's content."

She smiled. "Hey! Georgie! What do you think of that? You can play drummer boy."

He grinned and pulled those spoons out of Sarah's hands just as soon as she grabbed them. She was trying to usher him out the door, but he ran and hit the table with his spoons, and then the chair leg. And then he turned and looked at *my* leg.

"Outside," I commanded. "Go."

He went. And Sarah followed him, chuckling just a little.

"Don't let him chase the chickens," I called after her. "Or anything else."

"That was real nice of you," Katie commented.

I squatted down to wipe up the wasted molasses. "At least he's out of our hair and we can get the floor clean and the cake done."

"Don't you like Georgie no more?" Emmie asked me with such a serious face.

"I love Georgie. He's a wonderful little boy. But today, my mind is somewhere else, and there are things I just have to get done."

"Yeah, me too," she said without elaborating at all.

After we had all the walnuts and molasses off the floor and I turned my attention back to the cake recipe, Emmie scrunched up as close as she could beside me and waited till I looked her way.

"You know," she said, "seems like Georgie's kinda like me. Only louder."

"He's a unique individual," I told her. "Like you."

"Was Franky loud when he was little?"

I glanced at her face, not quite sure about the connections she seemed to be making. "I didn't know him when he was that little. Franky was just a bit older than you are now when I first met your family. But he was much quieter than Harry or Bert at that age."

"He thinks a lot," she explained. "Sometimes I think a lot too."

I didn't ask her for anything more, but

she kept right on talking.

"What if you was my real mama and not just my neighbor mama? Would I sleep over here all the time then, or would I go and visit Rorey and Berty and everybody sometimes too? Or what if Lizbeth had as many kids as all a' us, and they was runnin' around here all the time while she was teachin' school? We'd have lots a' messes then."

"Emmie, Lizbeth'll have to quit teaching when they have a baby. She almost had to quit just over getting married."

She frowned. "Babies is plenty good. But I hope she don't quit. 'Cause I wanted to ask her if I could go to *her* school. I know she wouldn't call me no dummy. An' maybe I could learn better there."

I was rather aghast. "Elvira Post didn't call you a dummy. Did she?"

Emma nodded her head in the affirmative, her little lip just beginning to stick out.

Katie was shaking her head the other way. "I don't think that's what she meant. But one day this week she did say it takes all kinds to make a world, the smarter and the not-so-smart, and we all just have to do our best work."

"But Teddy Willis said the not-so-smart

288

was me," Emmie cried. "An' she didn't even scold him, not one word!"

"Maybe she didn't hear him," I suggested.

"I didn't hear him," Katie agreed.

"Well, he said it! An' I wanna go to Lizbeth's school."

"Not surprising," I said, my heart suddenly heavy for her. "She's a wonderful big sister and I'm sure a fine teacher, but that school is in town, honey. Too far away."

"Not so bad far. Me an' Harry an' Bert'd go an' live with her if we didn't have Pa. I heard him say so once. An' Franky'd stay here so's he could work the wood. An' Rorey maybe too, so's she could be with Sarah. And then that would leave Willy an' Kirk, an' Joe when he come back from the service, an' they could handle the farm, leastways till they all get married, an' maybe one of 'em'd stay on even then."

"Did your pa say all that?" I asked her, more than a little surprised.

"Yeah. Only not today."

"Well, it may be well and good for him to rest his mind over what would happen with all of you, but you most definitely still have your pa, and I don't see how that's going to change for a very long time."

"I know. An' I don't want it to change,

e'cept for goin' to Lizbeth's school. But he said you never know 'bout tomorrow. What's he mean by that?"

"I'm not sure what he's talking about. Or why he'd tell it to you, for heaven's sake."

"I still wanna go to Lizbeth's school. Maybe I could stay with her sometimes even though we do got Pa."

I patted her hand, now wondering about her father. It'd been a very long time since we'd heard any talk of him not being there for his kids. "Emmie, honey, I'm not at all sure about you staying with Lizbeth. And that school's just too far for you to get back and forth every day. I'm sure your teacher wasn't meaning to call you a dummy or let anybody else do that, either. Most days you like school, don't you?"

"Yeah. I guess. 'Cept readin'. An' she's tryin' to make me do that all the time."

"That's what schools are for," Katie told her.

I was stirring up the batter. Emmie helped me fold the nuts in. "Can I put it in the pan?" she begged. "Can I, please?"

I almost said no. But it was so important to her. She loved to help in the kitchen. It seemed to be her most favorite thing. She'd choose cooking and washing dishes over most any game you could care to mention. "All right," I told her. "But let me help and let's be careful. I want this to look nice for Mrs. Howell."

"Mrs. Howell? Who's she?"

"The doctor's wife, remember? Only she's grieving now because he's gone on to be with the Lord."

She stopped and stared at me a minute. "Does that mean he's with Mama too?"

"Yes. With your mama too."

It seemed like only yesterday when I'd stood in Wilametta Hammond's bedroom with my shaking hands helping Mrs. Graham deliver little Emmie. And just a few short months later, Mrs. Hammond was gone. In the years since then, George had gone through spells of being angry at his wife and angry at God. But if there'd been any choice in the matter, poor Wilametta would never have left her struggling husband alone with ten children. Not in a million years.

Did George still miss her so dreadfully as he used to? Why would he start talking about what his kids would do without him? Especially in front of his seven-year-old daughter? Oh, it made me wonder.

I might have said something more to her. She might have said something more to me. But we suddenly heard a noise behind us and turned to find Samuel standing there, leaning against the door frame. I almost dropped the batter bowl.

"Samuel Wortham! What in the world are you doing up?"

"I wanted another drink of water, but it sounded like you had your hands full in here."

"Dad, I could've gotten it," Katie told him.

"It's all right. I'm doing all right." Slowly, more gingerly than I'd ever seen him walk, he made his way to the table and sat at the nearest chair. "If you wouldn't mind, just set it here in front of me, Katie."

She hopped to get it in a hurry. And I didn't know whether to be delighted for him or dreadfully upset. "Dr. Hall is not going to be very happy with you," I said. "I can tell how sore you are by the way you walk."

"Yeah. But it doesn't help anyone to have me stay in that bed."

"What if you've torn open that cut on your leg? Or aggravated something else —"

"Shhh." He took a slow drink of his water and then managed a smile. "I believe I hear Mrs. Pratt singing with some kind of drummer outside. Not a bad sound."

"Samuel . . ."

He looked at me and took a deep breath before speaking again. "I think Sarah's right. We ought to be in the house of God tomorrow."

I set the bowl down. "Are you sure?"

"I'm still here. After a barn fell on me, Julia. I ought to be going to worship."

"But Dr. Hall said —" The look in his eye stopped the rest of my words before they could come out of my mouth.

"He said I'd be all right. Didn't he?"

The doubt in me was suddenly squeezing at the pit of my stomach. "He said he's expecting so. That we'd be right to believe so."

"There you go. Then we ought to thank God."

"But . . . we can do that here."

"I want to be in church. I don't want to sit here making people fret. We never miss. Imagine, Julia, if we're not there. They'll be thinking it's serious."

I stared at him for a minute. "It *was* serious, Samuel. It *is* serious. Pastor knows how serious it could have been! And you don't have to do anything because of what people might think. They'll pray for you. They'll understand."

"I want to go."

His eyes looked so weary. His breathing

still pained him, I could tell. And I had no way of knowing whether he was still dizzy, except that he'd been holding onto the wall as he came in. "Oh, Samuel, are you sure? You're supposed to stay in bed."

"I'm sure. It's not like I have to walk the whole way or mount a horse."

"You must be the strongest man in the world," Emmie told him.

Samuel disagreed. "I imagine your father's having to be pretty strong right now, sorting it through in his mind what to do from here."

"Are you gonna help him make a new barn?"

"He'll have help." That was all Samuel would say about it. But I knew it'd be quite a while before he was ready for that kind of work. He was pushing things to be sitting in the chair in front of us.

"Maybe I should get you back to bed."

"Just a minute," he said slowly. "Let me sit here a minute till I get my legs on again."

Emmie laughed at him. "You can't take your legs off! Nobody can take their legs off!"

"You're dizzy, aren't you?" I asked him.

"It'll pass," he said with a quiet voice.

I tried to be happy about him getting up,

that he was feeling well enough to. But he *wasn't* well enough. And I wasn't happy at all. I tried to help him back to the bedroom when he was ready, but he wouldn't lean on me. He steadied himself in the doorway again, but that was all. He tried to act like it was nothing for him to get up and stroll around, but he couldn't hide the pain in his face.

"Oh, Samuel! How can you be so stubborn? We were just telling Sarah about obeying what the doctor had to say."

"I know. I just thought it over a little more. If I stay in bed, Juli, it'll scare the children."

"It'll scare them worse if you hurt yourself."

"Help me drag the bedroom rocking chair into the kitchen."

"What?"

"I don't want to be off in the bedroom, Julia. But Thelma and the baby are using the rocker in the sitting room."

"You need to go back to bed."

"I want a chair where I can lean my head back. But I want to be out around everybody."

I shook my head. "You can be so awful bullheaded."

He smiled. "So can you. In a good way.

Please, Juli. Help me get the chair."

He was breathing hard, holding on to me a little tighter. I knew I needed to get him settled somewhere. "Will you just sit on the bed and let *me* move the chair? Then if you feel like getting up again in a while, it'll be ready for you."

"All right. Fair enough."

He sat on the bed. But as I was pulling the chair, he slowly lay back and closed his eyes. I stopped immediately. "Samuel?"

"It's all right. Just getting my legs again. This room kind of whirls, you know."

"Oh, Samuel."

He peered over at me. "Need help with that chair?"

"*I'll* move the chair. Don't you budge. Not one inch! You just stay put a while. Do you hear me?"

He smiled. "Yeah. A while. Okay."

He sounded so exhausted. Why couldn't he see that he was scaring me just as much by getting up as he did when he lay so still?

"I love you," he whispered. "Thanks."

"For what?" I asked, giving that rocker a push through the doorway.

"Being bullheaded."

I looked up, and he winked at me.

He did get up and sit in the kitchen after

a while. I got him a pillow for behind his head and almost had a conniption when Georgie ran in and jumped on him and set the chair to rocking.

Delores walked in just as I was lifting Georgie off, and she took him out of my hands. "We're gonna have to get out an' go home," she said. "I can sure see that. Are you all right, Mr. Wortham?"

"He's just a little fellow," Samuel answered her.

"Maybe so, but he's still too big to be climbin' over banged-up ribs," she replied. "Now, Georgie, you've gotta leave Mr. Wortham alone. He's been hurt. You know that."

"Mommy!" he wailed, reaching toward the sitting room doorway.

"Nope," Delores said immediately. "I wouldn't be surprised if she was feedin' the baby again. Tell you what I saw, though, while I was out there lookin' around. Mrs. Wortham's got some ground cherries over past the well. You reckon she'd mind if we went and picked a few for her?"

"You don't have to do that," I protested.

"Nonsense. It'd be our pleasure. Wouldn't it, Georgie? You know how to pick ground cherries, don't you? Aren't you Grandma's big boy?"

He nodded with his little lip hanging out a bit. "Georgie big."

Delores helped herself to a couple of bowls. I wondered what the ground cherry plants would look like by the time Georgie got finished with them, but right then I didn't care. As long as the boy was occupied, that was fine with me.

Bert came hobbling into the kitchen, leaning heavily on one of Emma Graham's old canes. He looked like he'd napped again. His hair was sticking straight up on one side.

"You think Pa'll be back tonight?" he asked me.

"I don't know. But I expect at least some of the bunch will be here. They may be too tired to fix their own supper, and I'll bet if Willy and Kirk get hungry, they'll finish off whatever's left of the lunch we sent, long before suppertime."

He didn't say anything else to me, only went over and sat next to Samuel. The skinny oak cane slid to the floor with a clunk. "I sure am sorry, Mr. Wortham," he said with one hand fumbling down unsuccessfully for the crook of the cane. "I didn't want nobody to get hurt."

"I'm sure it's a lesson learned," Samuel told him. "Don't worry about it now."

"Are you doin' all right?"

Samuel didn't look all right sitting in a rocker in the kitchen with his head leaned on one pillow and another pillow against his side. But he wasn't about to tell Bert anything that wasn't positive. "Coming along fine," he said. "As a matter of fact, I was just sitting here thinking it was time I put my hand to something around here and quit wasting the day."

"Samuel —" I started to protest.

"Now just relax," he told me. "I didn't say I'd be running races. But if you could bring my polishing bag, maybe Katie'd carry me everyone's shoes and Bert and I could get them all shined up for tomorrow."

"Are you sure about this?" I asked him. Katie stood, waiting for his response.

"We can manage, can't we, Bert?" he said. "Polishing's a good sit-down job."

I might have argued that the arm movement could aggravate Samuel's ribs or that looking down at shoes might be a little hard on his aching head when he should be leaning it back, but Bert was smiling at the idea and I let it go. Maybe it would do them both good to be applying their hands to something. Especially Bert. And surely Samuel would know to quit if he got too tired.

Just as I expected, we heard our truck

coming back around suppertime. Robert came in and got the milk bucket. He was so pleased to see his father sitting in the kitchen that I thought maybe that was why Samuel had done it. It took a load off Robert's mind just to see Samuel out of bed. He and Willy went to start the chores together. I thought I caught a glimpse of Harry out the window, and I could hear Rorey on the porch, but she didn't come in. And it wasn't long before young Sam came walking through the door with his son on his shoulders and his mother-in-law following along behind him.

"I oughta take my family on home," he told us. "There ain't enough thanks to be said for what all you done for us, but —"

"It's just time," Delores finished for him. "Time we had Thelma in her own bed and little Georgie back over t' home again."

"Are you sure the doctor would want Thelma up and traveling so soon?" I asked with genuine concern. "It's not even been a full day."

"She's healthy," Delores assured me. "Don't you worry. Sam can carry her to the car, and once we're home, I'll have her straight to bed. I can stay a whole week, maybe two, an' she won't have to lift a finger."

I had to admit it might make things a bit easier for us. "You'll at least eat something here first, won't you?" I asked them. "So you won't have to fix something as soon as you get in the door?"

Sam and Delores both agreed. And Delores took Georgie in with his mommy and baby sister. Young Sam turned around a kitchen chair and sat in it.

"I'll be back tomorrow to see what I can do to help Pa," he said. "Ben an' Lizbeth stayed over there even though he didn't want 'em to 'cause he's takin' all this pretty hard, worryin' for winter an' everythin' else. He tried to send us all back over here, but Lizbeth wouldn't leave him alone."

I well remembered George's despairing behavior after losing Wilametta. He'd wanted to be alone then too. He'd taken to drink and come very close to suicide. But this was nothing like that, surely. A barn and outbuildings, and even the animals, were nothing like losing your wife. But I could tell it was bothering young Sam too.

"I'd a' stayed if it weren't for Thelma an' the kids," he told us. "Kirk an' Rorey wanted to too, but he made 'em come on over. Said he didn't want 'em in the house all night smellin' the smoke, but it ain't that bad."

"Are Ben and Lizbeth planning to stay the night?" Samuel asked.

"Yeah."

"That'll be all right, then. For now."

"I don't think Lizbeth'll go nowhere 'long as Pa's depressed like this."

"He won't stay that way," Samuel maintained. "It'll come out all right."

"I sure hope you're right, Mr. Wortham. He's feelin' pretty bad about you too. I oughta stop over there on the way home an' tell him you're up. That ought to ease his mind."

"You do that. Tell him I'm going to church in the morning and he ought to come too."

I was warming up leftovers when Delores came back in the kitchen and started pulling plates down from the cupboard.

"How many here tonight, Julia?"

I had to count. "Five of us, plus seven Hammond children is twelve. Then there's Sam's four plus you. That makes seventeen, right? Of course, Rosemary won't need a plate and Georgie ought to have a small one. The one with the rooster, please."

"Goodness," she said with a laugh. "That is a houseful."

"I guess we're used to it around here."

I started hearing footsteps on the porch and knew it was Franky coming in. He had a different sound to his walk than any of the other boys. He opened the door and came in just as young Sam was telling Samuel about finding what was left of the spade and the posthole digger in the remains of the burned-out barn.

"Maybe they'll be all right if we get some handles made," Sam was saying. "And there ought to be more to salvage where the east wall was. Lot a' tools was hanging up there."

"I can make handles," Franky said.

"Yeah. That's what I told Pa," Sam acknowledged. "But he wasn't wantin' to talk about that."

Franky didn't respond.

"What you been doin' today, anyway?" Sam asked him.

"Workin' on the cedar chest and chair me an' Mr. Wortham's s'posed to get out first a' next week. Got the chest done." His voice was quiet and his silvery eyes seemed far away.

"Well, that's a good thing," his older brother told him. "It was better you not being right there with Pa this afternoon."

"George isn't still blaming Franky, is

he?" I said in dismay. "After talking to the pastor?" Too late, I realized we hadn't told Samuel.

"Blaming him?" Samuel asked. "You mean for the fire?"

"I think he's tryin' to sort it out," young Sam told us. "Pastor told him Franky ain't one to lie. An' I'd have to agree with that. But then, Rorey ain't either. So I think maybe she just thought she had it figgered how it musta been —"

At that moment, Rorey walked in from the porch, and her brother stopped what he was saying.

"I know I must've missed some of what you're talking about," Samuel told us. "But accidents can happen, and there's no sense casting blame on anyone."

"Don't seem like everybody agrees with you," Franky said quietly.

Rorey looked over at him, and he turned his eyes to meet hers. Something unspoken passed between them. I wasn't sure what, and I wasn't sure if anyone else noticed it. But Rorey told us she was so awful tired that she didn't think she could eat any supper. She went right upstairs.

Franky was still a sight with his sooty clothes and bruises and his two hands still wrapped in bandages. Maybe Rorey was feeling guilty over causing him so much trouble. First with Lester. And then with blaming him for the fire just because she'd seen that he was awake. She ought to have known better than to jump to conclusions like that. Maybe she should be feeling guilty. I decided I'd better go up and talk to her after a bit and see if she didn't think she should apologize to her brother.

Little Georgie came sauntering back into the room, took one look at me, and commenced trying to pull on that apron again.

"You want a pickle?" I asked him. "They're better than noisy pans any day."

He shook his head and gave the immovable cupboard door quite a kick.

"Whoa, there," his father told him. "That ain't no way to act in Mrs. Wortham's kitchen. You tell her you're sorry this minute."

"So'wy," he told me with his big brown eyes looking my way. "Picka?"

"Oh, you do want one." I picked out a nice juicy pickle and handed it to him. He plunked down on the floor in front of the cupboard and started sucking on it.

"How's your hands?" Sam was asking Franky.

"It ain't nothin'. I wouldn't be wearin'

no bandages 'cept Mrs. Wortham insisted."

"Pa said you wanted him to notice."

"Nope," Franky admitted to his brother. "I almost took 'em off so he wouldn't see."

Young Sam shook his head. "Pa can be funny sometimes, we all know that. You shouldn't let it bother you, all right?"

Franky nodded.

We called in everybody to eat. Oh, what a tired and grubby bunch they were. And on a Saturday night! We'd be needing baths, church or no church. Usually there was no question but that we'd go. That's where Christian families ought to be on a Sunday morning. But this time I was hoping Samuel would change his mind. It was just too soon for him. Oh, how hard the ride would be over our bumpy country roads! It made me hurt for him, just thinking about it.

When most everybody else was eating, I went upstairs, thinking I'd better take this opportunity to talk to Rorey. Not just about apologizing to Franky but also about her feelings for the Turrey boy and that I'd have to let her father know when I got the chance. She wouldn't be very happy with me about that, I knew. Or with Franky and Sarah either, for talking to me. But I hoped she'd see that we all just wanted what was best for her.

I was rehearsing in my mind how to begin such a delicate subject as I opened the door to Sarah and Katie's room.

"Rorey? Can I come in a minute?"

She didn't answer. She was lying on Sarah's bed, already asleep. I pulled a cover up to her shoulder and left her alone.

Samuel didn't eat much. At first that bothered me, but I had to stop myself and consider what a blessing it was to have him doing so well as he was. It was silly for me to keep on fretting.

Little Georgie was yawning and running around behind and between chairs to keep from giving in to the tiredness. Finally his father swooped him up and said it was time to go. Pretty soon Georgie snuggled in his grandma's arms, I carried the baby, and young Sam picked up Thelma just as Delores had promised me he would. We walked on out and got them situated in their car. About half the other kids followed just to see them off.

"Now, don't you worry," Delores told me again. "I'll see that Thelma gets plenty a' rest."

"Thank you so much," Thelma told me.

"You're such a blessin'. And we'll keep on prayin' that Mr. Wortham gains his full strength 'fore you know it."

"Thank you," I told her and gave her a hug.

Emmie ran up to hug her oldest brother and plant a kiss on little Rosemary's forehead. Then she reached and kissed Thelma too. "G'night. Can I come see the baby tomorrow?"

"We'll see, sweetie, we'll see," Thelma told her.

They drove off, and we all waved and then headed back to the house. It seemed emptier, though we still had five Hammond boys and Emmie. Plus Robert and our girls. And Rorey.

Harry started a game of checkers with Berty, and I got Robert and Kirk to haul me water to heat for baths. Samuel got up and moved to a chair in the sitting room, and I had to admit he looked like he was walking better.

Everybody needed a bath, but we were all so tired that I figured it wouldn't hurt if we started each bath with whoever seemed the cleanest so we could reuse the water and save hauling more quite so many times. That meant Katie would be first once the water was warm. Or maybe

Emmie so we could get her settled down to sleep.

"Ain't no reason why we shouldn't be over to home tonight," Kirk said. " 'Cept Pa's all upset over everythin'. He said we oughta be where we can get up an' see to the animals first thing, but it ain't that hard to come over in the mornin'."

"It don't take all of us to care for the animals neither," Willy added.

"Sometimes your father's got to think," Samuel told them. "Don't worry. Lizbeth's got good sense. She'll know how to talk to him."

"She oughta bring him over here," Emmie declared. "I'd hug him real big an' tell him there's nothin' to worry 'bout 'cause Mr. Wortham's gonna help us build the barn back."

"You be quiet," Willy grouched at her. "Mr. Wortham can't build. Not hurt like he is."

"You wait and see," Samuel said to that.

I held my tongue on the matter, only giving Emmie's little shoulder a pat. "You'd be a real comfort to him, sweetie, but you can hug him tomorrow. Do you want me to read you a story?"

I knew she'd like that. I expected her to run and get our big book of Bible stories

for children. She especially liked everything about Miriam and Moses and the Is-
raelites leaving Egypt. But instead of going
to get that familiar volume, she looked at
me with solemn eyes and said, "What
about Franky's book? What's it about?"

I had forgotten all about the book
Franky'd taken such trouble to borrow
from Elvira yesterday. *Silas Marner*, if I remembered right. Kate went and got it off
the shelf.

Kirk rolled his eyes and muttered something under his breath.

"Are you sure you want to hear some of
this?" I asked Emmie. "It's not written for
children your age."

"Yeah, but Franky didn't get to hear it
yesterday, an' he had to fight an' ever'thin',
jus' to get it home."

"That's dumb!" Willy told her. "He
wasn't fightin' about that."

But Emmie seemed determined, surprising even me. "I don't mind to listen, at
least a little bit."

"Neither do I," Samuel said from across
the room. And that settled it for all of us.

Harry and Bert kept on with their
checkers game in the corner. Emmie snuggled between Sarah and Katie on the floor
with her dolly on her lap. And Robert,

Willy, and Kirk took up most the daven-port; they were all getting so big. Franky sat in the smaller chair to their right, and I sat in the only chair that remained, closer to Samuel in the rocker. He reached and squeezed my hand for just a minute. I saw his smile, but he suddenly looked so tired.

"Do you want me to help you lie down?"

"No. No, let's hear a chapter first. Then the water'll be hot. I'll lie down then and whoever can stay awake can get a bath in."

He was right to surmise that we were all pretty tired. What a night was last night! I hoped we never ever saw another one like it.

I knew that the boys on the davenport were less than thrilled at the prospect of listening along, but they had the decency to respect Samuel's word. So with ev-eryone gathered around the sitting room except Rorey, I started to read about the strange weaver and his reputation around the village of Raveloe. Franky sat in rapt attention, absorbing every word, and the girls were listening too, except that Emmie kept fiddling with the hem of Bessie-doll's skirt.

"How long is this chapter?" Willy asked after a while.

"Only three or four pages more," I told

him. But what pages those were. The story moved to young Silas Marner's past when he'd stood accused of a crime he did not commit. Betrayed by a friend and rejected by a misguided congregation, he was left to disgrace, with no one willing to believe his innocence.

Everyone in the room was quiet. Sarah sat looking at Franky.

I was about to ask her to go and see if the water was warm, but before a word was said she got up and disappeared up the stairs.

"Great book," Willy taunted his brother. "She musta thought Mrs. Wortham was gonna read chapter 2."

18

Sarah

Halfway up the stairs, I got to thinking about what Rorey might think and what Rorey might say if I just walked in asking her questions. Franky's book was hard to listen to, with hard words put together in ways that weren't easy to understand. At least for me when I was hearing it out loud. But then came the part about William Dane accusing Silas, when he surely must have done the wicked deed himself. And all I could think about was Franky and Rorey.

I walked the rest of the way pretty slowly, my mind trying to tell me two different things. Maybe Rorey was trying to cast the blame for her own fault on to her brother. Just like William Dane. Maybe she'd caused the fire her own self.

But she already told me the way it was. Lester didn't even come. She wasn't in the barn. She wouldn't lie.

I took another step, thinking of Franky fleeing his father's accusations and sitting alone in the woods. He'd never once tried to blame Rorey, despite what she was saying about him.

Because Franky was the one in the barn. Franky set the fire, a voice in my head was trying to say.

But I took another step, wondering why Franky hadn't just said that Rorey was lying about it. At least about some things. I knew she was. As I slowly climbed the last few steps toward my bedroom door, I knew Rorey was lying, as sure as Silas Marner's false friend had lied to get Silas in trouble. And I was feeling uncomfortable hot about it, because even though not everybody believed Rorey now, most of her brothers did, and mine did too. And so did her father when he wasn't trying real hard to please the pastor.

It wasn't fair, because Franky would tell us straight out if he really had dropped a lantern or something. Hard as that would be for him, he'd fess up. I knew he would.

I stood at the top of the stairs. The thought entered my mind that Rorey was probably sleeping and maybe I should just let her sleep. But I pushed the thought out of my head and opened the door. "Rorey?"

She rolled over on the bed but didn't open her eyes.

"Rorey, come on. I know you're not asleep." I went right over and climbed on the foot of the bed, bouncing all the way across so I could sit against the wall. I didn't care how much I jostled her in the meantime.

"Sarah, what are you doing?"

"You missed supper."

"I don't care. I'm tired."

"Maybe you just don't wanna be down there with my dad. And your brothers."

"What are you talking about?"

"Maybe you're feeling guilty. Are you, Rorey? Seeing them hurt?"

"Shut up. I'm tired."

"I know. Everybody's tired."

"Then go to sleep. Let me sleep."

"You didn't say nothing to Daddy, you know. Or Berty. Or Frank. I noticed that. Most everybody else had at least something to say. At least to ask if they're doing all right."

"It's mostly plain they're gonna be all right. Mr. Wortham's all right, isn't he?"

She looked absolutely awake now. I had her attention. But I wasn't sure of what I was seeing on her face. Anger? Fear? It seemed like both, and maybe a lot of other things all stirred in together.

"It'll be a while before he's really okay," I told her. "He's got busted-up ribs, Rorey. And a cut on his leg big as my hand, plus being knocked clear unconscious with something hitting him in the head. He coulda died, Rorey! My daddy almost died!"

"I'm sorry for him," she said real slow and soft. "I'm sorry he got hurt."

"So how'd the fire start?"

"I . . . I told you."

"Yeah. You were waiting up for Lester. And because it was so dark, you took a lantern —"

"I never said that!"

"You didn't have to. You were expecting him in the barn, so that's where you were, and maybe you heard a noise or something, I don't know, but somehow the lantern got tipped and it happened too fast to do anything much about it. Right, Rorey?"

"That's not what happened!"

"Yeah? Maybe Lester was on his way. You think he was on his way? But when he saw the fire, he prob'ly just turned tail and run off 'cause it'd be a whole lot more important to him not to get caught over there than to stay and help your family save what they could. Don't you think? Isn't that like Lester? Right?"

"Shut up, Sarah! You don't know nothin'!"

"Franky prob'ly just heard you like before. And so you decided to blame him because it would be easy, wouldn't it? Everybody picks on him anyway. Your pa and your brothers would believe you because they think he's clumsy and odd. So you figured you could tell them whatever you wanted and they'd listen —"

"I didn't make it up. Franky was in the barn! He was!"

I'd always envied Rorey's cute dimpled cheeks and strawberry blonde curls, but right now she looked so ugly to me I couldn't hardly stand it. "Sure he was! Trying to save your pa's animals. But the fire was already started. Wasn't it? You tell me! Right now!"

"Oh, Sarah, leave me alone!" Suddenly something changed in her. She turned from me and sat facing the other way, hugging at her knees.

"Tell me what happened, Rorey."

"You're gonna tell."

"You should've told already! What'd Franky ever do to you that you'd try gettin' him in so much trouble?"

"Shut up."

"No! It's not fair. Rorey, you know it's not!"

She turned around at me, and she hardly looked like herself at all, her face was set so hard and angry. "It's not fair for Franky to act like he's my pa or somethin'! It's not fair for him to act like he's so wonderful all the time and try to be your folks' favorite! And the pastor's favorite! But he sure ain't Pa's favorite, I can tell you that!"

"I know that. I think everybody knows that. But it don't tell me why, or what happened."

"I told you what happened."

"No, you didn't. You told me what you want people to think."

"Leave me alone."

"You know Franky didn't try to blame you or Lester. Didn't say a word about it."

"I don't care."

"You should. He could tell people you're lying. He knows you are. Unless he thinks you're so confused you don't know any better. Wouldn't that be something? You trying to get him in trouble, and him making excuses for you."

"Sarah, shut up!" She jumped off the bed. For a minute I thought she was going to run out of the room, but she didn't. She stopped at the dresser where Katie and I kept our clothes and turned back around.

"Franky's not so wonderful. Pa says we'd

still have Mama if it weren't for him.'"

Whatever I'd been thinking, whatever I might have said, those words stopped me cold. "What?"

"We'd still have Mama if it weren't for him. Pa would be happier, an' things'd be easier —"

"What are you talking about? She was sick. I remember. Mom went over to help, but there was nothing she could do. How could that be Franky's fault?"

"You just don't understand."

"Then tell me!"

She sat down on the floor, and my mind whirled about. Was she lying to me again? Or would Mr. Hammond really say such a thing? It made me wonder how he treated Franky when none of us Worthams were around to see.

"Pa said Mama used to be stronger'n him. Strong as an ox. She could throw hay or throw him if she wanted to. She could do work like two men. But that changed when she had Franky. Even 'forehand. She got sick as a dog when she weren't never so sick with the older ones, an' after he was born she couldn't hardly do nothin'. She never did get her strength up. Lizbeth had to start doin' most her work."

"Rorey, there's no way that could be

Franky's fault. It'd be real stupid to blame him —"

"Just listen. That ain't all. Couple weeks 'fore Mama took sick worse the last time, Franky dropped a whole basket a' eggs, an' most of 'em broke. We was needin' 'em awful bad, an' Pa got on to him over it. You know Franky. He just runned away. In the col' weather like a fool, an' it was freezin' rain outside."

"Your pa musta been too hard on him."

"He was sick a' us not havin' stuff 'cause a' Franky losin' an' breakin' everythin'! All a' us was! How would you feel if you was wantin' breakfast an' your brother busted up the eggs! We didn't have much a' nothin' else! You know that!"

"Oh, Rorey. He must've felt terrible."

"I don't know 'bout that. I only know Mama got up outta bed an' went lookin' for him, her an' Lizbeth an' Sam, an' she hadn't oughta been out. She took a spell or somethin' an' fell over by the woodshed an' she couldn't even get up. They had to help her in, an' she was still only worryin' over Franky. An' if he hadn't even run off, it never woulda happened! She never did get better, Sarah! She just got worse an' worse, an' if Franky wasn't such a fussbudget clumsy coward, she mighta been okay!"

320

I could only stare at her for a moment. "If you and your pa are holdin' that against him, I don't know what to think. All that was just accidents."

"Well, you don't know what it's like havin' him for a brother. Pa says he's bleary headed, all caught up daydreamin' in the middle a' somethin' regular like puttin' up hay, till he don't even know what he's doin'. Gotta watch for him all the time. Only thing he can do right is work wood with your pa."

I sighed. "So why'd you go blaming him, Rorey? Don't he have enough problems?"

She shook her head. "It wasn't even my idea. Lester said I should tell everybody Franky did it. He said they'd believe me on account a' the way Franky is."

I felt an awful tingly feeling down inside me, cold and sour all at the same time. "You mean Lester did come?"

She was quiet for a minute, looking at me strange like she hadn't realized she'd said that. "Yeah," she finally answered. "I knew he would, because he likes me, Sarah, no matter what you think. We was in the barn an' pretendin' it was a dance hall an' there was music playin'. I wished you'd a' seen. I was hummin' an' singin' 'Tea for Two,' an' Lester was twirlin' me aroun' like we was good enough to be in a show!"

"How'd the fire start?" I asked, feeling heavier than I'd ever felt in my life. Didn't she know all the trouble she'd caused? Wasn't she even one bit sorry?

"He was leadin' me, an' we was dancin', but then goin' backward I think my foot hit the lantern. We didn't mean to, Sarah. We didn't really do nothin' wrong."

She looked like the same Rorey sitting there in front of me. My friend for more than seven whole years. But I didn't feel like I knew her very well at all, and I was suddenly getting really hot about it.

"So he told you to blame Franky, and he run off without stayin' to help? And you let everybody risk their lives and think it was Franky's fault? You almost killed my daddy, Rorey. You almost killed him, and you haven't even said you were sorry! You haven't even cared!"

She stood up slow, staring at me. She took a step backward, looking strangely white. "No," she said. "I didn't hurt him, Sarah. That wasn't my fault." She turned and took a step for the door.

"Yes, it was! It was an accident, but it was still your fault! And you're the coward, Rorey Jeanine, because you didn't tell anybody! And you could have! You could have come right out and said you were sorry!"

She took off running down the stairs. I should have let her go. I should have just been quiet. But I was so mad right then that I didn't think it through. I wanted her to hear me. I wanted her to stop and tell me, or my daddy or somebody, that she was sorry.

"Lester doesn't care about you!" I yelled after her. "Or he'd have stayed to help your pa! He only wanted to make sure he wasn't gonna get the blame, that's all!"

I ran down the stairs after her, not even caring that surely the others were hearing me by now. She got to the bottom of the stairs and kept right on going. So did I. "Daddy and Bert and Franky all got hurt because of *you!* While you were standing there doing nothing! Franky was trying to save my daddy, and you're telling people it was all his fault!"

"Shut up!" she screamed at me. "Shut up!"

Suddenly Mom was grabbing at me, and Kirk was grabbing for Rorey. "Girls! Girls!" Mom hollered. "What on earth?"

Rorey broke away from her brother.

"*She* did it!" I yelled. "*She* set the fire! I'm just trying to get her to say she's sorry!" I tried pulling away from Mom, but Robert got hold of me too. Rorey went charging through the kitchen and out the back door with Kirk behind her. I didn't pay any attention to where anybody else was.

"Lester was there, Mom!" I cried. "They were dancing in the barn and kicked over the lantern like a couple of fools! But she told everybody it was Franky! Just because she hates him, and Lester said to and —"

"Sarah."

At the sound of my father's voice I stopped.

"Sarah, come here."

He was in the chair in the sitting room, right where he'd been before. I went toward him, suddenly trembling.

"Pumpkin, it was still an accident, wasn't it?" he asked me.

"Y-yes."

"Then you need to tell her you're sorry for yelling at her. And don't do it again."

"But Daddy —"

"She'll have to come to terms with the rest. And that's not your job. Is that clear?"

19

Julia

Kirk and Franky both followed Rorey. I didn't know where she was going. It wasn't toward home, that was sure. I didn't know if it might be better just to let her go and cool off a minute. Surely she'd be back. But nothing like this had ever happened before, and I wasn't really sure what she might do.

I thought about following after them, but I had Katie and Emmie in the washtubs and Sarah all in a huff and Samuel to think about. And Bert, sitting here in the kitchen soaking his ankle in salts and looking at me funny.

"Did she really?" he asked me. "Did she really cause the fire?"

"That's not something we need to concern ourselves with at the moment," I told him. "It was an accident, like Mr. Wortham said. No use casting blame." I looked over at my son. "Robert, you and

Willy follow after them, please. I just want to be sure she comes back here or goes home. That's all. Don't give her a hard time."

Robert didn't say anything. He grabbed his hat and went outside like I'd told him to. Willy, on the other hand, looked at me with a smirk. "Lester, huh? Lester come aroun' dancin' with Rorey an' burned down our barn?"

"William, I think you'd better leave that alone."

"Ain't no wonder he didn't want her to tell." He strode outside, and I prayed it was to look for Rorey. But I had a bad feeling about it.

"Harry," I called, knowing he was the only one of the boys besides Bert still in the house. "Harry, go with William. And if he starts toward the Turreys' house, do what you can to stop him, or come and tell us, please. All right?"

"Yeah." He grabbed his hat and ran out. And I wondered if I'd done the right thing.

"Seems like things is bad right now," Berty observed.

I couldn't even answer him.

Little Emmie came out from behind the draped sheet in the corner with her hair dripping wet and her eyes wide and round.

"Pa's gonna be real mad at Rorey, ain't he?"

"I expect," I said with a sigh. "And I sure hope he uses a little wisdom."

"Will he quit bein' mad at Franky?"

"I hope so. But it's not going to serve him well being mad at anybody."

Katie came out from behind the sheet with the hairbrush in her hand. "I wish the pastor was still here," she said.

Sarah was so exhausted she just sat on the floor at her father's knee. Finally I made her get up and take a bath. She didn't want to. She didn't want to do anything. But she did. And then I took her upstairs and helped her get settled in the bed. She was crying the whole time. I knew she was, though she scarcely made a sound.

"I don't think Rorey's gonna be my friend anymore," she finally said. "I'm not sure I even want her to be."

"We're like family," I told her. "After a while, we'll put this behind us, and you and Rorey will be able to get close again."

"Are you sure about that?"

"You're like sisters. I never had a sister, but I expect if I had, we'd always be able to find ways to forgive and go on."

"Katie wouldn't never have done something like that."

"Rorey's had some problems, Sarah. She's not always had an easy time of it."

"Well, same thing for Katie, Mommy! Her own mother just took off and left her with Uncle Edward when he was a scary, rotten bum! And it's not always been easy for us either! I remember when we didn't have nothing to eat but the daylilies and the dandelions and stuff. At least now we got chickens and milk and all, but so do Hammonds. It's not so different."

"Every family's different. And every person deals with things differently."

"But it wasn't right for Rorey to lie."

"No, it wasn't."

"She hates Franky, Mom. So does their pa. He blames Franky for his mama bein' sick, but it wasn't his fault. It couldn't have been!"

"No. It certainly couldn't." Anger at George Hammond surfaced in me again. Could he truly think such a thing? But I only hugged Sarah, and she held on to me tight.

"I'm glad I got good folks, Mom. I'm glad Daddy's not mean like Mr. Hammond."

I could've defended George. Perhaps I should have, and I almost did. George Hammond certainly wasn't always mean.

He'd become a hard worker, and he seemed to be good to his children most of the time. But when it came to Franky, I had to admit he'd been less than fair. And not just recently.

I knew Katie and Emmie were downstairs needing to get to bed too. But I took just a little more time with Sarah alone, praying with her, hugging her again, and singing a short little song I hadn't sung in a couple of years, at least.

"I love you, Mom," she whispered. "And I'm sorry I didn't tell you about Lester sooner."

"We talked about that already. And it's all right."

"No. There was more I didn't tell you. I knew they were going to meet in the barn last night. She told me not to tell, and I didn't, but if I had, her pa or you and Daddy would've got all upset and stopped him from coming over, and then there wouldn't have been a fire, and Daddy would be okay —"

"Sarah, sweetie, it's not your fault."

"Yes, it is. If I'd have told, it wouldn't have happened. I'm so sorry. I won't keep any more secrets. I promise I won't."

I leaned and kissed her. "Well, I guess you did learn a lesson."

"But do you think Rorey will learn a lesson too?"

"I certainly hope so."

I went down the stairs praying. For Rorey mostly. Somewhere I'd heard that the first time a young person does something really bad, a significant bit of their future and the choices they make rest upon the kind of response they get. I prayed that our response to Rorey would be what she needed.

Berty was already in and out of the washtub by the time I came down. I knew he didn't like a bath and probably hurried through it a little too quickly, but I didn't question him. He was sitting on one end of the davenport with his leg on a cushion. Emmie was on the other end.

And Samuel was up and gone from that rocking chair. I don't know why I didn't notice right away.

Katie was standing in the doorway looking awfully worried. "Where's your dad?" I asked her.

"He went outside. I'm sorry, Mom. I knew you wouldn't want him to, but we thought we heard yelling and he just got up and told us to stay here —"

"Oh no."

"I'm sorry, Mom."

330

"Honey, it's not your fault. Please just see if you can get these two settled for the night."

I ran out the back door.

"Samuel?" Oh, why hadn't he called for me or just waited till I was downstairs? He had no business running outside after Rorey in his condition. He'd been so dizzy, and hurting, and —

I had to stop myself. I had to stop and think that Samuel was just being a father. Even though most of these kids were not ours, we'd been acting like they were at least partly ours for years now. I couldn't really expect him to stay in his chair. *Lord, let him be all right. Let everyone be all right!*

"Samuel?" I called again. This time I thought I heard something from the direction of the barn, maybe on the other side of it. I hurried just as fast as I could.

Samuel was standing up, leaning on the pasture fence. Robert was beside him. Rorey was plopped down in the dirt in front of them. And Franky was squatted down at her side. I didn't see Kirk or William or Harry anywhere.

Rorey was crying, I could tell that now. But she turned her back to Franky, even though it was incredible to me that he'd even followed her out of the house in the first place.

"Rorey —" he said.

"I don't wanna talk to you! I don't wanna talk!"

"You may as well come back in the house with the others and get some sleep then," Samuel told her. "You're not doing anybody any good sitting out here."

"I don't wanna come in. You all hate me now!"

"Nobody hates anyone around here," Samuel continued. "You can stop that foolishness and get yourself to bed."

There was an edge to Samuel's voice. Pain, I knew, just from getting out here. But more than that, he was angry. I hadn't heard that in his voice in quite a while.

"But you're gonna tell my pa!"

"You're absolutely right I will. Every single word. An accident is one thing. And that would've been the end of it, if that was all. But you've yet to show yourself sorry, girl. And I won't tolerate you being hateful to your family. Not any of your family. Do you understand me?"

"Well, I don't have to stay in your house!" she sputtered. "I don't have to do what you say!"

Samuel responded instantly. "You're

right. Start the truck, Robert. We're taking Rorey home."

"I'm not going home! Pa'll kill me!"

"I don't know what he'll do. But it won't be *that* bad, and you're going home if I have to carry you."

"Samuel —" I started.

He turned to look at me, but I didn't say anything else, and neither did he.

Rorey stood up. I couldn't believe she could be so defiant. "I'll walk."

"No," Samuel answered her. "We're going to make sure you get there. And that your father hears what he needs to. Right now, I don't care what his feelings are for Frank. He's got some growing up to do himself. But he'll not tolerate you cussing your brother, not if I know him like I think I do. And he sure won't tolerate you laying blame where it doesn't belong or disrespecting me. So come on to the truck and let's get going."

I saw his hand gripped tight on the top of the fence, and I knew he was steadying himself. Robert knew it too. He hadn't left to start the truck. He stood right there, ready to support his father. And it was very clear that Samuel needed it.

"Dad, you better get back to bed." Robert sounded scared. "I'll take her.

I'll do it by myself."

He shook his head. "Julia, go with —"

He just sunk down, all of a sudden. He tried to catch himself on the fence, but how that must have hurt! He cried out with the pain of it, just a little. He'd have gone all the way to the ground if Robert hadn't gotten hold of him.

"Samuel!" I cried, rushing to his side. "You shouldn't be out of bed, let alone clear out here!"

I glanced at Rorey. She was only standing there, staring at us.

"Do you think we can carry him, Mom?" Robert asked. "If Franky helps?"

"I can walk," Samuel told us.

"You've walked too much!" I protested.

"Just hold me," he said. "Just help me along."

With me on one side and Robert on the other, we got him to his feet again. Franky came up close beside me, trying to help. Together we made slow progress across the barnyard. I didn't say a thing to Rorey. I didn't know if she'd run off. I didn't know what she'd do. But without a word, she followed us, all the way to the house.

It was hardest getting Samuel up the porch steps. He seemed to pitch forward, and I probably wouldn't have managed very well without Franky's help. My heart was pounding.

We went straight to the bed. Katie ran to bring us the pillows. Finally when we got him settled, he didn't say a word to me. He just looked at Rorey with the pain in his eyes.

"Are you ready to go home?"

"Please don't send me," she begged. "I'll stay here."

"No." Samuel shook his head. "Too late. You're going home."

I could see the tears at the surface of her eyes. I might have spoken on her behalf, that it wouldn't hurt just to leave things alone for tonight and talk to George tomorrow, but I knew he was right. The way she'd spoken to him, the way she'd acted, she hadn't left us much choice.

"I'll drive her," Robert said again. "Mom oughta stay here with you."

Samuel was breathing kind of hard. I took the cloth from the bowl at the bedside table and bathed his forehead with it. I hoped its wetness felt good to him.

"Maybe I should go," Franky said.

"Where are Kirk and William?" I finally thought to ask. "And Harry?"

"Kirk didn't come back in?" Samuel asked.

"None of 'em did," Katie answered.

"Oh no," I said aloud. "Samuel, what if they've gone after Lester? Now what?"

"They wouldn't," Rorey declared. "They wouldn't dare! Would they?"

"Willy would," I told her, and nobody argued.

"Maybe Kirk and Harry followed him," Katie suggested. "Maybe they'll stop him from doing anything too stupid."

"Let's hope so." I had such a sour feeling in my stomach. I should have gotten hold of that Willy and kept him in my sight. I very well knew what was running through his mind.

Samuel closed his eyes for just a second. "I'd go after them," he said with the pain in his voice, "but, Juli, I can't —"

"Honey, I know. I know. Please don't even think about getting up again."

"Maybe I oughta go after Dr. Hall," Robert said gravely.

"No," Samuel told him. "You drive by Turreys', and if those boys are there, you get 'em in the truck or get their father. Franky, do you think you can walk your sister home?"

"Yes, sir."

"I can go by myself," Rorey protested. "Or maybe I ought to go to Turreys'."

"You'll go with your brother," Samuel said again. "And you'll tell the truth when you get over there, or your pa will hear it from me and things'll go that much worse."

"Yes, sir," she said, her head sinking down. "I . . . I'm sorry. I'm sorry you got hurt."

Samuel was silent for just a moment. "Well. That's a good start."

20

Franky

Rorey didn't say much walkin' across the timber. I knew she'd do what Mr. Wortham said an' tell the truth once she got there, or she'd catch it worse. But I started wishin' it was Kirk or maybe Sam with her, 'cause I didn't figure it'd help matters to have me showin' up over there. Maybe Mr. Wortham had done that on purpose, I don't know, but me bein' there might just make everythin' that much harder for Pa to swallow.

She cried a little bit, an' I got to thinkin' on what Pastor said once about godly sorrow workin' repentance. I hoped that's what I was seein' in Rorey. I almost said somethin' about it, only I didn't figure it'd do much good right then. I'd kinda learned Rorey pretty good the last few years, and most a' the time she didn't want to hear too much from me.

A screech owl cried. Rorey jumped. And I told her it wasn't nothin' to be scared of. She slowed down some and quit walkin' so much off ahead a' me.

I got to thinkin' 'bout things and decided I didn't know Rorey so good as I thought I did. Nor Sarah Jean neither. I didn't think I ever did hear Sarah holler before, let alone be screamin' at Rorey. I wouldn't a' thought it to happen, not in a million years.

We got so far as the creek and Rorey stopped and stared down at the water all dark and ripply in the dim light a' the moon.

"What do you think Pa'll do?" she asked me.

"Can't say. I don't exactly remember you bein' in much trouble with him before."

She looked at me kinda scared. "What would he do if it was you?"

"Scream a while. You know 'bout that. What all else, I ain't for sure this time. I wouldn't worry too much, though, 'cause he favors you."

"Not no more'n Sam or Harry or Kirk —"

I didn't even answer. If she didn't know, there wasn't no use tellin' her. Rorey was no angel. Never had been no angel. But Pa wasn't one to correct her over nothin', nor even to notice her needin' correction. Lizbeth'd notice. But the last few years, 'tween school and then gettin' married, Lizbeth wasn't around much.

"How come you ain't never told the Worthams about Pa?" Rorey asked me all of a sudden.

"What about Pa? They see plenty of him."

"You know what I mean. How come you ain't never told 'em about him whippin' you?"

"He's lit in to Harry and Willy a few times too," I said, wishing she'd quit talkin' and get back to headin' home like we were supposed to.

"Not so much as you," she persisted. "I figured a long time ago you'd tell. Mr. Wortham, he'd set Pa down for a talkin' to. He's partial to you, an' he wouldn't like it."

"They're always dealin' with things. They don't need no more."

"Willy says you're too yellow. Scared even to tell, 'cause Pa'll lick you worse."

It shouldn't have been no surprise that Willy and Rorey'd been discussin' me like that. I didn't know what to say, so I didn't say nothin'.

"You think he'll beat me?"

"I don't know, Rorey. Won't be bad with Lizbeth there. She can rein him in pretty good, most times. But I reckon you'll jus' have to take whatever he gives 'cause he's your pa." I almost wanted to tell her she had it coming, but I didn't add that part. I guess I wasn't sure how I'd feel if he was really hard on her. And I didn't know why she was askin' 'bout the way he treated me. It never seemed to matter to her before.

She got up and started walking again. "Franky?"

"What?"

"Are you really scared to tell?"

Her askin' me again made me mad, but I wasn't gonna say so. "Are you?" I demanded. "I ain't heard you nor Willy sayin' nothin' to the Worthams 'bout it neither!"

"I guess we don't wanna talk about our pa."

"Well, I guess I'm the same way, then. The Bible says to honor your father and your mother, an' we only got Pa left, an' I ain't gonna go turnin' nobody against him."

She was quiet a while. We went on walking. "Once in a while Lizbeth asks me how Pa's been with you," she finally said. "I think she figures you wouldn't tell her straight."

"I sure wouldn't lie."

"But you wouldn't tell it all neither."

"Neither would you."

"Kirk thinks we oughta tell. 'Bout him drinkin' again. Sam an' Lizbeth an' the Worthams'd all be sore upset."

I took her arm and made her stop an' look at me. I guess I wasn't sure anymore what kinda stuff might be goin' through her brain. "Don't you be threatenin' him to keep from gettin' in trouble. Don't you tell him you'll tell if he does anythin' to you."

"Why not? Huh, Franky? Why shouldn't I tell?"

" 'Cause it wouldn't be honorin' him, especially not now. You take what you got comin' first if it's gotta be told."

"That sounds like somethin' you'd say."

"It *is* something I'd say, 'cause I done said it! And I mean it too! Maybe we oughta tell, I don't know. But not tonight. Tonight you gotta face up to yourself."

"What's that supposed to mean?"

"Examine yourselves, whether ye be in the faith. Prove your own selves."

"Are you talkin' Bible again?"

"Yes. Paul said that. An' plenty more. Now I pray to God that ye do no evil; not that we should appear approved, but that ye should do that which is honest —"

"Oh, shut up."

I did. 'Cause it don't do any good to give word to somebody hateful at it. But she changed her tune. At least a little bit.

"What's that mean, anyway?"

"I think it means we're s'posed to do what's right, not just so we can look like good folks but because it's right. Being honest an' all."

"You're a bother to listen to sometimes."

I guess I was feelin' ranckled more than I ought, 'cause I answered her back. "Is the preacher a bother too?"

"Sometimes."

She took off walkin' fast again, and I had an awful time keepin' up, but I sure wasn't gonna lose sight of her. "Slow down, will you?"

"Why?" she shouted back. "Ain't you glad I'm in a hurry? It shows I'm brave."

"Only shows you don't like to listen." I said that pretty quiet. I don't think she heard. Leastways, she didn't slow down. We come by the pond and Mama's grave, an' I was feelin' awful close to keelin' over. I guess I didn't realize how tired I was, and here she was runnin' me through the woods when nothin'd feel better than a bed. But I kept goin' till she finally stopped.

She just stood real still for a while. Then she turned around and looked at the graves behind us. Mama's under the birch trees with the flowers all around. And Mr. and Mrs. Graham's up on the hill above the pond. I didn't say nothin'. I just waited to see what Rorey was up to now.

"You ever think about 'em?"

"Sure. Lots. 'Specially Mama. But Mrs. Graham too. She was a real good friend to us."

"You killed 'em both. Did you know that?"

I'd heard a' such a thing as a spirit of lies, and I figured maybe that was what come on Rorey just then. There weren't no sense to it, for anybody with a thinkin' brain. I wasn't but eight years old when Mama and Mrs. Graham died. An' they'd both been sick a long time. I used to blame myself, 'cause crazy as it sounds, just a few days apart, I broke their clocks. Both of 'em. And even though Mrs. Graham was already dead when hers got broke, I'd felt awful bad and blamed myself. But the Worthams weren't a wit superstitious, and they taught me better. For a minute I wondered if Rorey knew about the clocks, but I didn't think she did.

"You made Mama sick. She was sick just birthin' you, an' then you made her sick

344

worse runnin' out lookin' for you that icy mornin'. You remember runnin' off, after you broke them eggs?"

"Yeah," I said kind of quiet. I hadn't thought on that in a long time.

"Well, that's when Mama started gettin' worse. An' Mrs. Graham wouldn't a' took worse if she hadn't come over in a snowstorm with Mrs. Wortham to see after Mama. It wore her out, an' she just couldn't handle it."

"She wanted to come."

"That don't change nothin'. It was your fault."

I didn't answer her for a minute. Then I just started sayin' the first Scripture to come in my head. "There is therefore now no condemnation to them that are in Christ Jesus —"

"Oh, shut up! If you ever wondered why Pa hates you, well, that's why! 'Cause a' Mama! He don't say nothin' much, but he still misses her so bad it 'bout makes him sick! He told me so! That's why he's drinkin'. An' thinkin' about goin' to meet her —"

"Did Pa say that?"

"Oh, shut up! You know I'm not lyin'!"

"I know you are. I just ain't sure how much of it."

"He don't like your smart mouth neither. You always think you know what's right."

"We better just go, Rorey."

"I'll go when I feel like it. Mr. Wortham said to see that I got there, not make me follow your lead."

"Pride goeth before destruction," I told her. "An' a haughty spirit before a fall. Better it is t' be of a humble spirit —"

"You're drivin' me crazy! Shut up! I oughta tell Pa that Mr. Wortham sent me over here with *you* an' that's punishment enough!"

I just started walkin', figurin' there wasn't another thing I could do. She could follow me or not, and face up to whatever consequences were to come of it. I guess I was pretty upset with her. I hadn't figured she'd ever be one to cry crocodile tears at me the way she'd done when she promised she wasn't gonna see Lester no more. But she was just fudgin' me so I wouldn't say nothin'.

I guess a piece of me was hoping Willy had got to Turreys' place before anybody could stop him. Then maybe Lester'd get some a' what he had comin'. But that weren't exactly the right way to think. And just the same way, I was kind of glad Rorey was gonna catch it for lyin' 'bout me. But I was sorry for her too, 'cause it's awful terrible to be lost outside of God's righteousness and I sure hoped she'd come around to seekin' forgiveness. Besides that, I know real well what it's like havin' Pa's yelling temper turned your way. And it kind of scared me not knowin' what he'd do.

She followed me after a little while. I didn't reckon she figured she had much choice, since Mr. and Mrs. Wortham'd be talking to Pa soon enough.

I thought about how they'd believed Sarah even though she'd been so yellin' upset. An' I wished there could be days when I could count on Pa believin' me. Did he really think I killed Mama? She'd told me once that birthin' me was hard, but that's the way a' things, she'd said. Can't be helped. She even told me she was glad I come out okay, 'cause she wondered there for a while if I would. Now I wondered how Pa felt about that. Maybe he wouldn't have mourned too bad if I'd have died.

But that was hard stuff to think, and I pushed it out of my head. I was glad Lizbeth and Ben had stayed with Pa because that meant he wouldn't be drunk. Nothing too awful crazy would happen. He might be mad at me for comin', at least till he knew Mr. Wortham had sent me. But he wouldn't never get mad at Mr. Wortham. We all owed him way too much.

21

Julia

I hated that the big boys were all gone and Samuel was hurting so bad and there was nothing at all I could do. Katie had gotten Emmie asleep upstairs. She said Sarah was asleep too, and I was glad about that because she needed it.

I prayed. I prayed that everything would come out all right tonight. We didn't need a bit more trouble. Berty'd gone to sleep on the davenport, and I was hoping that Samuel could sleep too. But I knew he wouldn't. He'd wait up till everybody was accounted for, just the same as I would.

Katie made me a cup of tea and warmed up what was left of the mullein and nettle tea for Samuel. I got him to sip it, but that was all. I don't know how he'd managed getting outside and all the way to the barn. He was hurting for it now. I checked his leg and I checked him all over and couldn't see anything worse, but that was small comfort, not being able to see on the inside.

"Can I do anything for you?" I asked him.

"No."

"Is your head the worst again?"

"Yeah." He kept his eyes closed, but I knew he wasn't anywhere near sleeping. "I'll be all right," he told me. "I just need to lie still a while. Things are whirling again."

"How's your side?"

He knew the worry in my voice. "Same. Juli, it's all right. Really."

I didn't believe him. And I knew that he knew I didn't. But he'd said those words anyway, partly because he wanted me to hear them and partly for Katie, who was still close by.

"Now the house is too empty," I said.

"Not for long." Samuel reached his hand toward me, and I took it, hanging on to him tightly.

"I hope those boys had the good sense not to go banging on Mr. and Mrs. Turrey's door," I told him. "What do you suppose they'd do?"

Samuel took a deep breath. "If Willy's spoiling for a fight, he'd go banging at

Turreys', all right. Or yelling till he gets their attention. But he may be in for a surprise if Lester's brothers are home."

That was an unsettling thought, to say the least. "Did we do the right thing, sending Robert?"

"He won't get in a fight over Rorey, honey. Or over George's barn."

"But he would over you."

Samuel was quiet for a moment, and then he shook his head. "I should've gone with him."

"No, you absolutely should not! You can't be up like that. Don't even think of it again, not till you're stronger."

"Juli —"

"We did the best we knew, sending Robert. You told him to get George if he needed help. He's sensible. And the Hammond boys listen to him. Surely it'll be all right. I shouldn't have doubted. I shouldn't have asked you about it."

He just lay back against the pillows with barely a nod. "Sorry about this, Juli. I don't guess I handled it very well."

"Oh, Samuel, stop. What could either of us do?"

Katie walked up and hugged on me, and then she hugged Samuel. "You always do the best you can," she said. "You always handle things fine. You can't help it if other people fly off the handle in all directions."

"Thank you," Samuel told her.

"The only one I'm worried about is Rorey," she continued. "If the boys all get in a fight, at least it'll be over and done before long. But Rorey thinks she's all grown up, and not even Sarah's gonna change her mind about that."

We were all quiet for a minute until the old cuckoo clock sang the hour to fill the void. *What a sensible girl Katie is,* I thought. *What a blessing to us.*

We prayed together. Samuel, Katie, and I, for Robert and the other boys to return home safely and quickly. And for Rorey to realize the folly of her ways that had caused so much pain.

"Do you think Sarah knew about this before tonight?" Samuel asked me.

"Not everything. She was far too upset to be able to hold all that in. Maybe Rorey told her about the fire when she went upstairs. Or maybe she figured it out somehow, I don't know."

I tried to get Katie to go to bed. I knew she had to be tired. I couldn't remember if she'd slept any through the day or not. Finally she laid herself down in one of the sitting room chairs, and I brought her a stool to put her feet on. "I wish the pastor was still here," she said again.

"He had to go. He had to be a comfort to Dr. Howell's family. But he'll be back."

Just the mention of the doctor's wife made me remember the cake I'd made still sitting on the counter and until this moment forgotten. Why on earth hadn't I sent it with Robert the moment we finished supper? I should've been thinking about that instead of reading from that book Franky brought.

But something about that book had started this whole thing tonight. Or maybe it was something about Franky. I remembered the way Sarah had looked at him before running up the stairs. That's what it was. She must have realized he was being falsely accused, just like Silas Marner. And she wasn't going to let it be.

Katie was asleep within a few minutes, even though she'd stayed downstairs on purpose to wait with us for the boys. I was glad she slept. She'd well earned her rest, and I had a feeling it would be better if she wasn't involved when the boys first came in. I would've moved her up the stairs, but she was too big for me to manage without waking her.

Every one of the kids has gotten so big,
I thought as I pulled a cover over Katie.
Robert was almost a man, and this would
be his last year of high school. None of us
knew what he'd choose to do after that.
Willy Hammond was the same way, and
Kirk was even a little older. Joe and Sam
and Lizbeth were already on their own.
And Sarah, Katie, and Rorey were already
teenagers. Or at least almost. Katie was
only twelve. But she seemed older than the
other two much of the time.

Glancing up at her peaceful face, I
thought about Sarah calling the three girls
triplets when they were younger. They'd
always done an awful lot together. But in
recent years, the threesome had been a
twosome. Either Sarah and Rorey, or Sarah
and Katie. Rorey and Katie hardly ever did
anything together anymore.

I went to get Berty a blanket, thinking
about Katie's mother still off someplace
trying to have a singing career. We only
heard tiny fragments about her from
Katie's grandma, who only wrote us at
Christmastime. Neither of them knew
what they were missing, not being around
to see Katie grow up.

But I was glad her father wasn't around.
Sometimes Samuel still dreamed about

him. At those times I wondered if I ought to tell the children more — they didn't know for sure that Katie was Samuel's half sister and not his niece or his cousin. We'd never talked much about it. Katie knew, or at least she had when we told her she was staying, but she'd never mentioned it again in the years since then. And she'd taken to calling Samuel "Dad" the very first week, maybe in an effort to fit in with Robert and Sarah.

Samuel's mother knew too. And I'm sure she wasn't exactly thrilled to learn about us taking in a child of her first husband's indiscretion. But she never answered us a word about it. Life had brought a lot of changes. Katie and us and Hammonds, all intertwined.

I walked into the bedroom and sat in silence at the foot of our bed. Samuel opened his eyes for just a moment, but he didn't say anything.

"Are you all right?" I asked him.

"Yes, Juli. And I want you to believe that. I can't stand seeing you stew."

I sighed.

"Come here. Please."

His eyes looked so in earnest, so serious. I moved closer, wondering what he might say.

"They'll be fine. It'll all come out fine. Okay? Come up here and lie down beside me. There's nothing we can do right now, so you may as well get rested up. We want to look strong and courageous for church tomorrow, right? Not frazzled and worn."

"How can you think of going to church tomorrow?"

"We have a lot to be thankful for. And a lot we need the church to pray for. Don't you think?"

"You know what I mean. It was too much for you, just going to the barn! You and these kids'll give me a head of gray hair before the weekend's out."

"Well," he said with a tiny smile, "you'll still be pretty when you're gray."

"I'm glad you can smile," I said, fighting back a sudden invasion of tears. "I'm glad you're finding something light, because I'm not! I feel like things are falling down around us. I thought the kids were growing up sensible. Katie said she was only worried about Rorey, but I'm not so sure any of them are doing as well as we thought, except maybe Katie herself."

"It's not so bad as that, is it?"

"I don't know. Maybe not. It's just that tonight looks pretty bad. And it doesn't help matters for you to talk about riding into town tomorrow over those bumpy roads, and climbing the church steps, and sitting in those hard pews! Oh, Samuel, you know I like church, but I'd be sitting there knowing you were hurting. I just don't think —"

He reached for my hand and pulled me a little nearer. "We don't have to go. Not if it's going to bother you. But I thought sitting still in the front of the truck, with a cushion or two I could make it. Tell you the truth, I don't think George'll go, and I wanted to be there to talk to some of the men. He needs help. More than I can give. He needs a barn up by winter, and I thought we could start planning a day —"

"A barn raising?"

"Yes. If you'd consent to feed a crowd. I'm sure some of the church ladies would help you. And for the men to gather on George's behalf, well, I can't think of anything that'd do him better good right now."

He was right. I knew he was right. "But you don't have to go," I told him. "You don't have to be the one to ask them. We can send some of the boys."

He nodded, just a little. "All right. If you'd feel better about it. All right."

"Church would do them good tomorrow anyway."

He smiled again. I climbed up beside him the way I had this afternoon and laid my head on his shoulder. He held me close. And I prayed for him again and for Robert and Willy and the rest. And Rorey, facing her father right about now.—And Franky. Maybe George would see it clear to apologize to him. I sure did hope so.

22

Franky

Rorey hesitated awful bad when we come in sight of the house. I can't say that I blamed her for that, but talking to Pa was something to get over with, no way around it. I took her hand just to help her keep her feet going, but she didn't like that.

"I'm comin'!" she protested. "Just leave me alone!"

I was the first one on the porch, and though we'd stopped talking by then, someone must have heard us, because the door swung open before we got to it. At first I thought maybe Robert had come here and told 'em we were comin'. But there weren't no truck. Just Ben and Lizbeth's car.

It was Lizbeth standin' there lookin' out. She didn't even look at us at first. She was just starin' out over the field. I thought I heard her whisper somethin', and then she seen me and jumped.

"Franky! What are you doing —"

She stopped real quick seein' Rorey behind me. Of course, it might have been a surprise us walkin' over here together at night like this. But Rorey had her head down all weepy, and I guess that's what got Lizbeth's attention.

"What's wrong? What happened?" Lizbeth was scared. I could hear it in her voice. She wasn't wantin' more bad news.

"Everybody's all right," I assured her. "It ain't nothin' like that."

Rorey sniffed. I hoped her tears was real.

"Who's come?" Pa suddenly shouted, and I could tell just by that much he weren't in no pleasant mood tonight. But after the kind of day and night we had, I couldn't be surprised.

"It's Franky and Rorey, Pa," Lizbeth explained. Ben came out and stood beside her.

"I told 'em to stay the night over there!" Pa yelled back. But then he came to the door too, and I could tell his first thoughts were like Lizbeth's. "What is it? Is Mr. Wortham takin' a turn for the worse?"

"No, Pa," I said. "He says he's makin' it all right." I didn't tell him about him almost fallin' outside and all the pain he was in. That wouldn't help matters just now, I knew.

"Well, then what is it?" Pa asked, sounding kind of rough again. I didn't answer this time. It was Rorey's to do if she was going to. It wasn't my job to tell.

"Mr. — Mr. Wortham sent us," Rorey finally said. "He said I had to come."

"Why?" It was Lizbeth asking. Pa just stared.

"I . . . I was so upset, I just didn't know to think on things right. And — I . . . I shoulda said somethin' sooner . . ."

Lord help. I could tell right now that Rorey was trying to find herself an out, and I felt sorry for her awful bad. If we confess our sins, he's faithful and just to forgive our sins. But that don't apply if we're tryin' to sneak out of it. So she was in trouble. I knew that. And trouble with the Almighty and your own deceivin' heart's even worse than trouble with Pa.

"What are you talkin' 'bout, girl?" Pa demanded.

"The fire," she said through a whole new bunch of tears. "The fire, Pa — it wasn't Franky. It wasn't. I shoulda told you . . . but I was scared."

"You come in and tell us now," Lizbeth said, and she sounded stern. I knew that if

Rorey really did tell the truth, even through a bunch of tears, Lizbeth'd see it clear. She was wise. I hoped Pa would be wise too, for Rorey's sake. Sometimes he was.

We went in, and everybody sat down on some of the chairs scattered around. I noticed that most of 'em was out of place, and so was the afghan that was usually 'cross the back of the rocker. And the teapot was settin' on the floor. I hoped they'd moved everythin' for some reason and Pa hadn't gone off the handle shovin' things.

Rorey just sat there wringin' her hands in her lap and lookin' miserable.

"Can you tell us what's going on?" Lizbeth asked me.

"Nope. Mr. Wortham said she had to."

Rorey gave me a sideways glance.

"Lord touch you," I said. And she frowned.

"Well, go on then," Pa prompted, and Rorey busted up with the tears again.

"I'm so sorry! I'm so sorry, Pa! I didn't tell you the truth! Lester, he told me I should blame Franky, and I was just so scared —"

"Lester?" Lizbeth asked. Pa folded his arms and didn't say a word.

"Lester Turrey come over last night. He wanted to see me. He wanted to go out to the barn, an' I did because he wanted to so bad. I didn't think it'd hurt nothin' just to talk or somethin'. I didn't think it'd hurt —"

She stopped and wiped at her eyes with her sleeve, and I just shook my head. *Let nothing that's covered not be revealed, and nothing that's hid not be known.*

"What happened?" Lizbeth asked. She was lookin' kind of pale, and Ben took hold of her hand. They were good for each other. That was somethin' to be glad about.

"He . . . he wanted to dance," Rorey started up again. "I shouldn't a' listened. But I didn't think it'd hurt nothin'! I wasn't really thinkin' good. So I let him. But . . . but . . . when he was dancin' me around, we hit the lantern, and it . . . it . . ."

"It burnt down the barn an' near all my livin'." Pa finished for her.

"I'm sorry! Oh, Pa, I'm so sorry! I wanted to tell you! But he — he told me not to, an' I was scared . . ."

Pa stood up, and even though he wasn't lookin' at me, I felt that same awful tight feelin' I always get. Rorey practically busted all apart, leanin' her head clear to her lap and cryin' her eyes out. I never seen such stuff outta nobody.

"So this boy come right over and talked you into dancin'."

She nodded, wipin' away at all the tears. "I'm sorry, Pa!"

"Why didn't you just tell him to go home or come an' ask me in the daylight?"

"Because . . . because he said . . . he said he really liked me and he didn't want to walk all that way home, an' I was scared to ask you 'cause you might think it was my idea. I was going to tell you, Pa. I was going to tell you, but then the fire happened and I was scared and Lester told me not to and I didn't know what he'd do and I thought you was gonna hate me —"

She busted apart all over again. It was kind of disgustin' to see. Lizbeth turned her eyes to look at me, and I figured that was all right. I figured she might be seein' what I was seein'. But then Pa started lookin' at me too.

"I s'pose you come so's you could say you told me so."

The tight in my gut started stretchin' clear to my toes. I had a awful time just answerin' him. "No, Pa. Mr. Wortham told me to come."

"And that was fine with you, I'm sure. Did you tell him you would?"

"Yes, sir, because —"

"Because you wanted to watch, didn't you? You wanted to see if I'd give Rorey a lickin' even though she's scared of some big cuss of a boy and heartbroke over all this."

There wasn't much of a way to answer. I felt like somebody was buryin' me under the ashes of our barn. I couldn't even hardly breathe. "No, sir. Mr. Wortham told me to come."

"Well, you can go on back! You don't need to be sittin' here starin' at your sister no more!"

"Pa!" Lizbeth protested. "What's got into you tonight? He's just mindin' Mr. Wortham. There's no call you bein' so hateful."

"I'm just tired of it," Pa said. "I'm just tired a' him actin' so perfect for the Worthams, an' then comin' over here like —"

I didn't think I could stand to hear whatever he'd say I was like. So I just stood up and turned around to the door.

"Where do you think you're goin'?"

I didn't answer. I didn't figure he ought to need me to. He already told me to go back.

"I ain't through with you yet."

"Oh, Pa, he can't help it!" Rorey suddenly cried. "Don't you know he always runs when things is hard? You know that! It ain't his fault I done what Lester tol' me to! He's got every right in the world to be mad at me. He'll prob'ly never ever forgive me!"

I couldn't hardly believe it. I wondered if she knew what she was doin' or if it was the evil one snarin' her soul. But Pa was lookin' at me like I was some foul thing.

"Ain't you the good ol' Christian that goes around spoutin' Scripture all the time?" Pa asked me. "You better well forgive. 'Less you're wantin' to be a hypocrite."

"Pa, there's no cause you givin' Franky this kind of talk."

Lizbeth was stickin' up for me. I felt so good about that, I almost couldn't keep from cryin' all of a sudden. But I didn't want Pa to see it. And there weren't nothin' at all I could say to him just then. So I went on for the door.

Blessed are they which are persecuted. The thought popped in my head sudden. I wasn't sure if I was being persecuted or not, but I was glad at least I hadn't answered back my pa. I guess God'd forgive me for walkin' away from him like this.

Lizbeth kept sayin' somethin' to Pa, but I was feelin' too fuzzy headed even to hear. I grabbed for the porch rail on my way out and kind of misjudged, I guess, because instead of gettin' hold of it, I whacked my hand on the side. It hurt. And funny thing was, I was glad about that hurt because it seemed to take away some of the hurt in my gut just for a minute.

I didn't really want to go and tell Mr. and Mrs. Wortham what just happened. I didn't know if I could without endin' up in more trouble over it when Pa found out. After all, Rorey'd confessed, all right. She'd said she lied about me, and that her and Lester started the fire after meetin' together in the barn without gettin' nobody's permission. She'd said everythin' she was supposed to say. And got Pa thinkin' I was some kind of hypocrite for thinkin' she oughta get in trouble.

Blessed are ye, when men shall revile you, and persecute you, and shall say all manner of evil against you falsely, for my sake. Rejoice, and be exceeding glad: for great is your reward in heaven: for so persecuted they the prophets which were before you.

All those words come rushing in my

mind. I remembered they were part of what's called the Beatitudes; we learned 'em in Sunday school a couple of years back. But they made me feel awful bad right now, and the crying I was trying to avoid kind of spilled out. Because I knew I wasn't bein' persecuted for the Lord's sake. Pa wasn't mad at me over lovin' the Lord. He just plain didn't like me, and that weren't for nobody's sake but my own.

I heard footsteps behind me, and at first I thought it was Rorey. I wasn't going to turn around. I didn't care what kind of thing she'd come up with to say. But then as I went across the yard and the footsteps just got closer, it didn't sound so much like her. Nor Pa neither, 'cause these feet were lighter. I turned around, and it was Ben reachin' out his arm.

"Frank, Lizbeth told me I ought to follow. She probably would herself, but she's still trying to talk some sense at your pa. I hope it takes."

I didn't say anythin'. I just kept on walkin'.

"Are you all right?"

"Sure," I told him. "Ain't nothin' wrong with me but a little burn and a nail scratch. I wouldn't be wearin' no bandage e'cept Mrs. Wortham insisted."

Ben was quiet kind of long, and I kept walkin'. But he followed me. "The last I knew there was something more than that," he said. "Something about somebody beating you up yesterday."

"That's like old hist'ry by now."

"Frank," he told me kind of low, "your big sister loves you."

I almost choked on the stupid tears. "I know it."

"It's not right the way your pa does with you."

"He's just Pa."

"Tonight he's just wrong."

I didn't say nothin'. I figured Ben would go back in the house and be with Lizbeth. I figured he'd turn around real quick 'cause we were almost to the timber and he'd already said enough to make me feel at least a little better. But he didn't turn around. He followed me right into the trees. I wondered about Lizbeth handlin' Rorey and Pa both. But if anybody could, she could.

"Has he been like this all your life?"

"I don't know."

"It's worried Lizbeth some that he might've gotten worse after she left."

"She . . . she just had a way a' makin' things all right," I managed to say.

"I'm sorry."

That was a mighty strange thing for him to say, and I told him so. "Seems like you hadn't oughta be sorry over her leavin', or it'd sound like you's sorry to be married. I ain't sorry 'bout that. I think it's fine, Lizbeth bein' so happy."

"She's not always happy."

I turned around to look at him, even though I hadn't wanted him to see that my cheeks were wet. "What do you mean? Why ain't she happy?"

"Well, besides worrying about all of you, she's been a little upset with me lately."

I could feel my fists foldin' up, even though I knew good and well that wouldn't be no proper way to deal with nothin'. "What for?" My voice sounded kind of mean, even to me.

"I've been wanting children. Lots of children. I guess I asked her one too many times if she didn't think it was time to get started on that."

"That don't seem to be somethin' that's my business."

"Maybe not. But I just wanted to ask you, Frank. Do you think it might be because of your pa? Or all of you not having enough? Do you think maybe she's worried that I won't be fair?"

I was close to chokin' again, just tryin' to

figure why he'd be asking *me* somethin' like that. "Maybe she's tired. Maybe she don't wanna have to deal with so much as Mama had or go through the pain a' birthin'. She was with Mama for the younger ones, even though they always shooed the rest of us outside. Most girls maybe don't know so much about it as Lizbeth knows."

"You're probably right. Thanks."

"I didn't do nothin' solvin' the problem. You's still of one mind and her the other."

"Maybe. But just understanding a little better helps me."

We went walkin' on without talkin'. I wasn't really sure why he stayed with me. But it felt good, and he felt like family. Like we had a good understandin'. I'd felt that way with Mr. Wortham plenty of times, and with Sam or Joe once or twice. But I didn't ever remember it with my other brothers. Nor Pa. Not even once.

23

Julia

Finally we heard the truck in the driveway. Samuel was trying to sit up, but I told him to stay put right where he was. I'd make every one of those boys come and answer for where they'd been.

Robert was the first to come in. Maybe they'd talked it over and decided he ought to, because by far he looked the best.

"I found them," he told me. "They're all right."

Then Harry came in with his shirt all ripped in the front and Kirk with what was going to be a black eye to rival Franky's. Willy was the worst. He was messed up all over. My heart was pounding, and I was upset for them and angry at them all at the same time.

"You went and fought. All of you. You went and fought at Lester Turrey. When you know that won't solve anything! And they're not even churchgoers! What are they going to think of Christians acting that way?"

"It was just gonna be me," Willy said. "But you sent Harry along."

"To stop you!"

"Well, he didn't figure it was right what Lester done."

"An' I was gonna go get Pa, on account of Rorey," Kirk explained. "But I met up with 'em in the timber an' I remembered Lester's brothers. I didn't figure they could handle it just the two of 'em."

"What about you?" I turned to Robert. "Did you get yourself involved too?"

"I just went to bring 'em home," he said. "But there was five of 'em. Didn't look like they'd get away without help."

"Oh, Robby."

"Well, Mom, don't you think Willy's right? Don't you think Lester's got it coming after what he did? And he's the one who's too much the coward to own up, and blaming it on Franky. That's the stinkin'est thing I ever heard!"

"Even if there was five of 'em, we done all right," Willy added. "You oughta see 'em. They look worse than us."

"That is not the point! Didn't you hear what I said?"

Exasperated almost beyond words, I ushered them all in so Samuel could take a good look. He didn't seem as upset as I was.

"Well, I can't say that I'm surprised," he told them. "I suppose I might've had some hotheaded days when I was younger when I'd have done the same thing. But that doesn't make it right. You all understand that, don't you?"

Robert and Kirk nodded. I couldn't see a sign of regret from the other two.

"Sometime, hopefully soon, you'll think about this a little more and realize that fighting's usually not the best way, even if it feels right at the time. I'm not sure yet what to do about this. I guess it'll wait till morning when we've all had some rest. Was Lester's father home? What did he say about it?"

"Nothin' at first," Kirk told us. "I guess he figures a fight'll happen now and then. But he got tired of it toward the end and come out with his shotgun."

"That's when we left," Robert added. "I was glad I could pull the one kid off of Harry so we could go."

I had a hard time restraining myself from saying more. But Samuel just told them to go and wash the best they could in the bathwater that was left in the kitchen and get themselves to bed.

"The world's gone crazy around us," I said as the boys were leaving the room. "Every last one of them, even Robert."

"Well, there was a sister involved for three of them, not to mention the barn. And for Robert, you told me about that already."

"That doesn't excuse them."

"No. But I doubt there's a man in the country who wouldn't understand it."

"Samuel . . ."

"I know. I'm not endorsing fighting to solve your problems. I'm just saying the way things were sprung on them, we can't be surprised. And we'll have to take that into consideration. I'm sure George will."

"Oh, George picks and chooses what to take into consideration! He wouldn't give Franky half a chance to explain himself, and Franky was innocent all along! And I suppose with this he'll say his boys were just being boys and look the other way."

"I don't know. But I sure will talk to him. He owes Frank an apology, but so do those young men in there, and I think they know it."

"Well, I hope they're gracious about it! I get sick and tired of them tearing him down."

Samuel nodded. "You better get some sleep, Mrs. Wortham."

"Not till the boys are settled. Hard telling what they might come up with if we leave them on their own."

"I wouldn't worry about that. They're too tired for anything else tonight."

Samuel seemed to be right. All four of those big boys could barely drag themselves through washing and getting up the stairway. Harry didn't even try. He just plopped himself down on a blanket on the sitting room floor. The other three were about to head up to Robert's room when we heard someone else on the porch.

We weren't expecting anybody, and at first I jumped, thinking it might be some of the Turreys wanting to finish what got started. But it was Franky who came in, With Ben, which surprised everybody.

Franky didn't talk to us. He just went in and lay down on the floor beside Harry. He'd worked so hard all day and all last night. I knew he was exhausted. But before the other boys went upstairs I heard Robert tell him he was sorry.

"I shouldn't have blamed you," Robert said. "Should've known you wouldn't lie."

"What happened to you?" Franky asked them.

Kirk laughed. "Guess we decided that if you can get yourself busted up by Turreys, so can we. It's the least we can do."

Pretty soon they'd gone upstairs, and I didn't hear another peep out of them. I made Ben a cup of coffee, and he sat and told Samuel and me all about how things had gone at the other house.

"Do you need to go back?" I asked him.

"Yeah. Probably. Lizbeth'll be needing a hug or two, I expect. But she didn't want Franky alone tonight. She'll be glad he's over here."

"Thank you, Ben," Samuel said.

Later, after Ben had gone and the house was quiet, I lay beside Samuel again, both of us very still.

"Not long ago I asked Franky how things were with him and his pa," Samuel said softly. "He just said about the same."

I laid my hand across his arm. "I have a feeling it's been worse than they've said. For one thing, they all talk about how clumsy Franky is. But he's not that way over here."

"You think George makes him anxious?"

"He would me, if I had to listen to that kind of talk."

Samuel sighed, and his breath sounded so heavy. "When Franky had the broken leg, we almost kept him. Even after he was up on it again. Maybe we should have. Maybe we should have insisted that he stay with us. George didn't seem to care."

"But Franky did. Franky wanted to go home."

"I'm going to ask them again. I'm going to talk to both of them."

That thought and those words just floated on the air around us, and we both drifted into dreams. I saw Samuel's mother again, pouring her box of letters all over the kitchen floor. That was all I remembered when the cuckoo clock woke me at about 3:00 a.m. Samuel was shivering a little in his sleep. I pulled the blanket up over him, and he shuddered and pulled away from me. I wondered if he might be dreaming about his father again. Those dreams were never good.

I got up slowly and was careful to check on all the children. It was chilly tonight, and I wanted to be sure they were all covered. When I got to Franky, I found him all curled up in a ball. He was crying. At first I thought he was awake, but he wasn't. I just kissed his bruised-up cheek, pulled a blanket up to his chin, and left him alone.

Sarah was crying too. Or at least she had been. At least one cheek was damp. I

378

prayed that none of us would have any cause for crying after this. I prayed that Rorey and her father would have a change of heart, whether it was Lizbeth or the Spirit of God who prompted it. And I prayed that the morning would find us all doing better, rested and ready to go on from here with good judgment and forgiving hearts.

Before I lay down again, I picked up Franky's borrowed book, *Silas Marner*, and turned to the back page. It was with some surprise that I found the line at the top stating that Silas had brought a blessing upon himself by acting as a father to a motherless child. I was glad to find a happy ending, since the book had started out so dark. But I couldn't help thinking that Samuel and I had done that, for Katie, and in a sense for all the Hammonds, even though they still had George. And Samuel was wanting to do more for Franky, if he needed it. If he'd let us.

I set the book on the shelf and tiptoed past sleeping children and back to bed. Samuel was asleep. But he had the barest hint of a smile on his face, and when I lay beside him he put his arm around me without even waking up.

24

Sarah

Sunday morning was busy. And I could hardly believe I'd slept through my brother and three of the Hammonds taking off last night and coming back all beat up. They looked awful, but Mom insisted that at least some of the boys were going to church. And me too, she said. Because I should.

I kind of wished Mom and Dad were going, but I was also glad they weren't when I saw how tired Dad still looked. I don't guess he'd slept as long as I did.

Katie was trying to feed people, and Mom was trying to get everybody fixed up. Fresh bandages on Franky, even though he didn't want them. And Bert's foot soaking again, even though it was feeling so much better today. Harry needed his hair washed and stuck down because it only wanted to stick straight up. Willy and Kirk kept putting cold cloths on their faces where the bruises were the worst.

I got to thinking that if Charlie Hunter still came out to pick us up like he used to before Dad swapped work for Barrett Post's old truck, whoever was going to church would surely end up making him wait. It seemed to take longer than usual just getting chores done and everybody dressed. But then, to look at us you could hardly wonder why. Only Mom and us girls didn't look banged up some way. Every single one of the boys had managed to get himself looking terrible. Even Robert, who didn't look so bad as the rest, had a bruise and a cut on his chin that came from Lester Turrey's older brother swinging at him hard. I figured if the doctor showed up now, he'd shake his head at us for sure.

Mom told me what Dad wanted us to say to the folks at church. Robert and me and Franky were almost ready to go when Willy said he didn't want to go. Kirk didn't either, but then a car came pulling in our drive that made them both change their minds. It was Orville Mueller telling us that Mr. Turrey had gone to town early to find Ben Law, the sheriff, and tell him about Hammond and Wortham boys at-tacking them last night. I guess they didn't want to be home if Ben Law came out. Or I guess they thought it'd serve them well to be found in church.

Katie and Emmie came along too, and that left only Bert home with Mom and Dad. It seemed strange driving to church without them. I kept having to tie and retie Emmie's scarf all the way there because of the blowing wind and because she wouldn't leave the tie ends alone. She must have asked us six or seven times if Rorey would be there.

"I don't know," I told her. "She'll be there if your pa comes. Or Lizbeth."

I guess nobody expected to see us. As soon as we pulled up, there came a big crowd hugging at us and asking all kinds of questions, especially about Daddy. I think most of them thought that the boys' bruises came from fighting the fire somehow, so the boys were all kind of like heroes until Benjamin Gray started telling people otherwise after talking to Harry.

Sunday school was strange without Mom, because usually she taught one class. But today all of us in Mom's group were put in with Bonnie Gray's class. That was Benjamin Gray's mother, and also Rachel's. She was just a little older than me and she liked my brother, I could tell. She sat beside me and asked me maybe a dozen questions that she didn't have the nerve to ask Robert directly.

Choir was strange without Mom too, since she sometimes helped Mrs. Pastor with it and sometimes sang standing right next to Katie and me. Emmie sat with Rachel Gray while we were up singing. I didn't know why Emmie didn't want to sit with her brothers.

Robert and Franky had talked to the pastor before church ever started, and he called them up to tell everybody what Dad wanted to ask. And the men of the church had a vote right then and decided to come and help the Hammonds raise their barn the very next Saturday. Some of the men even said they'd help getting the lumber.

Franky cried. I never did see him cry in church before, even though I knew he took it more serious than most people his age. Everybody thought it was because he was so happy that the church was willing to help. And I'm sure that was part of it, but I had a feeling that wasn't all. Rorey wasn't there. Neither was her father or Lizbeth. And I knew Lizbeth would be, if she figured their father was in a fit enough frame of mind to leave. So I guessed he wasn't, and I raised my hand and asked for prayer for him and Rorey both. Katie and Franky both smiled at me for that. So did the pastor.

When we got home, we found out that Ben Law really had been sent out, but when he heard the whole story, he didn't think Hammonds and Worthams were any more to blame than the Turrey boys were. So he just left a warning for everybody about fighting, and he even said he was going to talk to Lester special about how an accident so serious as that fire needed to be reported honest, even if he didn't mean any harm.

Franky curled up and slept on the davenport before we even got any dinner, and Mom made everybody be quiet and let him sleep. Katie said he was long-suffering, whatever that meant. Robert said he'd been the one to tell the preacher what Dad wanted, on account of Robert almost always getting tongue-tied around Pastor Jones.

I prayed for Rorey again, but we didn't see her all day. Dad stayed in bed like he was supposed to, and Dr. Hall came that afternoon and said he'd be okay if he just let himself take it easy and not do too much until he was healed.

Mom went to see Mrs. Howell. Robert

drove her, and they took the cake, even though it wasn't warm and Harry'd took a corner off before he knew who it was for. The funeral was going to be Monday while we were at school. I was a little bit glad of that, because I didn't really want to go.

School was strange on Monday, mostly because it seemed like everybody already knew as much as we did about what had happened over the weekend. Two of Lester Turrey's little brothers and two sisters were there, but they stayed away from all of us. They wouldn't have had to, especially the girls. Because none of it was their fault. I gave Rose Turrey an apple at lunch because she looked so sad and she was sitting all alone.

But the strangest thing about school was that Rorey didn't come. Willy and the rest did, all but Kirk, who was working field again, and Franky, who schooled with Mom at home. Even Berty came, because Dad let Robert bring us in the truck. He sat there with the old cane between his legs and even gave a safety lesson to the class, that nobody ought ever run in a burning building.

But Rorey wasn't there. Katie said she was probably ashamed. Millie Mueller said

Rorey's pa had probably grounded her so she couldn't even leave the house. I didn't know which it was or how I felt about it. I missed her and was glad she wasn't there, all at the same time.

That whole week was the same — Rorey didn't come to school one day. Lester showed up on Wednesday when we were heading home, wanting to get hold of Willy or somebody alone. But we were all together, so he just left.

The older Hammond boys went home some, but Emmie and Bert stayed with us. Franky too, because Daddy told him to until he had a chance to talk to his pa. But Mr. Hammond didn't come over, and Kirk said he was acting sour most of the time and that Rorey sure enough was grounded, though Mr. Hammond would let her go to school if she wanted to.

Sam Hammond went over there a lot, and they cleaned up all the rubble and got the roof of the house fixed. One night Willy came bringing some of the tools they found. They were all black and charred with the handles burned off. Willy said their pa was asking if Franky could make some handles. I think Franky started that night, since Mrs. Calloway and Mr. Porter had already come to get their cedar chest and chair.

You should've seen all the people on Saturday. Almost the whole church, and even some people who didn't go to our church. Some folks had brought lumber, and that was a big help, but Daddy'd asked Robert to get the lumberman to bring the rest on credit. I think Mr. Hammond was bothered by that, but he was happy to have all the help just the same. Even the pastor came, though he spent part of the time sitting down with Rorey and her pa.

It was the first I'd seen Rorey all week. She strolled around the yard with Emmie for a while and then helped Mrs. Miller cut up some apples for the biggest apple salad I ever saw. But she didn't want to talk to me.

Mom tried to talk to her. She even gave her a hug. But I could tell Rorey was glad to get away.

Daddy couldn't work too hard. The other men wouldn't let him. But they joked all day about him and George Hammond being the bosses. Dad watched and looked over the paper that showed how they were going to put up the barn. But after a while he had Mr. Hammond sit down with him alone, and they had a real long talk. I wish I knew what they'd said. Because even after the talk was done,

Franky didn't stay at his home that night. Berty did. Emmie too. But not Franky.

That Sunday, Daddy came to church. Mom packed pillows around him in the truck and even brought one inside the church for him. He just teased her that he wasn't fragile, but he moved different, and we all knew he was still a long ways from right. The dizzy kept coming back, and some bad headaches, and his side was paining him more than he let on, I think, and that made him tired.

But I was proud of him sitting in church. I was real proud Dad had saved Berty and got the Hammonds a barn again and everything else. That Sunday, Mr. Hammond came to church too, and Rorey sat right beside him. She even came to Sunday school class and sat in her regular seat, right by me.

"Lester's mad at me," she whispered.

I didn't answer such words as that. "Katie and me are reciting a poem by William Shakespeare at school tomorrow," I told her. "You ought to come."

But right then Mom asked if anybody remembered Psalm 116 that we'd read a couple of weeks back, when she was there last. Franky raised his hand, and when she nodded, he started quoting it right out.

Rorey rolled her eyes. "There he goes again."

"Yeah," I told her. "Don't you wish you could remember stuff as good as he does?"

Rorey looked away. And I smiled and turned to listen. Because it really was a wonder, and those words even seemed to fit him.

"I love the Lord, because he hath heard my voice an' my supplications. Because he hath inclined his ear unto me, therefore will I call upon him as long as I live . . ."

25

Julia

The first Sunday that Samuel was back in church, we stopped at Charlie Hunter's service station on the way home even though we knew he'd be closed. He'd told us we'd be more than welcome to use the telephone. Samuel was finally going to call his mother. I'd almost forgotten about the letter by then, and pretty much decided I must have thrown it away. I'd been so tired that day.

Samuel stood with the telephone receiver in one hand, leaning his back against the wall. I prayed that his mother would be gracious. I prayed that she'd be proud of what he'd done and tell him so. But she wasn't home. I could tell he was disappointed. Then we went on to our Sunday dinner.

Samuel didn't eat much. He went to lie down without me prompting him. I'd been so glad that after a week he seemed to be feeling better, but that afternoon I knew he wasn't feeling well at all.

He still seemed weak Monday morning. He got up for a while but then had to lie back down again. I told him surely he'd just done too much over the weekend.

Barrett Post came by early to tell us that school was let out for the day because his brother, Elvira's husband, was doing poorly and had to see the doctor. Elvira was looking to retire by Christmas, he said, and the board was wanting a young unmarried woman to take her place.

Picking what was left of the ground cherries with Kate, I prayed for Clement Post and Samuel. I thought Samuel might like it if we went to town to call his mother again. But I didn't want to mention it yet. Not till he seemed to be feeling a little better. I almost sat down and wrote another letter, in case we couldn't get to the phone, but then I thought I'd better not. Samuel wanted to talk to her himself, and besides, I ought to just believe that he'd be fine to go into town as early as this afternoon. I ought to have faith for him to be well. He'd had one painful week, despite how much he tried not to show it. And I believed that surely from here on out he would be feeling better.

As I was picking cherries, Franky sat under the apple tree with Sarah, doing some ciphers. She'd offered to help him since she was home. I wondered how that was going. Sarah didn't quite understand how he could tackle three, four, or even five digits in his head but struggle so severely with simple problems on paper. Some days I didn't even bother with paper, but I knew she was right that he needed to be able to write down his charges for the work he did, as well as read someone else's.

"It's just numbers!" Sarah had told me. "That's not so hard as words. Why can't he read numbers?"

He did some. But he was forever confusing twos and fives, or sixes and nines, or the plus and multiply signs, even though his vision was fine. I didn't understand it either. But it made the arithmetic almost as hard as the reading.

Emmie went and joined them for a while, and Sarah told me later that Emmie could add and subtract just fine in her head but scarcely knew any of the numbers on paper. I began to wonder if maybe Emmie was right, that maybe she and Franky were a bit alike.

"Franky's the only one who hasn't been home overnight yet," Katie pointed out to me. "His father can't still be mad, can he? He didn't even do anything wrong."

"No, he didn't," I agreed. "And George knows that. He even apologized."

She looked over at me with her face so sad. "But he still doesn't want him, does he?"

How could I tell her something like that? How could I come right out and admit that I didn't know how long Franky would be spending nights with us?

"Honey, Franky's father seems to be having a difficult time. And I guess he's just being difficult in the middle of it. He only said he wanted a break for a while, that's all."

"From Franky?"

"I know. It doesn't make much sense."

She glanced over toward the apple tree. "Rorey's the only other one who hasn't been back and forth all week."

"She's having a difficult time too."

Katie glanced down into her bowl of ground cherries with their greenish-brown husks and gave them a shake. "Looks like more with the husks on. Too bad this isn't even a mess."

"We'll have enough for preserves when

393

we finish. Not many. But some is better than none."

"I thought Georgie'd trample them all." She stood and pushed a strand of dark, wavy hair behind one ear. "Mom, I think somebody's coming."

I looked down the lane. Sarah and Franky were looking too. A car was coming. Charlie Hunter? It'd been so long since he'd driven out this way that I wasn't sure. And he wasn't alone. Of course, he had a wife and two sons now, but I could think of no reason why they'd be coming to call, especially during hours when Charlie was normally working.

As they came up our drive, I could see that the woman in the front seat was not Millie Hunter. She was a good deal older and wore a generously brimmed straw hat. And there was a man in the back. He stepped out first.

"Julia!" Charlie called out the window. "Brought you some kin, straight off the train!"

Kin? My heart started pounding, and I almost dropped my bowl of cherries. Off the train?

There was something vaguely familiar about the man who had been in the backseat, but I still didn't realize who he was. I had no living relatives except Samuel and the children. And Samuel's family was so far away, in more ways than one.

But as he came stepping toward me, I thought of the cheery best man at our wedding. Samuel's cousin, the only cheery relative Samuel seemed to have. Dewey? Come all the way out here? He was the reason we'd moved to Illinois, although he'd had to start over back East not long after we got here. And we hadn't seen him since then.

"Dewey?" I called, feeling sure and yet not sure all at the same time.

"Good to see you, Julia!"

He kept on coming in my direction. But the woman with the hat just got out of the car and stood watching. It wasn't Dewey's wife, I knew that. Had he brought his mother? She was nearly as difficult as Samuel's mother.

Suddenly I felt cold and scared inside. Samuel's mother. Joanna.

I had to push myself to walk in their direction. What could have brought them? Especially her. She'd never been to visit us. Not even when we lived closer. We'd had to go and seek her out when we had Robert and Sarah, or she never would have seen her grandbabies. Joanna just didn't visit.

Dewey came right up and enthusiastically pumped my hand. "A man we talked to at the train depot directed us to your friend at the service station across the road," he explained. "And he was good enough to drive us all the way out here. I was expecting to hire out a taxi car. Didn't realize Dearing wouldn't have one."

I just stood with my hand still holding his, almost too surprised to speak. Katie had followed me, and Sarah was suddenly at my side. Franky and Emmie came up close too.

"This is . . . quite a surprise," I managed to say.

"Well, yes. We thought it might be. And we were worried for most of the trip. It was a great relief to hear from your friend that Samuel's been up and about some. How is he today?"

I just stared for a moment. This didn't seem real. They knew? They knew Samuel had been hurt? But I didn't mail the letter. And we didn't call.

"Mom, who is he?" Sarah whispered.

I suppose that might have been less than polite, but I wasn't behaving much better, just standing there staring. "It's your father's cousin Dewey," I said. "And . . . and your grandma."

Sarah's whole face lit up. "Grandma? Oh, I prayed you'd come!"

I looked at my daughter in shock, and then I thought I understood. Sarah had mailed that letter. She must have.

Sarah didn't wait for her grandmother to approach us on her own. She ran over and took hold of her hand. "Thank you!" she cried. "Thank you for coming!"

I held my breath, almost expecting Joanna to pull away or say something unkind. But she only stood still for a moment, looking surprised at Sarah. And then she said her name. "Sarah." And it was a voice I didn't know. I stepped closer as her eyes turned to me.

"Julia, I hope we're not intruding. But after your letter, we . . . I — I just felt like I needed to come."

"You're welcome," I told her, feeling that she needed to hear that assurance immediately. "You're both very welcome here."

"Is Samuel inside?"

"Yes. He was lying down."

Her eyes were deep and sparkling with a hint of tears. They didn't look like Joanna's eyes. Not the Joanna I had known before, who with one glance could make me wish I had somewhere to hide.

"Sarah's grown up so tall and beautiful," she said. She turned to Franky. "And this, this must be Robert."

"No, ma'am. I'm Frank."

"Frank? Oh. A neighbor."

"Yes, ma'am. And this is my sister."

Emmie smiled, but that was all.

"Are you the boy my Samuel saved?"

Franky stood tall and proud, his ciphers book in one hand. "No, ma'am. That was my brother. And we're grateful. Mr. Wortham's a hero."

It was so unlike Joanna to say something like "my Samuel" that I began to wonder if it was really her. But it looked like her. Except for the kindness in those eyes.

"It didn't surprise me to hear it," Dewey was saying. "I just hope it's the last time."

"Do you think it'd be all right for us to go in and see him?" Joanna was asking me almost timidly. "I don't want to disturb him too much if he's resting."

"Oh, goodness," I said, snapping out of my shock. "Yes, of course. He'd want to see you. Right now. Come on in, please."

"Do you want me to get Robert?" Franky asked quickly.

"Yes," I told him. "Yes, that would be nice. Thank you."

I was beginning to turn and show them to the house when I noticed Joanna's eyes suddenly on Katie.

"Are you Katie?" she asked with something solemn in her expression.

"Yes, ma'am," Katie answered. She spilled some of the cherries out of her bowl without even noticing. Emmie scrunched down and started picking them up.

"I'm Samuel's mother."

Katie nodded. Then slowly she reached out her hand. "Pleased to meet you."

"You do look like Samuel. Both Samuels."

I was glad for her to shake Katie's hand, but I was still not sure what to think. Samuel had dreamed something like this. I guess I'd dreamed something about it too. And I wondered if she had a box of letters stowed away in Charlie Hunter's car.

Charlie was unloading several things from the back.

"Thank you so much for bringing them," I told him.

"My pleasure."

Dewey grabbed all he could of their bags in his long arms, and Sarah hurried over to help him.

Charlie had to get back to work. "Have a nice visit," he said. Then he waved and was gone.

There was nothing to do but show them in. I wondered how long they would stay, but I wasn't sure I dared to ask. I didn't want to do a thing to risk spoiling Joanna's pleasant frame of mind. Even if it didn't last and she got persnickety again, I wanted Samuel to see her like this. I wanted to watch her greet him like a mother should, maybe for the first time in his life. Even if it did feel like a waking dream.

They followed me up to the porch, and I was so proud of Emmie holding the door for them. Franky was already gone, running out to the field to tell Robert his grandmother was here. I almost wished I could see Robert's face.

"You can set your bags anywhere," I told them. "Samuel is on the davenport, right this way. He's been sore, but he's stronger, doing all right."

"I'm glad," Joanna said. "The letter frightened me. I kept thinking he might've been lost. And me never telling him the things I should."

I tried not to stare. *Lord God, only you can make this kind of change in a person, if it is truly real. Does she know you now?*

I thought Samuel would hear us as we came in. But he was lying so still, his eyes

400

closed, and I knew he was asleep, with a bed pillow under his head and a cushion hugged to his side.

"Samuel?" Joanna called his name softly, and I couldn't help but think of her jagged, ugly voice taunting him the day I met her. *"Who is she, Samuel? Speak up, or she'll think she's got hold of a stammering baboon!"*

He woke, turning his head at the same time, as if looking for the voice. I saw the stark change in his eyes. Surprise. But past that, I saw the familiar wariness in him as he began to lift his head. He was always on guard with her. Always.

"Samuel, don't get up. Don't let me trouble you. Just lie right there. Please."

He laid his head back down, his eyes turning to me in question. But then Dewey stepped into his view.

"What's this I hear about you walking through burning buildings?"

Samuel smiled a tiny smile. "Dewey."

Dewey leaned forward, about to greet him with an embrace. But he stopped. "Don't want to hurt you, pal," he said.

"It's all right," Samuel told him. And they hugged. These two had played together. These two had been the best of friends, enduring together the tumultuous ways of both sets of parents. And they'd become good men. I was glad for them. I was always glad to hear from Dewey. And I was so glad to see him again.

Joanna stood watching without a word. I could remember her hugging Samuel only once, at our wedding. And that had been stiff and mostly because people had expected it.

"Son?" she said, sounding timid again. Dewey turned around and reached to give her hand a squeeze. That gesture surprised me as much as anything else.

For a moment nobody said anything more. Samuel and his mother only looked at each other. I saw his eyes soften, and I knew he was seeing the same difference I had seen.

"Mom," Samuel finally said. "I —"

"No. Don't say another word."

Like a sudden veil, the hurt was in Samuel's eyes again. "Juli, some water —"

"I'll get it!" Sarah ran for the kitchen.

Joanna stepped just close enough to reach and touch Samuel's hand.

"Son, I need you just to listen. For just a minute. Please."

She had tears in her eyes. Samuel did too. Just a little. He was still not sure of what he was going to hear. I wasn't either.

But I knew it would be different from anything we'd ever heard from her before.

"I'm glad . . ." she started. "I'm glad you're all right. I called Dewey and asked if he might be able to come with me. I'm so glad he could. It's such a long way. But I'd have come alone if I needed to. Oh, Sammy . . ."

She lowered her head. Samuel carefully took her hand in his. "It's all right, Mom."

"No. Nothing's been all right. For years now. And I'm so sorry."

I saw those words wash over Samuel. Words he'd never heard but had needed for so long. He didn't move. He didn't say anything. He closed his eyes for just a second, and when he opened them they were awash with tears. I noticed suddenly that Katie was crying too, and I took her hand.

"Can you forgive me, Samuel? I was such a poor mother. And you should've had so much better."

He reached both arms to her and pulled her into his embrace. At first she was taken off guard a little. She was stiff, but then she stretched her arms around him and held him. "Thank God you survived," she whispered to him. "If you'd gone — if you'd been killed and I never made it right — oh, Sammy, how could I forgive myself? I was such a drunk. I was so caught up —"

"Mom, you're saying *was* . . ."

She lifted herself up from him. I was waiting just as anxiously for her answer as Samuel was.

"I'm trying to change. I . . . I am changed. At least a start."

"Joanna," I dared ask, "do you know the Lord?"

"I'm trying to know him. Trying to learn. I want a piece of what you've been trying to share with me for so long. I've been re-reading your letters. All of them. Over and over. And then when the new one from Julia came —"

She stopped for just a second, and Samuel looked at me.

"I was scared I was too late," she finished. "Too late to tell you that I love you. And I'm sorry. And none of it, none of it was your fault."

Samuel took his mother in his arms again. He closed his eyes and he whispered, "Thank you."

I didn't know if he was telling her that, or God.

Joanna and Dewey stayed two weeks.

Two strange and wonderful weeks in which it felt like we were discovering a new kind of treasure. Joanna told us how Samuel's old letters about God in our lives had kept touching her, drawing her back to read them again and again, for months now. And how Sarah's little note moved her to tears, especially since she'd been ignoring Sarah's letters for so long. *"We love you,"* Sarah had written. *"And God loves you too."*

It had been enough to spark something hungry in Joanna, and she wept and called Dewey and made her plans to come out here and wept some more. She brought every letter with her, in one of her bags, and started reading them again on the train, asking Dewey how Samuel had learned what he did, how he'd managed to become a Christian.

Dewey was young at the things of God. He'd only been in church three months himself, but he recognized a need and did his best to answer the questions. And then when he didn't think he had any more answers, an ordained minister got on the train and sat down right in front of them.

The rest of the ride was like church. That minister prayed with them both before he got off the train, just two stops before Dearing.

We had a wonderful visit with Samuel's mother and Dewey. Better than we could have imagined. And made so much better, just knowing the miracle God had wrought. When it finally came time for them to go, we took them to the train ourselves with hugs and kisses.

After that, it seemed like things were getting back to normal. Elvira's husband was well enough so that everyone was back to school, though they'd had six days off while Joanna was here.

Some of the men from the church came out again and helped George put up fence so the Hammonds could have their animals back home again. George seemed to be in better spirits then. He came over and spent some time with Franky in the woodshop, complimenting him for the tool handles he was so carefully making. Franky went home that night, but only for one night.

Rorey came over that day, very solemn and quiet. I knew why she'd come. I knew she wanted to make amends. But she was having a hard time finding any words to say. Finally she just brought Samuel a bouquet of the last of the fading wildflowers, the way the girls used to do when they were little. Sarah hugged her, and then

Rorey told them both she was sorry.

Katie was thinking more and more about her mother, I could tell. She wrote her grandmother a long letter asking lots of questions. And some days later, she was excited to get an answer. But if her grandmother knew where her mother was right then or much of anything else, she didn't tell us.

Sam Hammond had been around a lot helping his father whenever he could, in between WPA jobs. They got in what late hay they could, but there was nothing any of us could do about the loss of the field crop. Sam brought Thelma and the children out the Saturday after Joanna and Dewey left. It was amazing to see how much Rosemary had grown in such a short time.

Little Georgie was as energetic as ever. I tied the pan cupboard shut again, but he didn't even try to pull the apron loose this time. Instead, he waited till no one was looking and opened an entirely different cupboard. In a matter of seconds, with a delightful array of clanks and thumps, he had my mixing bowls, sifter, and canning lids spread out across the floor. Oh, how he laughed! Sweet triumph. I had to laugh with him.

Samuel tried to resume his normal activities. The dizziness was gone and his head-aches were fading. But his ribs were not healed. Moving still hurt, lifting things hurt, and I had to get after him a few times to take it easy. He still tired so much more quickly than he had before. Bert was walking fine. Franky's hands were doing fine. But Samuel still worried me some-times, when I saw the weariness or the pain in his eyes.

He kept assuring me he was all right, that everything just took time, and the doctor said basically the same thing. But it was hard for me, nonetheless.

Emma Grace decided that just as Franky was especially good with wood, she must be good at something too. And she decided that something was cooking. She pestered me every time she was over to let her help me cook or bake something. She wanted me to read all the measurements and di-rections aloud and let her do as much by herself as she could. Oh, we had some frightful spills and mess after mess to clean up. But it was worth it, and I began to see her as a whole extra pair of reliable hands. It wasn't long before she could devil eggs and fix potatoes and green beans, among other things, all by herself. Soon she was telling Elvira Post my oatmeal cookie recipe from memory. Teacher and I were both impressed.

It started getting chilly sooner than I was ready for it to. Lizbeth came out and helped me can dock greens, the late sweet corn, and a box of tomatoes that Louise Post brought.

Thelma might have been right about the hard winter coming on. All the woolly-worm caterpillars had dark coats, and the geese went south earlier than usual. The garden had been so miserable, and not even the apples or berries had come on strong this year, so I didn't have near so many filled jars on the pantry shelf as I would have liked.

But we'd always made it, every year before, and I could be just as confident that we'd make it this time too.

I guess I needn't have worried, because Samuel kept improving. He did more than I realized, till he was back to a full day's work with me scarcely noticing the change.

One day I saw him splitting logs. I'd been having Robert do all that kind of work, so I went out across the yard to caution him. At first he just looked at me. Then with mischief in his eyes, he dropped the splitting maul, picked me up, and went twirling me around.

"Samuel! You shouldn't be —"

He paid no attention. He just laughed and I let him. I was so glad to have him strong and well again that I just wanted to enjoy the moment. But I guess the moment got a bit long when he stopped his twirling and held me in his arms. We kissed, and I didn't even notice Robert coming up until he cleared his throat.

"Uh, Dad. Mr. Turrey just drove up, and he's wanting to talk to you."

We hadn't heard a vehicle. Samuel walked around to the side of the house to see what Mr. Turrey wanted. I looked a minute and saw that he was alone. I didn't go over there, but Samuel told me later that he'd said he'd been to talk to George too and wanted to know if there was something Lester could do to pay us back for the damage he'd caused. I wondered why he hadn't come sooner, when George was rebuilding and Samuel was laid up the way he'd been. But George hadn't gotten everything rebuilt yet, and we soon set Lester to work putting up the new pig house. George made sure Rorey was at our house whenever Lester was there after school hours. She didn't care. Something about burning down a barn had put a damper on their relationship, much to our relief.

Franky tried something new, carving a dove with spread-out wings on a wooden plaque. It was beautiful. He gave it to us, and I proudly hung it in the sitting room. He started another plaque with a cross and flowers to give to his father for Christmas. I hoped George would be delighted.

Joanna wrote to us every week. It was strange at first. She'd only ever written us once before. But it was so nice to know what was going on in her life now. We started praying fervently for her second husband, Samuel's stepfather, who owned a tavern and wasn't pleased with her new desire to go to church. We answered all of her letters. And we wrote to Dewey, and Samuel's brother, Edward, and to Katie's mother, sending that letter on to the grandmother in hopes that it would someday reach her. We told every one of them of our love and God's continuing love for them.

The first snow came early. Samuel and George butchered together as usual. It was a hard day for George, feeling like he was going backward just to survive when he'd wanted to feel like he was getting ahead. We were cosigned on a loan for the barn lumber, and all of us were thankful that Mr. Felder at the sawmill was patient.

Twice Pastor Jones made a payment for us. For a long time I didn't know where he'd gotten the money, until Pastor eventually told us it came from Ben Porter's parents wanting to bless Lizbeth's family.

Rorey, Katie, and Sarah sang together for the Christmas program at the school. Their performance was so beautiful that they did it again for church the following Sunday. "O Holy Night." And Rorey had never sung with them before. She had her difficult times, when her attitude was terrible and she was far from a help to her father or anyone else. We prayed for her and hoped she'd come out all right. At least she wasn't trying to see Lester Turrey anymore, or any other boy, so far as we knew.

I wondered about George Hammond sometimes. He seemed so much quieter. We had all his children with us more often than we really wanted to. I thought he was too withdrawn, and Samuel spoke to him about it more than once. But he assured us he just needed the quiet sometimes. He visited the woodshop again to see the chair Franky was working on for Lizbeth. Franky and his father finally talked that day, for a long time. And I never saw George yell at Franky again, though there were plenty of times they just kept their distance.

Katie's birthday was an extra happy day because Joe was home for the first time in months. Everybody was out. Sam and Thelma, Lizbeth and Ben. We had a big dinner, a big cake. And no fire. Lizbeth told me that she thought she might be expecting. She asked me not to tell anyone yet, and she promised me that I wouldn't have to deliver this child, unless I really wanted to. She had no qualms about letting the doctor take care of it.

Sarah told me she thought the fire had actually been good for us, looking back. That maybe it had helped her and some others grow up and change a little for the better. Maybe she was right. I know God used the whole circumstance and even our need that winter to stretch my faith and remind me once again of his faithfulness. Every time I look at Samuel now I can thank God he's still alive, that we had a miracle, a double miracle that brought his mother to be truly a part of our family. In this life and the world to come. We could go on thanking God forever for that, and it would still not be enough.

And that is just like God. Unending. Source of miracles. Breath of life. He holds our days in his capable hands.

About the Author

Leisha Kelly is the author of two inspirational fiction series. She and her husband live in an old house in small-town Illinois where they are busy with the ministries of their church and the education of their two children.